SARAH GARDNER BORDEN

Games to Play After Dark

Sarah Gardner Borden holds an MFA from the Warren Wilson
Program for Writers. Her fiction and nonfiction have appeared
in a variety of journals, including *Open City, Willow Springs,*
the *Chicago Reader, Other Voices, Literary Mama,* and the *New
Haven Review.* She lives in Brooklyn.

*games
to play
after dark*

SARAH GARDNER BORDEN

VINTAGE CONTEMPORARIES
Vintage Books
A Division of Random House, Inc.
New York

A VINTAGE CONTEMPORARIES ORIGINAL, MAY 2011

Vintage is a registered trademark and Vintage Contemporaries and
colophon are trademarks of Random House, Inc.

Library of Congress Cataloging-in-Publication Data
Borden, Sarah Gardner.
Games to play after dark : a novel / Sarah Gardner Borden.
p. cm.
"A Vintage original."
ISBN 978-0-307-74090-8
1. Married people—Fiction.   2. Marital conflict—Fiction.   I. Title.
PS3602.O6858G36 2011
813'.6—dc22
2010053422

Book design by Ralph Fowler

www.vintagebooks.com

150098039

For Anya Gardner and Stella Rose

*games
to play
after dark*

I

KATE AND COLIN met at a party thrown by Kate and her West Twelfth Street apartment mate, Darcy, a party Colin turned up at only by happenstance, knowing neither Kate nor Darcy and tagging along with a friend of a friend. They were recently out of college and young enough so that it didn't matter whether one was invited to a party or not. Strangers would wander into strange apartments and get themselves drinks and make out with other strangers on ripped sofas in the dusty corners of candlelit rooms.

Darcy had majored in art history but now worked as a paralegal at a high-powered law firm in Midtown by day and chased investment bankers by night. While Darcy put in long hours for lawyers, Kate did financial projections for Liz Claiborne. She and Darcy swapped clothes and went out every Thursday, Friday, and Saturday. They ate pasta with tomatoes and basil at restaurants with the doors open to the sidewalk in the summer. They went to bars where Drew Barrymore hung out with her guitarist boyfriend or where a friend's band was playing. They poked around flea markets, bought scarves of Indian silk, drank coffee from blue-and-white paper cups, averted their eyes from a man defecating on Houston Street. They fiddled with the apartment on the weekends and once in a while had someone come to clean, a sweet, thin Polish woman with recurring bruises on her face and a deep, abiding love for Elvis Presley. They did their laundry in the basement and sent the dressier things out for dry cleaning. Mondays, they opened a bottle of cheap white wine and watched *Melrose Place*.

On the day of the party they tidied up and then spent the afternoon at Balducci's, where they bought, among various snacks and ingredients, a tremendous ham. They put the groceries away and got dressed. Darcy pulled back her hair and poured herself and Kate a glass of wine and tied on an apron. Recklessly, she was attempting several complicated recipes from the Union Square Cafe cookbook. She prepared Roman-Style Marinated Olives and Bruschetta Bianca and set them out in the living room. Kate put on a secondhand pink velvet minidress and knee-high black boots. She applied makeup and buzzed in the first batch of guests. Darcy drank more wine and made Parsnip Pancakes and began to garnish each one with a tiny dollop of sour cream. Kate received cluster after cluster of guests, some she knew and some she didn't. The party had been conceived of as a dinner party but it seemed to be morphing into something resembling a fraternity party. Kate retreated to the open kitchen and watched Colin, whose name she had not yet learned, hold the door for two slurring, shrieking girls on their way out. This manly young man holding the door, with his blue-checked button-down shirt and nice manners, looked as though he did not belong at this suddenly dreadful party. His glasses gave him a stern, righteous look. His hair, blond, was already thinning. In spite of the latter, she found him handsome.

Darcy still had Creamy Polenta with Mascarpone; Red

Oakleaf and Bibb Salad with Gruyère, Garlic Croutons, and Dijon Vinaigrette; Mashed Turnips with Frizzled Leeks; and Stuffed Chicken Breasts with Herbed Goat Cheese to go. The buzzer persisted. People leaked from the living room into the bedrooms. Friends meandered tipsily into the kitchen to say hi. Darcy was dropping things and beginning to break a sweat.

"You could serve the sour cream on the side," Kate suggested. "You could put it in a cute little bowl or something."

"But you know how that is; when a bunch of people are dipping the dip gets all ick." Darcy's face had begun to fall apart a bit and her stockings had run. She charged around the kitchen in her high heels with her pinned-up vermilion hair coming down.

"You could put a spoon in the dip and then they could use the spoon to put the sour cream on their pancake and then the ick would be avoided."

"But they won't know what the spoon is for!" Darcy cried.

"You could put up a little sign. Directions. You could make an announcement."

The buzzer rang. "Will you get that? Will you get that?" Darcy asked. When she felt anxious, which was often, she said things twice.

Kate buzzed the guests in but did not bother to greet them. She went back to the kitchen and Darcy—both disheveled, both staggering toward catastrophe, both running roughshod over their original intentions.

Darcy finished putting sour cream on the pancakes—the final dollops panicked and sloppy—and began skinning turnips with a vegetable peeler. Kate watched, tending to the buzzer and drinking her wine. Every so often a turnip would slip and shoot out of Darcy's palm and land in the prehistoric muck of the sink.

"Is Luke here? Have you seen Luke?" Luke, a trader at Goldman Sachs whom Darcy regularly put out for, was clearly blowing off the party. But every time the buzzer rang Darcy's spine would snap into place and her face would fly open—then everything would go loose and shut down again.

"Is it Luke? Is it?" Darcy swept aside the turnips and opened a jar of peppercorns and blitzed half the jar in the coffee grinder.

Kate looked out into the hallway. Raucous guests were carrying the ham into the bathroom, setting it on Darcy's digital scale. "Don't worry about Luke. Plenty of cute guys here."

"I haven't even started the chicken." Darcy dumped the ground peppercorns into a coffee mug. Reaching for the salt she overturned the open spice jar, and dozens of tiny peppercorns leaped onto the linoleum floor, where they jumped joyfully for a full minute.

"What can I do? This?" Kate stepped up to the sink and took the turnips. She stood at the sink, as Darcy had, but when it occurred to her that they lacked a disposal and therefore a definitive reason to peel vegetables at the sink, she moved aside and began to peel the turnips right onto the counter. She searched for a clean bowl in which to put the peeled turnips but there wasn't one. She attempted to wash one but the water in the sink rose forebodingly. She poked at the drain for a minute or two with a wooden cooking spoon. Darcy wiped her eyes with a checkered dishcloth and opened a sheaf of goat cheese and began to smash it, in its wrapper, with damp chopped herbs.

The buzzer again. Kate shook out her wet hands.

"Is it Luke? Is it?"

"Sorry, honey." Kate poured herself more wine.

Darcy sagged against the fridge. "He doesn't love me."

"No. He doesn't love you," Kate answered, carelessly. She stood with a turnip in each hand, considering the sink. Registering her own utterance, she whipped around, as if realizing, too late, that she'd knocked something fragile off a small, interfering table.

"I'm going to pass out, I think," Darcy said. She put her head down on the counter.

"Wait. Not yet." Kate brushed Darcy's sweaty bangs out of her face and went to her own bedroom and got a Valium, one swiped from a stash she'd discovered two Christmases ago in her mother's medicine cabinet. She fed the pill to Darcy.

Darcy slid against the cabinets to the floor like she'd been shot. Colin rounded boisterously in, swinging two handfuls of empties. He registered Darcy, Kate, the sink. He put down the bottles and reached in and unclogged the drain, as if he weren't afraid of taking on something chaotic and feminine.

"YOU LIVE HERE?" he asked Kate.

"I do."

Darcy, bearing the pancakes, had gone out to join the party. Kate and Colin were straightening up the kitchen, washing dishes and wrapping the now obsolete goat cheese and herbs and raw chicken breasts. She put things away in the lower cabinets, he in the higher ones. He was tall, though not unapproachably so, both his height and build reassuringly average.

"You don't look like you live here."

"No?"

"You're pretty. And . . . you smell good." He closed the fridge and stood with his back to it, legs apart, hands in pockets. His eyes were blue behind the glasses.

"It's kind of a dump," she admitted. "But . . . not usually this bad."

"What happened?"

"This was supposed to be a dinner party. You know. Civilized."

"Oh, well."

"I guess we're not ready for that."

"Guess not."

Later they put Darcy, flattened by Valium and wine, into bed in her ravaged stockings. They collected bottles and tossed stray food. They piled glasses in the sink. They wiped off the ham and wrapped it and put it away. Then they went to Kate's room. She showed him her high school yearbook, her CD collection, and the IKEA cabinet she'd assembled herself. He kissed her and pushed her up against the wall and then down on the bed, where they struggled for a while. Her dress came off. Her boots and stockings came off. Her hair came down. He produced a magnificent erection. They ground against each other. Colin, on top, supported himself in the gentlemanly manner with his arms. Contraception was mentioned. Kate rummaged tipsily around Darcy's medicine cabinet and her own. Withdrawal was suggested by him and rejected by her, it being a delicate time of the month. To compensate, she took him in her fist, then her mouth.

. . .

IT WAS IMMEDIATELY CLEAR to her that if she gave him the opportunity to love her he would—and while she felt, dimly, that her motivations were devious somehow next to his, her character suspect beside his seemingly honest and upstanding and simple one, that she looked on their entanglement as an experiment, an adventure, while he looked on the same as a righteous endeavor, she wasn't sure she could resist. He wanted her, and her narcissism flowered expansively under the hot orange light of his craving. She told him of her mother's anxiety, the other men she'd been with, her father's temper, the time she'd strayed from her family in a Moroccan bazaar, the time she'd had a pea stuck up her nose for an entire summer. Colin told her how it had flooded on the day of his communion, how he'd been held at gunpoint by a hitchhiker, how his father's skin had turned yellow before he died last April. Later she learned that he wore his socks inside out because he didn't like the feel of the seams, that he ate his hamburger first and his fries after.

She felt diagnosed somehow, at the start of a long healing process—she felt split open and figured out; everything about him was like a warm curious hand inside her, making sense of the rubble and confusion, turning things over and putting them back where they belonged.

THEY DATED ALL WINTER and spring and summer. They held hands and watched a white Bronco tear down Southern California freeways. They spent whole weekends in bed, screwing and sleeping and recounting their dreams upon waking. They freely swapped love, trading it back and forth like second graders with stickers. They opened constantly to each other, ready always to receive each other and any accompanying inconveniences. They spent Labor Day at her mother's house, eating at midnight in Greek diners and driving hours for fresh strawberries and a disappointing flea market. Back in her room, after a movie and dinner at Thomas Quinn's Bar and Grill, Kate's mother asleep already, Colin asked Kate if she'd marry him. They lay on her girlhood bed, playing cards—she dressed in a denim skirt and a soft brown Indian blouse. When he asked her Kate laughed because she couldn't believe he was serious, but then she said yes.

This was unprecedented—amazing. She felt as though she'd suddenly landed a starring role in her own life. She found herself desperately thirsty, the kind of thirst she used to get with her hangovers when she was a teenager, and she and Colin walked over to the gas station and bought three different kinds of fruit punch, and back at the house she drank some of each, from a tall glass filled with ice. She couldn't get enough of it— her teeth hummed and she was almost sick.

"I didn't even realize I *wanted* to get married," she said. "But I do! I want to see you every day. I want a pink bathroom and a mirror at the end of the bed. And an Oriental rug in the living room. And a really nice fridge. I want to make birthday cake. And babies. I want to have a happy family. That's it. That's my dream. I didn't even know until right now."

Parties were thrown for them; they were baptized with cards and presents and attention. They were celebrities— everyone believed in them, supported them verbally and fiscally, took an almost civil interest, as if Kate and Colin were candidates in a political campaign. In October, Darcy and Kate visited Bergdorf and Saks and Vera Wang. Kate waited for

Darcy on the steps of the New York Public Library, drinking sweet and light coffee from a paper cup. She wore a striped, pointed woolen hat, a brown tweed jacket patched at the elbows, corduroys of a darker brown, and a giant diamond ring on the correct finger. The ring marked her—she could not get used to it; she could not accustom herself to the responsibility of something so valuable and she kept touching it and twisting it, making sure it was still there. She looked up and down Fifth Avenue. Her nose ran a little; she sniffed and wiped it, making a fist. The diamond, turned around, pressed into her palm. An elderly woman in a fur coat and hat passed Kate on her right, emanating even in the cool clarifying air a strong odor of expensive perfume. Her face was a powdered, crumpled, exquisite little thing. Soon, Kate thought, she would be legally tied to someone who would accompany her into old age. She imagined that in her forties she would wear her hair shorter and somehow be tan; that when she reached her sixties she would grow the hair again and wear it up, the way her grandmother had. Colin would thicken around the shoulders and wear monogrammed velvet slippers given by her for their thirtieth anniversary. They would live in New York and subscribe to the ballet, during which Colin would sleep.

She had intended to shop for the dress alone—especially she did not want her sweet but alarmingly passive mother in tow—but early this morning, a Saturday, before getting on the F train uptown on a wedding errand, she had prodded Darcy awake and requested her company—partially simply to validate the experience—seeing herself, though with awe, as an impostor in the white dress, an understudy called upon to play the crucial role on opening night, hoping the audience and her producer—Colin—wouldn't find her out.

Two smooth hands covered her eyes. Kate grabbed one wrist and pulled at it.

"I am so psyched to be doing this with you," Darcy said. "Where to first?"

Sober and showered, with her bright straight hair and pale skin and strong Slavic features, she looked as though she'd been chipped from the cold air.

"Bergdorf. Can you stand it?" Kate asked, locking her jaw.

They caught a cab going up Madison Avenue. A man jumped out of their way as they pulled from the curb. Darcy cranked down the window and shouted, "Nitwit!" Kate finished the last of her coffee and crumpled the sides of the cup together, spilling a few sweet remaining drops.

"My mother is on my case because you're getting married," Darcy said. "She scoffs at the whole idea of women needing to get married but then it's still totally important to her."

"My mom is that way too. Ostensibly liberated but actually a doormat."

"I'll stop complaining. This is your day."

"Oh, please. I don't want it." Kate paid for the cab and they got out in front of Bergdorf Goodman. The interior was dense with perfume and flowers and Kate sneezed as they waited for the elevator. Darcy examined the store directory and when they boarded she pressed the correct button.

"Bri-dal," she sang in a falsetto voice.

They stepped out of the elevator and found their way to the inner sanctum of wedding finery. Gowns billowed sideways from racks, animated by crinolines and proximity to one another. A plump, delicate little woman drifted from the pouf, her hands clasped inquiringly: "May I help you?"

"We have an appointment," Darcy said, grandly.

Kate wished she'd worn something besides the brown corduroys and hoodie that had been so comfortable this morning. Darcy wore a long droopy soft skirt with leggings underneath, sneakers, and a frayed sweater that smelled of mothballs, but her height and gorgeous hair allowed her elegance anyway.

The woman showed them dresses in varying degrees of flounce. There were fairy-tale-princess skirts with layers of net below; there were lace bodices and beaded necklines and heavy ivory satin. ("For a redhead," their fairy godmother intoned.) There were pristine Waspy white A-lines and dramatic overblown ball skirts and sexy satin sheaths with bows on the behind and mermaid fishtails about the knees.

"What are you doing for Thanksgiving?" Darcy asked, flipping through dresses. "Wanna come to my parents' house?"

"Going to Colin's. His mother's."

"Wow. That's serious."

"Darcy. We're engaged."

"Oh, right." Darcy pulled a dress off the rack and held it up in front of herself and looked in the mirror. She frowned and batted at her hair. "I forgot. Hey! Look at this one! And this!" She fingered the dresses boldly, running her palm possessively along the lengths of the waists. Kate picked up the dresses as Darcy let them go. There were so many, too many choices. Whatever she picked she'd get it wrong. On one dress she liked the bodice but not the neckline; on another she liked the neckline but not the waistline; on another she liked the skirt but not the sleeves. She pointed out four gowns and the fairy godmother brought them in her size. Two other fairy godmothers were tending to a Locust Valley type and a cropped, jockish type, both with matching mothers. Kate and Darcy went with the dresses into a softly lit room with a tumbler of water and two glasses on a small table. Kate stood on a pedestal in front of the mirror and Darcy did up dozens of pearl-shaped buttons. All the dresses were too long for Kate, so they fell over the pedestal all the way to the floor, making her look tall.

"Why does this matter to me?" Kate said. "Why don't I just give the wedding money to charity?"

Darcy reached up to pull a loose piece of hair off Kate's face. "How will you wear your hair? Up?" She piled the hair up on top of Kate's head and held it. "You look like a goddess."

"Really? Do I?" Kate took over the hair. She turned her head and looked at herself in profile.

"You should be very proud of yourself."

Outside, the jock and the lockjaw marveled over their own and each other's daughters.

"Just look at that!" the lockjaw exclaimed.

"Exciting times," the jock said. "Exciting times."

AT THANKSGIVING, Colin's mother cornered Kate in the pantry and said, "Colin is a lovely person. I know I'm biased, but he is."

Kate nodded. She'd escaped to the pantry to refresh her drink, a martini. Fresh ice cracked in the shaker she guiltily held. A fleet of Cornish game hens (her future mother-in-law's bird of choice) marinated on the counter.

"He will never hurt you. He will never abandon you." She looked at Kate as if anticipating thanks.

Kate chose an off-the-shoulder A-line dress and white satin heels and a Cynthia Rowley purse to match. Her mother booked the church and the club. Kate shacked up in Colin's Upper West Side apartment. Darcy cried, helping her pack her shoes and dresses and wine-bottle lamps. At a Turkish restaurant, over an awkwardly wide mosaic table, Kate and Colin conducted a discussion of their future. Kate had imagined they'd live in the city, downtown, of course, but Colin, who worked in private equities, had been offered a better setup at his company's Stamford branch. Taxes, he said, family, quality of living. His sister was pregnant and this was giving him ideas. Kate saw them forming daily, energetically, like mold on fruit. She saw him looking into strollers on the street. The other night, another couple's baby had woken up and started to cry as the adults sat down to dinner.

Colin looked at Kate. "Don't you want to just go in and pick up that baby?"

"No. Not really."

"I do," he said.

"Well, you should."

"Maybe I will. Don't you want to?"

"No."

"You're not ready," he'd said indulgently.

She could see that doing what he wanted was compelling for both of them, and that to resist would interfere with the sexual chemistry that served as foundation for their bond. "Okay," she said. "I don't care where I am," she said, "so long as we're together." But later that night, doubt moved in her. They'd gone to bed. He'd fallen asleep quickly but she stayed up and worried. Was he afraid—if so, of what? She did not want to admit any vulnerability in him. So she smothered the fear under thoughts of wedding plans, spooned him, and went to sleep.

IN HER CHILDHOOD ROOM at 123 Livingston Street, a stylist from the Richard Penna Salon pinned Kate's hair up and applied powders and creams to her face. Then Kate and Darcy waited together in the girlish room, listening to Shawn Colvin, sipping at glasses of champagne, Kate pacing delicately back and forth in front of the full-length mirror.

"I have to pee," Kate said. "Should I go now or later?"

"Now. You don't want to be thinking about it during the ceremony."

"Okay."

Darcy held up Kate's skirt while she went. Then, sorting out crinolines, Darcy discovered a loose button.

"I think it'll hang on through the party."

"But . . ." Kate twisted, trying to look.

"I shouldn't have told you."

"Where's my mother?"

"Downstairs, I think . . ."

"She has sewing stuff; she can do it. Will you get her?"

"It's no big deal, really; you have so many other buttons."

"But it's right at the waist. Please just get her?"

Darcy exited the room and returned a few minutes later.

"Your mom left for the church already."

"Are you *serious*?"

"I think she has things to do there."

"I can't believe this." Kate groped at the loose button. She rustled over to the bed and despairingly sat on it.

"I'll do it! Where do I find the sewing stuff?"

"Her bedroom, bureau, first drawer."

Darcy fetched needle and thread. "Oh, don't cry," she said. "You'll mess up your makeup."

"I know." Kate plucked a tissue from the box on the bedside table and poked at her eyes.

"It's fine. It's totally fine. I can do this."

"I know. It's just that I feel like I want my mother to do it. I know it doesn't matter."

"Shush. Stop crying. Don't be a hysterical bride." Darcy pulled her gently off the bed. "Stand up; turn around." She unbuttoned the gown all down the back, then knelt behind Kate and began to tend to the delinquent button. "Deep breath. Don't cry."

"Okay. I'm not." Kate closed her eyes and breathed through her nose.

"Remember those peppercorns? Bouncing?"

"That was ridiculous."

"I know it was." Darcy's manicured fingers probed and labored. "You know what I think? I think that Colin is going to have fun with these buttons."

An hour later, Kate's father walked her down the aisle to Bach's "Jesu, Joy of Man's Desiring." She had ignored her father throughout the engagement—she had avoided him at various dinners and parties; she had averted her eyes as Colin and he talked golf at the bar of the Fairfield Tennis and Swim Club, identical amber-colored drinks at hand. She sensed his amusement over the whole affair, and she did not let him catch her alone or look him in the eye. Evasion proved easy. She seldom saw him anyway. She could count on one hand her visits to the apartment he'd rented since divorcing her mother. Kate ignored him as he took her arm and gave her away. She would not let him mess this up. Her current sense of joy and victory was a glass vessel she was carrying on her head down a long cluttered hallway. He would not distract her from this task. He would not! If she looked at him, talked to him, met his eye, she would trip and the glass would break.

2

HE TEACHES HER to ride a bike, running along beside her and pushing her off into the grassy sections of the park until she can pedal on her own. He teaches her to drain the boiler and replace a fuse. At his brother's place, in their hometown of Galveston, he teaches her to load and fire a rifle. He teaches her mnemonics: for the order of the planets, the color of resistors, the digits of pi. He writes them out on index cards and sticks them to the fridge:

My Very Educated Mother Just Served Us Nine Pizzas.

Bad Boys May Ruin Our Young Girls
But Violet Goes Willingly.

I Took A Quick Glimpse At Bright Stars Far North.

They perform backyard experiments. They turn milk to stone (chemical reactions) and conduct a tennis-ball moon bounce (conservation of motion). They make lightning with aluminum, Styrofoam, and a sock. They build a volcano with clay, baking soda, vinegar, and an empty bottle.

At the Payne Whitney Gym he teaches her how to throw a punch. He tells her: Stand with your feet shoulder-width apart, one in front, knees bent. Keep your thumb outside your fist. Swivel your body. Use your weight.

He teaches her how to drive: around the block, then up and down Whitney Avenue, then on the Merritt Parkway, then on I-95. Always drive defensively, he says. Pay attention. Don't speed. Wear your seat belt. Yield anyway. Know your blind spots. Create space around your vehicle. Signal your intentions. Slow down in rain or snow. Watch the road. Don't look at the tree you're about to crash into—look where you want to go. Steer through a skid. When in doubt, both feet out.

They inhabit a single-family house in a residential section of New Haven, Connecticut, birthplace of the hamburger and the cotton gin and the automatic revolver, home to Yale University and Pepe's Pizzeria and acres of depreciating industrial real estate and scores of disaffected inner-city youth. Kate's father, Dennis Allison, teaches physics at Yale, and her mother, Edie, works for human resources at United Illuminating—an occupation that seems to embarrass Kate's father a bit—and manages all other aspects of life, aspects having to do with the household and two children, Kate and her brother, Miles. Kate's mother shops and cooks, she makes phone calls and calculations and doctors' appointments and lunches, and if necessary she sits up late in the kitchen sewing on buttons and paying bills. On other evenings, exhausted from holding the family together, she crawls into bed early with a mystery novel or a biography. She believes that books exist for entertainment or education, not psychological or spiritual enlightenment.

The house, 123 Livingston, a three-story Victorian painted a whimsical lavender by the previous owners, occupies the edge of an extensive and overgrown park, which rises at its eastern reaches into a massive rock. The rock contains hiking and bike trails, a tower and a telescope, and, along with I-95, divides the academic side of town from what the academics think of as the slums. Eastwood Park surrounds a pond, basketball courts, a hill for sledding, and a playground. Beer and soda bottles litter the playground, as do cigarette butts and roaches and used condoms and the occasional syringe. As a preschooler, Kate frequents the park in the company of her mother or a sitter. As a grade-schooler, she bikes and hikes the trails in the company of her father.

Occasionally muggings or rapes occur. Once: a young babysitter, a neighborhood girl with professor parents, out walking her charge. The attacker drags them off the trail and into the surrounding brush. He parks the stroller against a tree—the toddler shocked from sleep, crying—and throws his coat over the awning. The girl's coat he arranges under his knees. Kate hears the story on the local news and around her school and at a faculty dinner party given by her parents. She likes to sit on the back stairs when her parents have company and listen to the conversations: forgettable, pleasant ones and horrible, valuable ones. The man, Nelson Young, is arrested at a Dunkin' Donuts in Fair Haven and shuttled off to prison. The girl, Matilda Hellerman, does not go away to Princeton as planned. She stays home and crops her hair and keeps it that way, short as a boy's. The word is she gorges daily on brownies, that she buys sanitary products in bulk and sucks her thumb. She develops acne. She becomes obese. Kate, as she waits for the bus, spies her walking the family dog down the block, singing wistfully under her breath. Kate spots her also at the Italian market, filling her basket with sweets, grotesque and troubling amid the young mothers pushing double strollers, the graduate students in plum-colored T-shirts and jeans choosing peaches and corn carefully from the wide wicker baskets, the professional women rushing in after work to get something for dinner before closing time, which is supposed to be seven but really happens at six forty-five because the Italian girls put the cardboard sign up early, impatient to leave.

Kate's father dislikes whimsical colors, so he and Kate's mother are saving up the money to paint 123 Livingston a sober off-white or a sensible dark red. One year they tore off the porch, which was falling down, and rebuilt it. The following year they installed a slate walkway. Beside the walk rises a massive copper beech, which supports a swing and keeps the front rooms cool in the summer. Certain funds go toward the tree's maintenance. Once a month a man is paid to mow the lawn, and his wife is paid to clean the house. Kate's mother has decorated the latter in a typically shabby Waspy fashion, little purchased, much inherited: sconces, wrought iron and gilt, outfitted with electric bulbs; tiny silver bowls; swimming and riding trophies; paintings of horses and ducks and foxhunts; needlepoint pillows; trim, firm couches and chairs covered in tapestry prints. From Kate's father's family: a stag's antlers mounted on a polished piece of wood; above the fireplace, an antique rifle. On the first floor, the kitchen, dining room, study, and living room lead one into another and surround the front hallway. The second floor holds four bedrooms and three bathrooms: the parental suite, a guest room, and separate bedrooms and bathrooms for Kate and Miles. Kate's father stores his scholarly journals on the third floor, the attic. Industriously, he piles them away, great blockades of brilliance and intellect. Kate's mother teases him, saying that she believes if he has journals left to read, he won't be allowed to die like everybody else.

Every now and then a mysterious local somebody makes rounds at night and leaves small gnome statuettes on certain porches and doorsteps. The condition of having received a gnome, as well as the action of planting the gnomes, is known on the street as "a gnoming." "I was gnomed last night," one neighbor will say to another. "And you?" Some people find the gnomings delightful. Kate's father does not. He takes as dim a view of gnomes as of whimsical colors, and upon discovery of a doorstep gnome he curses and hurls the gnome to the sidewalk, where the little fellow rolls and cracks.

In the other houses around the park, also three-story Victorians painted whimsical colors, live Yale faculty and the more affluent townies: doctors and lawyers and bankers and small-business owners. The neighbors on the left, two men who live together, teach respectively in the drama program and the medical school. When invited along to the Frankenstein house, as Miles calls it, Kate and Miles poke around the basement while the adults drink cocktails upstairs. A century ago, the basement functioned as a sort of laboratory. Glass jars fill the shelves and preserved liquids and substances, some labeled, fill the jars. A collection of tiny bones. An eyeball, too large to be human. A chicken foot, a hawk's foot. Green sludge. A sheep's phallus, a rat's brain, a cat's kidney, a deer's heart. Fungi. Petals, stones, seashells. Hair, teeth, nails. More sludge, jars and jars of terrifying unidentified sludge.

The non-Yale-affiliated neighbors on the right have allegedly changed their family name from D'Amato to Anderson for business purposes. Max and Ella D'Amato-slash-Anderson have five boys, all close in age, like brothers in a fairy tale or a British children's novel circa 1900. Along with Miles and Kate, they attend Whitney Hall, the private K–12 school.

Though Kate occupies herself mainly with Topher (at her age, the youngest), she adores all five of them and finds reasons to choose Topher's house over hers for play. "My mom's got a headache," she tells him. Or, "My brother will bother us." Or, most often, "My father's working in his study."

While Max Anderson runs his contracting company, Ella Anderson stays home and supervises the rambunctious but cheerful household. Topher and his brothers wrestle and tussle, rolling over backs of couches, toppling lamps, disrupting cushions, and crashing down on coffee tables. Ella scolds from the next room, and Kate stands back, watching and wanting to jump in. Injuries abound, some from the roughhousing, others from various team sports. Back and forth from Yale–New Haven Hospital the boys go, ankles and wrists and shoulders bandaged, skin stitched. At dinner, which the Andersons sit down to every night as a family, tender expressions pass between Ella and Max over the roast chicken, the mashed potatoes, the beef bourguignon. Unlike Kate's mother, Ella makes a production out of dinner: Billy Joel on the stereo, sauce splattering the stove, little rags of meat dropped underfoot. Kate and Topher might sit at the counter and watch, eating raw sliced carrots and chips, and if need be jump up to wave a broom in front of the smoke alarm. Topher's father, instead of shutting himself in his study, watches the game, whatever it is. He follows the Red Sox, the Patriots, the Whalers, the Celtics. Like all the fathers, he stays away from the dishes. Topher and Kate set the table. Then Kate eats and eats. Ella and Max exclaim over her appetite.

Skinny little thing!

Watch you pack it away!

Where do you put it!

Tell us!

Kate and Topher might watch a sitcom after dinner, or they might go up to Topher's room and turn off the lights and tell creepy stories and count the fluorescent stars stuck to his ceiling. On a weekend, they might have a sleepover—then they might sneak back down to the kitchen in the witching hours and conduct a knockdown-drag-out food fight, which they wake early to clean up.

At Kate's they play Connect 4, Monopoly, Clue, backgammon, Dungeons & Dragons. They read books (*Half Magic, The Adventures of Tom Sawyer, The Book of Three, The Phoenix and the Carpet*) and lie in the sun on the back patio, ants crossing the pages like the black letters come to life and walking impatiently away. They go around the yard with Kate's father's magnifying glass. They make a geyser with Mentos and bottled diet soda. They put soap in the microwave and watch it blow up into gigantic crispy bubbles. They fry eggs on the sidewalk. They see movies, comedies with Eddie Murphy and Rodney Dangerfield and Tom Cruise. Kate's father mixes up the titles on purpose, to tease them. *"Trading Money,"* he says. *"Easy Business. Risky Places."* They play Freezing Han Solo, a game of their own invention that entails placing Topher's Han Solo figure in a butter dish filled with water and storing the butter dish in the freezer.

At Topher's they entertain themselves with the basketball hoop, the gigantic television, Atari, and glimpses of his brothers beating off in the second-floor bathroom. A new lock has been added to the door, the old one taken off, but the hole the old lock once occupied still needs filling and sealing. All four older brothers visit the bathroom (which Kate tries to avoid actually using) at regular intervals: Nick, Bobby, Sebastian, and Rudy, one after the other, stealing away with their father's *Playboy* or their mother's *Cosmopolitan,* the latter of which they then return to the stack on the coffee table. Nick and Bobby and Sebastian prefer to face the sink, and so the lock hole offers a limited but satisfactory profile view of the action. Rudy, however, provides Topher and Kate with a full frontal, leaning back against the stacked washer-dryer, his pants open, free hand clutching the magazine. The creased skin of his testicles runs to dark gray, almost black—its texture recalls that of the copper beech in Kate's front yard. Kate notes how he moves not just his hand against his thing but the skin along with the hand. He twists, at intervals, around the top, as if opening a jar—opening and opening, and eventually the substance inside spurts out, thick pale fluid accommodating a flight of ambitious creatures.

Watching, Kate wants to jump in, like with the wrestling, just to be included. "Let me try," she says at the Atari, shoving Rudy aside. And he kindly lets her. She wants to beat him at that and here, also, she wants to. She feels sorry for him. It seems such a struggle. And besides Topher, she likes Rudy best of all the brothers. He is consistently thoughtful and gentle with her. Years ago, he came to her rescue on the playground when a group of older kids ran off with her winter hat. And the other day: Ella sent him over to Kate's with cinnamon buns and he found Kate in the basement, doing laundry. Her mother, though she still does Miles's laundry, is encouraging Kate to learn to do her own. So far she has shrunk her favorite jeans and dyed all her whites pink. Rudy knocked on the wall at the top of the stairs and called down to Kate, as if to a rare and excitable house pet. "Hey," she called back. "Here." She piled her basket with clean, dry laundry and stood at the bottom of the rickety wood steps. He descended, trailing one forearm against the drywall.

"My mom made something for your mom. I put it in the kitchen. On the table."

"What is it?"

"Cinnamon buns."

"Buns!" She laughed. A pair of newly pink underpants shook loose onto the floor. Topher would have teased. But, solemnly, Rudy picked them up and placed them on the top of her pile.

Like his mother, he enjoys cooking, and spends hours looking through her issues of *Gourmet,* the fact of which regularly sends Kate into hysterics.

"Will you make this!?" She points to a recipe for Raspberry Chicken.

"Or this!" Shrimp Curry.

"Or this!" Dilled *Blanquette de Veau.*

"Maybe. Maybe, maybe."

Rudy throws down the *Cosmo* or the *Playboy* and mops himself off and Kate and Topher rush to Topher's room, wait a bit, then find and scour the magazine of choice. Topher pays special attention to the *Playboy*s, while Kate skims through the provocatively titled *Cosmo* articles: "Twenty Things He Wishes You'd Do," "Fifty Nifty Sex Tips," "How to Touch Him Where It Counts," "Dirty Games to Play After Dark." On a weekend, if they are patient and attentive, they might listen outside closed doors to Nick pounding away at his girlfriend,

Suzy Brenner, Bobby at Marion Ross, Sebastian at Allison Bell, or even Mr. Anderson at Mrs. Anderson. Ella Anderson chats throughout the activity—the boys' soccer practice is mentioned, the dry cleaning, the dishwasher, as if the sex act naturally recalls other domestic concerns. Allison Bell whispers: "Like that," "Not yet," and "Fuck me." Marion giggles. Suzy Brenner shouts, "Give it to me, baby! Give it to me! Give it to me!" Suzy Brenner has long straight blond hair. If Kate and Topher climb out onto the sloped roof of the kitchen addition they can see right into Nick's bedroom. They can see Nick and Suzy kissing and taking each other's clothes off on the bed, then Suzy doing something energetic to Nick's crotch under the covers. They can see her hanging backward off the bed—they can see her on her hands and knees, Nick slamming against her from behind, a fist around the beautiful hair.

Back in Topher's room Topher does a little dance of what appears to be victory. "That's gonna be you someday. You know it, baby!"

"My hair is dark," Kate says, coldly.

"Well, you better chop that hair, Rapunzel, if you don't want—"

"Shut up. Shut. Up."

THE PHYSICS DEPARTMENT HOLDS a holiday party, which Kate and Miles and their mother attend along with Kate's father. Afterward, along with the head of the department and two other tenured professors and one graduate student and his girlfriend, they dine at the Q Club. Kate ends up next to the graduate student, Jack Auerbach. His shaggy dark hair intimidates her, as does the gap between his two front teeth. She sees that underneath the tablecloth he keeps a hand on the girl-friend's leg, as if afraid of misplacing her.

"So, you dating yet?" he asks Kate.

"Jack," the girlfriend says. "Really?"

A waiter brings bread and sweet cold butter in the shape of a star. They order their food. The adults go through several bottles of wine. Kate's father puts a roll on the end of his fork. He hits the tines with his fist and the bread flies across the restaurant, onto another table. The professors laugh. He flips more rolls. "Every trajectory," he says, in Kate's direction, "is an orbit interrupted."

Eventually, the waiter comes over.

"Kate," her father says. "You hear the man?"

Kate puts her nose into her Shirley Temple. Everyone looks at her. Jack says, "Quite the arm for a little girl." He places the last roll on his fork and shoots it down the table right into Kate's father's Bordeaux.

In the car, on the way home, her father driving quite drunkenly, Kate's mother objects. "Why must you bully her like that?"

"Who? Like what?"

"Kate. Blaming her for the bread."

"Relax, Edie."

"I understand that you were teasing, but I think you embar-rassed her."

"No! He didn't!" Kate cries. To have her embarrassment discovered and discussed would only add to it. "I didn't mind!"

Her mother twists in her seat. "Really, Katie? Because you seemed like you did."

"I didn't. I liked it."

"I don't believe you, Katie."

"It was funny. I'm going to do it in the cafeteria."

"Oh, don't do that."

"Listen to your mother," Kate's father says.

Kate's mother asks, "What's Miles doing?"

"Sleeping," Kate says.

"I heard the most horrible story on the news today," her mother says. "This poor girl got on the back of her boyfriend's motorcycle, went riding without a helmet, poor dumb thing; they ran into the back of a truck; she split her head right open."

"And?" Kate's father asks.

"Dead."

"The boy?"

"No helmet either. But okay. Just this and that. Kate," her mother asks, turning again, "are you wearing your seat belt?"

"Yes."

"Is Miles wearing his seat belt?"

"Yes."

"Any daughter of mine," Kate's father says, "went riding on the back of a motorcycle with no helmet, *I'd* crack her head open."

"Oh, Dennis!"

"What."

"Dennis, what a horrible, horrible thing to say."

"Well, aren't you the shrinking violet."

"Like you didn't ride your motorcycle without a helmet every day from Los Alamos to Santa Fe when you were twenty . . ."

"Kate, my darling. Light of my life. Don't follow my bad example."

"Okay, Daddy."

"As a matter of fact, stay away from bikes altogether. And the guys who ride 'em." He turns onto Livingston Street.

"That Jack is a nice fellow," Edie says.

"And talented." Dennis pulls up to the house and kills the engine. "I've got my eye on him."

3

COLIN TOOK THE POSITION in Stamford and they bought a Cherokee with thirty thousand miles on it and rented an apartment in Bridgeport, a one-bedroom on the first floor of a teal blue three-family house reminiscent of the Livingston Street house: the white walls, the plaster, the dark oak trim, a china closet with iron latticework. Their first night in the new place they slept on the pullout in the living room, and Colin wanted to call his mother but Kate wouldn't let him. Darcy found a new roommate and applied to MFA programs. Like a traveling circus, the wedding hoopla moved on to someone, somewhere else. Colin and Kate were alone, surrounded by dozens and dozens of glass bowls.

A month or so into their marriage, they took a belated honeymoon to Eastern Europe, stopping on the way in London to visit Colin's sister, Moira. On the plane they were separated—overbooking, a situation with a mother and baby. This seemed like a bad sign to both of them. Colin spoke with a flight attendant, then tapped the shoulder of the man Kate had ended up next to, a courteous bearded Indian fellow. "Wonder if you'd mind switching seats with me. So that we could . . . so that I could sit next to my wife. It's our first trip together," he explained.

The man agreeably moved from his window seat. Later,

waiting for the bathroom at the back of the plane, Kate spotted him squeezed between a sprawling teenager and a heavyset older man. She wished Colin had refrained from requesting
the favor, feeling uneasily that much had been given to them
already—their being young and well-off and lucky to have
found each other and in love and lucky to be going on this
adventure together. But she went back to her seat beside Colin
(he the aisle, she the window) and held hands with him when
the plane landed.

They took a cab to Maida Vale, where Moira and her husband, Paul, lived with their new baby boy. Moira opened the
gate, holding the baby, and offered tea. She directed them to
their room. They unpacked, showered, lay down on the bed.
Kate rolled on top of Colin and unzipped his fly. "We'd better
wait," he said. "We just got here." They went down to the
kitchen where Moira moved around from sink to counter to
stove, rinsing and chopping and cooking. She wore a long skirt
with a ruffle and a white button-down shirt. Her shape, post-
partum, seemed barely recognizable as female, distended in all
the wrong directions, as though she had put herself through
the dryer on the highest, hottest cycle.

Didn't she care? Did she?

"Want help?" Kate asked. She pointed to the stove.

"Don't worry. Sit." Moira set a bottle of white Burgundy
and three glasses on the scuffed wood table. They sat. They
drank the wine. The baby lay on his back under a mirrored
contraption and kicked his legs and arms.

"Liam's in his office," Paul said.

Liam, Kate observed, at five months had not yet grown into
his looks—in fact, he struck her as the ugliest baby she'd ever
encountered. He had pale red hair and demonically bright

blue eyes and a squashed face. His fat little hands grabbed at anything and everything—Colin's nose, Kate's earrings, his mother's bosom, his own tiny package.

"I'm making biryani," Moira said. "Lamb. Kate, you're not a vegetarian, are you? I should have asked."

"Nope. Not me."

"She barely eats anyway," Colin said. "Look at her."

Liam kicked on the mat and began to cry. Moira swept him up and sat at the table and took out her breast. Gigantic blurred purple veins led from the base to the nipple, which disappeared suddenly, mercifully, under the baby's head. Sucking sounds commenced. Kate drank the wine rapidly, feeling squirmy. She recalled her mother bringing Miles home from the hospital and sitting up in the parental bed, nursing him.

Moira put Liam against her shoulder and patted his back and put him down and returned to the stove, bordered prettily by blue-and-white tile. An earthenware jug held cooking utensils. A bouquet of drying herbs hung from the iron pot rack. An empty dog bed occupied the corner by the back door. "Where's the dog?" Kate asked. "What kind?"

"We had a Great Dane. Alice. But then we had Liam. And she was too much work so we gave her away." Moira shrugged and made a regretful face. "It's ready," she said.

They ate and finished the wine. Paul went to put the baby to bed and Colin and Moira and Kate cleared up. Kate took to the wooden cutting board with a sponge and soap and Moira came up behind her and removed it from her hands. "Never use soap on wood," Moira said.

"Heh, heh," Colin said. "Wood."

Upstairs, Liam wailed.

"Why do they have to cry?" Moira said. "I wish they didn't. I'd take him into the bed if Paul was okay with it. But." They followed her up the stairs. "Try to sleep." Then, "So good to see you two!" She embraced them both. Kate leaned warily but curiously into her large, milky bosom. "Sweet dreams!"

Twenty minutes later they were occupied under the covers, pushing aside each other's sleepwear (Kate's a silk slip she'd gotten for her bridal shower, Colin's a T-shirt and boxer shorts). He kissed her breasts; she made her way down his torso and put her face in his groin. Moira knocked on the door. "Sorry! Towels!"

"Wait, stop," Colin whispered.

Kate opened her mouth on him, slid him down her throat.

"I have washcloths and hand towels and regular."

How insufferable Moira was! How officious, how interfering!

Colin grabbed Kate's head, conflicted. "Stop," he said again.

She continued. What better way to render the competition irrelevant?

"Should I just leave them here?"

"Yes. Please."

"We decided on the Globe Theatre tomorrow. What do you think? Colin?"

"Yes! Great!"

Moira retreated. Colin removed his hand from Kate's head and reached down and pinched her behind. Teasingly, but hard. "Get thee to a nunnery." He moved his hands in her hair. "But first, keep doing that."

.   .   .

IN THE MORNING she pulled on tight corduroys and a tighter T-shirt. Moira had a baby but Kate had a body. Colin snored on his back. She shook him. "Wake up."

"Not now."

"Resist the jet lag."

They followed the smell of coffee downstairs. Moira stood again at the sink, washing a pacifier. She turned as they shuffled in. "Harold Eagleson died," she said to Colin. "A heart attack, last night." She looked at Kate. "He was like family. We grew up with his kids. Janie, Charlie, Meg."

"The one who fucked the maid," Colin said to Kate.

"Oh, Colin." Moira shook out the pacifier and dropped it into the dish rack.

"I'll get in touch." Colin poured coffee for Kate, then for himself. He sat next to her at the table and put his hand on her leg.

"Such a shock."

"How old was Harold?"

"Seventy-five. Give or take."

"And a heart condition. So. Not really a shock."

"You're being mean." She looked at Kate. "He can be mean sometimes, you know."

Paul walked in, holding Liam against his shoulder. Moira reached for the baby and unbuttoned her blouse.

"It's too bad about Harold. Just not a shock."

The purpose of this conversation, of most conversations managed by Moira, Kate had decided, or at least those that happened around Kate, was to point out Kate's adjunct status in the family. The purpose of the whole visit, the whole detour to London, Kate suspected, was the exploration of this fascinating dynamic. Encounters, even the simplest ones, between Kate and Moira presented certain challenges and discomforts, yet also certain thrills. And Colin on some level seemed to enjoy pitting Kate and Moira against each other, throwing them in the ring like mud wrestlers in slick bikinis— his own sister!

"Well, the Globe's out, I guess," Moira said. "It's raining, anyway."

"Yep." Colin reached for the newspaper.

"You should write them," Moira said. "They wrote us when Dad died."

"Can't I just call?"

"A note is better."

"Can I use your Mac then, later?"

"You should *write* it. With a pen and notepaper and your very own hand."

"I'll help you," Kate said.

Colin took her hand and drew her onto his lap. He kissed her neck.

"You guys are too in love," Paul said. "Can't watch. Train wreck."

Moira cooed at Liam. She stroked his pale head and guided him onto breast number two. Milk sprayed the kid's face.

Kate read her book and Colin read his newspaper. She peered over his arm. He was deep into an article titled "After a Year, Santer Wins Friends, But Not Headlines."

"I should really read the paper," she said. "Who's Santer?"

"You take it when I'm done."

"I just always feel like I'm so behind already. Like it's a class I've skipped all semester and there's no way I can catch up.

Like I just won't understand what's going on if I jump in now."

"Newspapers," Colin said, "are written for people like you."

THE RAIN STOPPED and Moira decided an outing was best after all, and so they left the house at noon and took the underground to Notting Hill and walked up and down Portobello Road. They stopped at a market on the way home and shopped for dinner. Then Kate and Colin sat at the kitchen table with Moira's notepaper, light green with a rough texture and ragged edges, and two purple felt-tip pens. Colin wrote their names in a heart. He drew legs on the heart, then a penis. Kate giggled.

"Don't waste it, please," said Moira, from her everlasting stance at the sink.

Paul lounged in an armchair by the window, reading Colin's discarded *Times.* Kate smoothed out the notepaper. Resentment nudged at her, on Moira's behalf and toward Moira herself. Water ran, the dishwasher chugged, noises Kate associated with Livingston Street and her mother and the kitchen and the fridge and the mnemonics: *Bright Stars Far North. Violet Goes Willingly. Eli the Ice Man.*

Colin rolled the pens away and got his favorite fancy ballpoint from his coat. He cracked his knuckles and hunched over the paper, sighing. "Just say how sorry you are," Kate said. "Et cetera, et cetera."

"I know," Colin said, but his tongue went between his teeth and he filled the page haltingly. Kate checked the wall clock: six-thirty. She waited for someone to offer her a drink and when, by seven, no one had, she opened the fridge and poured herself a glass of wine.

"There," he said, and slid the paper and pen across the table, and she began to write out the letter, and he watched her do so, and they carried on like kids copying homework. Then Colin took Liam in his lap and sang a little song to him, about a man who lived in the moon and played on a ladle. It surprised Kate that he knew such a song.

"He looks like you," Moira said to Colin. She leaned over Liam and peered at him like a scientist examining the results of a lab test.

"He doesn't," Kate said. "Not at all. He doesn't look like Colin at all."

"Oh, he definitely does!" Moira said.

"I don't see it," Kate said.

"Well, he is related to me. Let's hope he doesn't end up with my hairline."

"He has your chin, Colin. Your nose."

"Yup. Mom's chin. Dad's nose."

"And I have the opposite—isn't that funny."

"He looks just like Liza's kid. They *look* like cousins."

"So great to see those guys at the wedding."

"All babies look alike," Kate said.

"No, this one is a Doyle. No question." Moira tickled Liam's little foot.

"You, Liza, who else?"

"You're next, maybe. And Daniel's getting married."

"That's right."

"I chatted with her. Sweet."

"Think his eyes will stay blue?" Colin asked.

"They will. Paul's are blue. Blue is recessive."

Paul spoke up from behind the paper. "They say blue-eyed men pick blue-eyed women in order to be sure of paternity."

Moira looked closely at Kate. "Uh-oh, Colin. Her eyes are brown."

"I'm not worried," Colin said.

"Your kids will have brown eyes then," Moira said. "Brown is dominant."

"Right."

"Are you going to raise them Catholic?"

"What, our kids?" Colin blew a raspberry on Liam's cheek.

"We're atheists," Kate said to Moira.

"Atheists or agnostic?" Paul lowered the paper.

"We're not observant. And anyway, Kate is . . ." Colin looked at her.

"Episcopalian," Kate said.

"You'll have to send them to me," Moira said. "For their religious education."

Kate stood, gathering her wine and writing supplies. "I think I'm going to go upstairs and finish this."

She hoped, expected, that Colin would follow her. That he would take the pen and paper from her and write out the second letter himself. Instead he continued his misplaced worship of Liam.

"Okay. Later," she said.

He glanced up. "Don't lose that pen."

"What?" She stood in the doorway. He passed his nephew back to his sister.

"It's my favorite pen."

She threw the pen at his head.

"Jesus! Kate!"

She ran upstairs. He ran after her. She rushed into their room and slammed the door behind her. He banged it immediately open and followed her in.

"What the fuck . . ."

"I copied that letter for you! And no thank-you, no nothing!"

"I was going to—"

"I help you with your homework and you're too fucking self-righteous and self-important to even thank me; you just assume my entire purpose in life is getting your back; you're too busy getting a hard-on over your nephew—"

"Kate!"

"That kid is ugly, ugly! He doesn't look one bit like you!"

He put his hands on her shoulders. "What the fuck is wrong with you?"

What *was* wrong with her? She hated Moira at the sink. She hated herself hunched over the letter.

"That kid . . ." she said. How to describe his special ugliness? "Remember that *Seinfeld* episode? Elaine? And the rabbi? And the baby?"

He pushed her. She fell backward onto the bed.

"I should leave you."

"Yeah, you probably should." Behind her sinuses she felt the shameful pressure of tears.

"Right this minute."

"And *then* who's going to suck you off? Moira?"

He slammed the door behind him.

"Stop slamming the door!" Moira, the patron saint of suffering, called up the stairs.

Kate wished she could take it back. She regretted everything.

What had come over her?

No. She'd meant it, all of it. She would say it again.

She put on her jacket and slipped down the back stairs into the early dark illuminated strangely at the corners of the sky. She walked to a bus stop. She felt terribly lonely, as if she'd left her soul behind in the warm but horrible house.

She waited and got on the next bus. She went up the narrow stairs to the upper level. It was wonderful up there. The other passengers seemed civilized and compassionate. She admired their drab skin, their terrible teeth, the unkempt hair and nails of even the fashionable ones. They looked at her as if they recognized her wicked ways and forgave them. She took a seat by the window. Shops and lights passed below. She saw rooftops, gardens lying dormant, smoke lifting from chimneys.

Once, only once, had her mother protested the division of labor at 123 Livingston Street. United Illuminating had downsized her department, leaving the remaining staff to pick up the slack. Miles was tiny and teething. Dennis was writing a book. A storm had torn a gutter from the northern side of the house. Their city-issued trash bins had disappeared and Public Works had refused to provide replacements unless a case report was filed, in person, at the police station on State Street. The hot-water heater had gone bust and it was February. Kate had been sick with a fever, home from school. Edie had taken a day off from work, then scrambled for sitters. Dennis's brother and family were scheduled to visit. An argument erupted after dinner one night—raised voices, tears from Edie. Kate sat at the kitchen table making up homework. Activity commenced in the front hallway, the activity of Edie putting on her coat and boots and banging out the front door. Minutes later she returned, for Kate, as it turned out. They got into the car and drove downtown and saw a movie at York Square. Then for a week or two Edie went on strike. The sink filled with dishes. Laundry piled up in bedrooms and hallways and outside the door that led to the basement. Trash accumulated in the kitchen and the Tuesday-morning collectors ignored the loose bags Dennis dragged grouchily out to the street. No dinner, no hot water, no clean underwear.

Finally Miles's day care called and a roach crawled out of the sink. The same Friday. On Saturday morning Edie gave in and tackled the mess, to everyone's—even Kate's—relief.

Next to Kate on the bus a man ate a Cadbury bar. She asked him, "Is there anything to do on this line?"

He looked up. "Well, there's shopping. The mall. Stop after next."

"Anything else?"

"Skating at Marble Arch."

She saw the skating rink ringed by light in an odd little park. She ran off the bus and followed the lights. She had to go through the underworld of an underground station to get there, under the avenue, then up into a tent where another helpful Cadbury-wielding Brit pointed her left. She felt drunk—maybe she was. How much wine had she had, and how little had she eaten? Not since lunch and then just a side of chips. In a warm busy carpeted room, boys and girls and men and women occupied upholstered benches, strapping on skates. She pushed a few pounds across the counter and then she was unzipping her boots and hooking up laces. She stashed her things in a locker (briefly, she recalled her old high school) and wobbled toward the rink. She stepped on and tentatively pushed forward. The morning's rain had pooled on the ice and everyone was falling, but exuberantly. They slid through water and slipped and landed on their sides, backs, knees, and behinds. A father tried to get his son to break his hold on the rail. A small girl windmilled forward, shrieking. Kate tensed her thighs and turned her feet in and out, swizzling, until her muscles loosened and her feet began to know where they were. Rock music blared from giant speakers. Spectators thronged at the edges. Around and around she went, darting, dodging small children, sluicing through puddles. Water soaked the ends of her jeans and the denim flapped heavily around the skates.

She skated until the rink closed, then found her way home on the bus. Later, in bed, pacified by fellatio, Colin hugged her shoulders and rubbed her back. "I'm sorry."

"No, I'm sorry. My chaos, and you, an innocent bystander."

He wasn't, though. They both knew that. He was by no means innocent. Neither was; neither wanted to be. "We're confused," they told each other, but they knew; now they knew for sure that each had found in the other an accomplice.

THEY TOOK A TRAIN from Krakow to Budapest to Prague. It was then that she began to apologize indiscriminately—for talking too much, talking too little, wearing too much makeup or wearing none at all. Colin accepted the apologies, squeezing her shoulders. "It's okay," he said. If she shifted and dug her elbow into his side, if she handled him too roughly, if her teeth grazed his skin, then he'd object, wanting another apology, her soft and supplicating voice. But she sensed his uncertainty, a normal touch of uncertainty that had developed, at Moira's, into something more serious. So she apologized for that too— she apologized for both of them.

Every night they went out to eat and hear music. He ordered the drinks and picked up the check. She let him do the talking, which meant she seldom got what she wanted. They sat close to each other in banquettes and drank chilled vodka and ate nuts from a bowl. They clinked their glasses together. Under her knit dress Kate wore a pink lace bra and pink lace underpants to match. When she got up to go to the restroom, men examined her. In the mirror over the sink she saw that she was beautiful. She retouched her red lips. She wet her eyelashes. She pinched her cheeks. She pushed her loose hair off her face.

They finished their drinks. She put a hand on Colin's thigh, then his crotch. He left money on the table. They stumbled out onto the street, his arm around her hips, and kissed in a doorway. He put his hands under her dress. He pulled down her stockings and pink lace.

"We shouldn't be doing this," she said. "Who does this?"

"What?"

"Who gets married?"

"People get married all the time."

"I feel like I'm going to ruin you."

"Why would you do a thing like that?"

"Not on purpose . . ."

"I won't let you."

"We could still get this whole business annulled."

"Are you fucking kidding me?"

.   .   .

THEY RETURNED to Bridgeport, to the wedding gifts and the packing boxes and the teal blue house. And then, for a while, years and years, in fact, it seemed as though things were going to be all right.

4

KATE SWIPED A RAG through the cabinets and put down contact paper and organized the wedding gifts. She wrote thank-you notes and took her wedding dress to the dry cleaner's. She put a pink lamp in the window and Colin set it with a timer. Together, they hung drapes and venetian blinds. They hung tiny pictures in gilt frames. They disguised their ratty couches and chairs with Indian bedspreads and pillows. They merged her CD collection and his books on tape, her pink ceramic bowls and his Indonesian masks, her novels and his *Wall Street Journals*. They shopped for towels and sheets and then a bed: a sleigh bed that reminded Kate of the hill in Eastwood Park and how she'd torn up her face once sledding right through a dry bush.

She found a job in the financial-planning department of Silgan Holdings—manufacturers of metal food containers with a sidebar in cardboard and plastic—and started right after Christmas. Then she and Colin drove to Stamford together weekday mornings in the Jeep, stopping for coffee at the nearest Dunkin' Donuts. The weekends they spent having sex and going out to eat at a diner in a deserted neighborhood on the other side of the highway, a place Colin claimed was dangerous for a woman to visit alone. That was what they did and that was enough. All Kate knew of where she lived was the apartment, sex, the diner, the feeling of the highway all around. She wore old corduroys and cleaned out the coffeepot with kosher salt. She drove to Home Depot and lost herself in the long aisles, examining nails, bolts, hammers, sandpaper, picture hooks, lumber, pliers, power drills, screwdrivers, levels, clamps, pots of paint and wood glue and polyurethane and spackle. She built shelves in the kitchen with plywood and strips of metal, and she stacked the shelves with cookbooks organized by cuisine, a French wire utensil basket in the shape of a hen, and ceramic flour and sugar jugs that later became infested with moths.

Colin's promotion had bestowed upon him a private office. When Kate called him at work, he answered the phone quickly and sounded lonely. To protect him from his solitude, she called him three times a day until he got irritated. She discovered that he was the type of person who faithfully consulted the phonebook and unplugged the toaster and all the lamps when they went away for the weekend. Sometimes when they left the apartment together she had to go inside again for something she'd forgotten, and when she came back out he'd ask her, "Did you reset the alarm? Did you lock the door?" Sometimes Kate found this funny and sometimes she didn't. He discovered that she was the type of person who forgot a pork chop in the oven for a couple of weeks. When he wasn't home, she called information and cleaned the CDs with her spit.

Above, in the second-floor apartment, lived a British journalist and his six-year-old daughter, who stayed with him Wednesday through Sunday. The journalist, Wes, was in a custody battle with his ex, whom he referred to as "the woman who used to be Lucy's mother." Kate could hear him fighting with her on the phone, fighting with such bitterness and fury that at first Kate thought he was rehearsing for a play. Wednesday through Sunday she heard Lucy practicing piano: "Mary Had a Little Lamb," "Three Blind Mice," "Für Elise." In the attic apartment lived Andie and Brice, a twenty-something couple from Colorado. Brice was a forestry student, Andie an artist-slash-masseuse, heavyset and shy around groups of people.

The landlady, a widow with four teenagers, clearly cared little for the house, which had advantages (the low rent) and disadvantages (broken appliances, unreturned phone calls). Once in a while she had her teenagers come over and mow the yard and the two struggling patches of grass on either side of the front steps.

In April, Andie knocked on Kate's door and invited her to help with a garden. They got into the Jeep and drove to a nursery. "What should we get?" Kate asked, looking around.

"What works in this climate?"

"I thought you would know." She imagined Andie to have intimate knowledge of all things earth-related. "You're, like, nature girl."

Andie shrugged. "We lived in the mountains. Our backyard grows wildflowers."

"This looks tough," Kate said. She pointed to a bush with shiny prickly leaves. "Not so pretty, but—"

Andie read the information on the plant's white plastic tag. "Yes. Good."

They loaded the back of the Jeep with perennials and impatiens. They scattered the impatiens and lined the larger plants up next to one another in even rows, the plants like people lined up for coffee—the shiny investment banker, the willowy artist, the housewife, the college student. Colin planted new grass in a barren patch of the yard, grass that ended up thriving and making the other grass look bad.

May nourished the garden with constant rain. Then in June the world opened up, inviting everyone to be a part of it. "I'm bored," Kate said. They sat on the couch in the living room, watching *Seinfeld*.

"Already?"

"Maybe just with my job."

At Silgan, the work itself of little consequence to her, and New York with its mighty relevance removed from her daily life, she had begun to feel some existential angst.

"What about teaching or something instead?" Colin asked. "All those young minds."

"I don't want to *teach*!"

"Whatever makes you happy."

"I'm afraid of children."

"You won't be when they're ours."

"Isn't there anywhere to eat around here besides the diner?"

"There's gotta be."

"Let's see a movie tomorrow."

"Okay. Nothing artsy."

She got up and shook out the local weekly. "How's this? 'U.S. Marines take over Alcatraz and threaten San Francisco with biological weapons.' Nicolas Cage, Sean Connery."

So the following evening they set the alarm and locked the door and stepped out into the muggy evening, and then they got into the Jeep and drove down long hilly bending heavily populated roads toward the Showcase Cinemas. It was an election year and political flags cluttered front lawns alongside children's toys. Colin turned the car onto the Post Road and they passed the Lender's bagel factory and the Sears and the Super Kmart. He said, "What about that place by the Dunkin' Donuts?"

"The faux hunting lodge?"

"Yeah. The steakhouse."

They pulled into the parking lot, fragrant with the smell of doughnuts frying next door. They went inside and sat in a booth. Framed French posters adorned wood-paneled walls. "Salad bar," Kate said. "Priceless." A blond waitress with a bouffant hairdo and a big smile took their drink order. Kate's pinot grigio and Colin's Guinness arrived within minutes. And soon after, the food: teriyaki sirloin and the prime rib, baked potatoes on the side.

Kate put her hands around her wineglass. She leaned back in the booth.

"I'm so happy," she said.

The blond waitress served another round of drinks. Then dessert, Mississippi Mud Pie. They made it to the theater in time for the previews.

At home, after the movie, Kate tackled Colin at the bathroom sink. He spit Crest and saliva into the drain. "Hey, there."

She squeezed him around the torso, and then hammered at his back. "That was fun, wasn't it?"

"What?"

"*The Rock*! So good!"

"Hell, yeah." He shook out the toothbrush and turned around. She punched him in the gut. "Um, what the fuck was that?"

"Just a love punch."

"Love punch, huh?"

He picked her up and threw her over his shoulder.

"Where are you taking me?"

"Where do you think?"

They rolled around the sleigh bed. She gasped and moaned.

"Keep it down. It's Saturday. Lucy'll hear us," he said.

"She won't."

"Try to be quiet."

"I don't care."

"I do."

He put his hand over her mouth. She hooked one leg over his shoulder.

"Okay, will you stop now?"

"No," she said, from behind his palm. "I won't."

The following Wednesday, as Lucy banged through "Für Elise," Kate said, "Do that thing."

"What? What thing?"

"From the other night."

"What?"

"That thing with your hand."

"This?" He did it. She jammed her nails into his back. He pressed harder over her mouth.

"Oh, yeah? Is that how it's gonna be?"

And so it went. Lucy graduated to Pachelbel's Canon, to Mozart's Minuet in G. Kate moaned and hung on to the bed. She murmured into Colin's hand.

"What? I can't hear you."

"Mmmmmm . . ."

"You want it hard? Is that what you want? Is that what you're trying to say? Okay. I'll let you talk."

Though normally, in the context of their shared experience, seventy percent of most everything seemed funny, in bed nothing did—not the ungainliness of genitalia, not the extremity of certain positions, not even hearing one's spouse carry on like a porn star.

He lifted his hand.

"Yes. Hard."

"Yeah?" Hand over the mouth again. His other hand holding her wrists. A natural, he was.

"Oh, yes. Like that."

Week after week, the blond waitress smiled and rushed their drinks. A black man shot the white men who raped his nine-year-old daughter and a handsome, heroic young white lawyer got him off. Aliens attempted to take over the earth and were thwarted by a disenchanted scientist and a feisty young air force officer. A good guy and a bad guy switched faces and the bad guy killed the only person capable of reversing the operation. A prison transport plane was hijacked by the convicts on board and a Desert Storm vet in jail for manslaughter wrested control of the plane from the other, nastier convicts and landed it on the Las Vegas strip. Harrison Ford faced down a terrorist. "I am the president of the United States," Ford declared. The audience laughed. Colin prodded Kate in the ribs and, crunching popcorn, whispered jokes about the Force.

One Thursday in August during prime-time repeats she reached over from her side of the couch to rub his stomach. "Not tonight, baby," he said. "Long day. Long week. And listen, little Lucy."

Bach jingled above.

Kate grabbed his package and squeezed it. He pushed her off the couch, onto the floor, where the rug burned her elbow so badly that it bled. She got her way.

The air began to smell of apples, and squash appeared in bins outside the Stop & Shop. Darcy quit her paralegal job to begin art school. Colin and Kate continued to go to the steakhouse and a movie on Friday nights but Kate wore corduroys instead of flowered cotton dresses and the movies aspired to have more meaning. There was a John Cougar song on the radio that Kate liked and she searched for it as they drove to work or around doing errands. They built fires in the white-painted brick fireplace, which worked without a hitch or even a cleaning, and Colin's favorite shows began to premiere. He watched the television in the living room and when he laughed Kate ran in from the kitchen or the bedroom or the study, wanting to hear the joke, wanting to laugh too. He brought her flowers on their first anniversary and she persuaded him to lick wedding cake (defrosted) from her nipples. On a public radio station Kate discovered a show that played jazz and big-band music from six to midnight on Saturday nights. She got to know the sound of Artie Shaw, Glenn Miller, Billie Holiday, Sophie Tucker, and the crackling of old records coming through a tiny metal portable radio Colin had received for his communion. She brought the radio into the blue bathroom while she took a candlelit bath. They shopped for Halloween pumpkins and laid newspaper down on the living room floor and carved them, and Kate giggled over Colin's pumpkin face, which had the same personality as his handwriting, generous and goofy and sweet. They put the pumpkins on the porch and became disillusioned with them when they saw Wes's far more spectacular pumpkin: a Byzantine production of mosaic-style diamond-shaped cutouts. Andie, who knew everything, caught Kate on the stairs and told her Wes had used a pattern. On Halloween Kate and Colin filled bowls of candy and ran to the door when the bell rang, slipping on the rugs and watching each other with the children. Around eleven they turned off the porch light and retired.

"I meant to dress *up*," she said. "Oh, well. How's this." She tied her nightshirt up around her waist, her hair into a high ponytail, and posed at the end of the bed. "You be the captain. I'm Jeannie."

"Wow," he said. "I love you. I mean, I really love you. Come here."

"Yes, master."

She put her head down into her crossed arms and he entered her from behind. "That good, baby?" He ran a hand over her shoulders, her breasts, her back.

"My ass."

"What about your beautiful ass?"

"Hit it. Hit me. Hit me on the ass."

He smacked her. And smacked her again.

"Harder."

Again. He grabbed her hips. His pelvis slapped her behind in counts of two. Their breathing ripped at the dry atmosphere, the nosebleed-making skin-cracking winter interior drought and chill.

"My hair," she said.

"What about your hair?" He reached around and twisted her nipple. "You don't want me to mess up your hair?"

"No, no . . ."

"Well, too bad, just wait and get a load of what I'm going to do in your hair when I'm done fucking you."

"No, pull it. My hair, pull my hair."

"Like that? You mean like that?"

He wrapped the long layers around his wrist. Her head snapped back. He jerked it from side to side.

"Yes, yes . . . ow, yes . . ."

THEY ATTENDED HIS COMPANY holiday party. For the occasion, Kate bought a red dress at the Saks in the Stamford mall. The dress, a soft jersey, fell off the shoulder in a Grecian sort of way, hugged her breasts and waist, then flared out slightly to end at her knees. She lit a candle and sat on the bed with her legs up on the bureau as she applied makeup, listening to an album of rock and hip-hop artists covering traditional Christmas music. She put on lip gloss to match the dress, sheer hose, high heels, rhinestone earrings. Then she put on a secondhand black twill coat with black soft synthetic fur at the collar and hems and went out into the bright cold night and got into the Jeep with her young, capable husband. All the way to Stamford she could not get over herself—she kept glancing in the passenger-side mirror.

Had she remembered to blow out the candle?

Yes, she had.

"I'll give you a tour," he said, when they got to the party. He procured punch in plastic cups. He showed her his office, petite but private, with a view of other office buildings. He showed her the kitchenette and the copiers.

"Very cool. My office doesn't have those."

"Ha, ha."

"Really, honey."

"I'll show you how it works." He stuck his hand on the screen and made a copy and handed it to her.

"I'm awed by your technological prowess."

"We have different-colored paper too. I'll show you."

"I'm wet already."

"Come on."

She blew him in the supply closet.

WINTER SETTLED into the town off the highway. Colin picked Kate up at work and they drove home through a bad neighborhood and pulled up to the apartment; then, half an hour later, the house was warm and Colin was in front of the TV with a bourbon on the rocks and Kate was in the shabby little kitchen with an apron and the Sabatier knives, teaching herself to cook. She consulted recipes and made pork chops with apples, Hungarian goulash, tagliatelle with raisins and chicken. She made meatballs and meat loaf and flank steak and mashed potatoes and creamed spinach and veal tonnato and couscous with raisins and pine nuts and duck with green olives. She made mole sauce and red Thai curry and tandoori lamb. She threw lemons down the disposal and lit candles to protect her eyes from the onions. Waving a broom in front of the smoke alarm, she recalled Ella Anderson. She opened windows and the door to the yard. Then the smell of Andie's incense drifted down the back stairs to Kate and Colin's apartment and mixed with their garlic and candles and coffee, Wes's lamb chops and cats. Wes's furious phone calls continued. Kate was amazed that after months of this, he still had the energy to be so angry. Often he shouted, "Liar! You're a liar!" Kate asked Andie what the issue was, exactly. Why couldn't they share Lucy, as they'd been doing? She said that the ex-mother wanted to move to Oregon with her new boyfriend and take Lucy with her.

On the first Thursday of every month Brice and Colin went bowling and Andie and Kate met at one or the other's apartment and talked and drank wine and ate Terra Blues potato chips. Andie was going to an acupuncturist named Tamara whom she described as "the most spiritual person I've ever met." She made references to a mysterious illness but Kate couldn't figure out what it was and she didn't want to ask because she was afraid Andie had already told her and she'd somehow forgotten. Andie said that sometimes she cried, getting her treatments; that certain memories were stored in the body and the needles woke and released the memories along with the pain. Kate asked her if she and Brice considered themselves happy. Andie said that happiness was not something she ever thought about. She'd accepted the fact that adult life was just a long process of healing the damage done to you as a child.

"What happened?" Kate asked. "I mean, to you?" Like a psychiatric patient, she reclined on her living room couch while Andie sat cross-legged but upright in an armchair.

"I was raped."

"You *were*?"

"I'm okay," Andie said. "It was a long time ago. But yes."

She told the story: a sleepover, the friend's older brother, a forced "confession" to the family priest, a subsequent rejection, later in life, of the Catholic Church, etc., etc.

"It's why I keep the weight on," Andie said.

"Why?"

"I used to be thin. But I didn't like men looking at me. Now they don't."

"Doesn't . . . Brice look at you?"

"Brice?" Andie shrugged. "He's my husband. He's my best friend."

"Nothing like that ever happened to me," Kate said.

"No trouble? Ever?"

"Nothing much. My dad was strict. But I needed that." Kate sat up suddenly. She reached for a potato chip and looked at it. "I don't know why I feel so strange sometimes."

"Even massage can help," Andie said. "Come up tomorrow for a session. On me. You shovel the walk."

So Kate climbed the stairs to Andie's apartment and stripped down to her underpants and lay on a foldout massage table in the kitchen. Andie dimmed the lights and lit candles and put on Enya. She rubbed oil between her palms and dug into Kate's back. "Let go," she said.

"Of what?"

"Let your mind wander."

"Okay. Going to try."

"What are you thinking about right now?"

"Thinking about . . . bills. Have to pay 'em. Tonight. Ugh. And about how good this feels."

"Well. Think about the bills if you need to." Andie kneaded and pushed. Kate thought about the bills. She thought about a café she used to spend time at in college, about the dusky pink walls and the radiator at her knees in her favorite seat and the lattes and the Billie Holliday the owner had obsessively played. She thought about a life-drawing class she took her senior year and about her college boyfriend, who'd cheated on her with the model. She thought about a deer hanging by its legs in the garage in Galveston.

"Relax," Andie said. "Every day is a task. But at night, count your blessings. Don't think too much. Don't look too hard. Let your life find you."

THE FOLLOWING SUMMER, Kate and Colin's second since the wedding, Darcy came to visit wearing glitter and bangles and heels, grime in her enhanced hair. She got off the train full of stories and energy and drama. "He can't commit to anything," she said about her new guy. "I mean, in other ways he's been great. He's been to shrinkage with me. He's been communicating. He bought a new mattress and everything, like I told him to."

"Mattress . . . ?"

"He was fucking around. I told him I wouldn't fuck him on the same mattress he'd been fucking around on."

"I see."

"It's not as if I'm like, 'Marry me, marry me.' But there comes a time, you know? So I'm giving him an ultimatum."

"Another one?"

"One last one."

"You're a catch," Kate said. "I would marry you. If *he* won't marry you . . . I'll divorce Colin and *I'll* marry you."

"Fun!" Kate turned off the highway. Darcy squeezed her thigh. "Well, at least if Jesse and I break up I won't ever have to eat Indian food again. We go out for Indian food three times a week. I get chicken or shrimp or vegetarian. Jesse, every time, the same lamb vindaloo. The same! He would eat lamb vindaloo every single day if he could. I'm starting to *smell* like Indian food. My body odor, everything. They plop down this disgusting meat, and this pile of greasy rice, and he just plows right through it . . . astonishing. And he wonders why he's getting a gut."

They sat in Kate's living room drinking wine.

"What is it like?" Darcy asked. "Being *married*? Is it fun? Is it weird?"

"I don't know. Both."

"I love your bracelets!" Darcy cried. Kate had taken to wearing silver bangles. "Oh, I miss you!"

Her visit reminded Kate and Colin that New York was not so far away. So when Colin picked Kate up from work on a Friday instead of going home to the apartment they would drive to the station and catch the six twenty-two.

The train would be crowded, going in. By Stamford sometimes all the seats were taken. Then Kate and Colin would stand by the doors and lean into each other against the rail. He would put his arms around her and rub her back and she would lay her head against his chest and look through the grimy glass doors at the inner-city kids playing basketball in cement lots, their bodies loose as water, skin like coal brushed orange in the summer dusk—then, when the weather changed, dark in sweats and snug knit caps. Kate saw a house built into the bay, a restaurant she'd gone to once with her father, over Fourth of July weekend—they'd watched the fireworks and talked about the constellations right there at the far table on the back patio with the train overhead, maybe some other girl watching them, seeing them from the window, briefly, swaying raptly in transport. Maybe that other girl, watching Kate and her father, had wanted her guy as badly as Kate wanted Colin, holding on to him on the rickety train, one hand exploring his neck, his face, his head, his vanishing hair.

Another year went by and the blond waitress disappeared and the movies became less interesting and there was nothing

left to hammer or hang or build or organize and Kate and
Colin wandered from room to room like bored teenagers.
Kate lay with her body half on and half off the bed and noted
how long it took her to fall and whether Colin pulled her
back up and onto the bed before this happened. She rearranged
the candles on the sideboard and he checked on the basement
or watched golf or went to get a sandwich. Though neither
said anything about it, both realized that some of their pen-
chant for each other—so alarmingly quickly!—was falling
away. The sex got rougher, as if to compensate. And every
once in a while they would fight, badly, fights that recalled the
Liam fight, and the center, the object, of their fights would
shift, frustratingly, so that neither Kate nor Colin could determine later what the fight was really about. They screamed at
each other, not caring at all that Wes and Lucy and Brice and
Andie could hear them. Kate broke a plate and Colin broke
a horrible wooden fish given to them by Kate's Philadelphia
relatives.

Sometimes just for something to do they drove out to the
shoreline, looked at the water and in the windows of houses,
stood in bookstores and flipped through the bestsellers and
told each other, "Listen, listen to this," shopped for cider and
taffy and pumpkins, and sometimes these things surprised
them by substituting well for what they actually wanted. The
oil heater broke and for a week they spent the evenings in bed,
under the down comforter and the matelassé bedspread. Kate
read a novel and Colin read the *Wall Street Journal* and magazines with George Clooney on the cover. They listened to
NPR on the radio and played pillow tag. They had interesting,
peaceful conversations about topics that had nothing to do

with them. They had ordinary, affectionate sex that week, which was nice but only reminded them of the other kind.

"WHAT IF I LOST ALL of my hair," Colin said one weekend morning—abruptly, from behind his paper. "I mean, all of it. Would you still want me?"

Kate thought about it. She got up from the kitchen table and loaded her coffee cup into the dishwasher. "Maybe not. I mean, I would still love you but I might not want you. Not the same way."

"That's not right," he said. "That's not how you're supposed to feel."

"What if I gained two hundred pounds? Would *you* still want *me*?"

"Yes."

"You would not!"

"I'd worry about your health."

"Total crap. You know it."

"I guess we see things differently."

After all these months together, differences in their individual perceptions seemed out of the question. "I will then," she said. "I'll gain the weight."

She opened the cabinet and reached for a package of Mallomars, Colin's childhood favorite. She crammed one in her mouth. Then another. He watched her, curious: How many Mallomars could she actually manage? He wouldn't stop her—he wanted to know.

She threw the cookies back into the cabinet. "You get the idea."

. . .

WES FOUGHT LESS FREQUENTLY with the woman who used to be Lucy's mother. He found a girlfriend, a ravishing Indian woman who taught foreign policy at Georgetown and came to stay with Wes on the weekends. She smoked outside on the porch at night, because of Lucy's asthma, and she smiled at Kate and Colin when they came home from their movies out and Saturday-night dinners. At night, they heard sounds of love above them, which compelled them to amp up their own routine—Wes was, after all, almost forty.

THE BASEMENT FLOODED and the paint peeled off in scabs. The landlady didn't bother to send her teenagers over anymore. The block association put together a petition against the house and all the tenants signed it, even Lucy. Darcy finished art school and Kate and Colin went into the city for her thesis exhibition. Her thesis was a six-foot black-and-white photograph of her vagina, printed on poster board.

"It's amazing," Kate said, looking at it.

She could see the labia's every wrinkle and fold, the clitoris swelling above, the hairs twisting exuberantly about one another.

"I totally agree with you on this one," Colin said.

Darcy sashayed up behind them and put her arms around Kate's waist. "It's Freudian," she said. "The child looking up the mother's skirt."

"I guess the mother doesn't wear underwear," Colin said. In the face of culture he tended to become silly.

"Oh, shush," Darcy said. "It's art."

"It looks so *powerful*," Kate said.

"Not what I'd want to run into at the Bridgeport train station on a Tuesday night," Colin said.

Darcy pinched him. "You wish."

They stayed at Darcy's that night and drove home the following morning. It was spring again. They got coffees from the deli and cruised north on the FDR. The East River shimmered alongside. They merged onto I-95. They were sick of all their music so they listened to the radio.

"I feel melancholy," Colin said. "I don't know why."

"It's okay," Kate said. I do too, she could have said, because she did. She rubbed his leg. Then his crotch. Then, to cheer them both up, she unzipped his pants and loosened her seat belt and blew him en route.

Later they went out to dinner at their favorite of the downtown Bridgeport Italian restaurants, the kind of place with wall-to-wall carpeting and a drop ceiling and salad included with the meal and more pasta in one serving than a person could reasonably eat. They parked and detoured around the block because it was still light out and, in Connecticut, the week for cherry blossoms, and cherry trees bordered these few particular streets. A light wind moved about, blowing the blossoms off. The trees bloomed, then lost their delicate crop immediately, the petals spinning and circling all week, the air in constant motion. Kate and Colin held hands. White blossoms caught on their hair and arms and shoes. Colin twisted Kate's fingers around his own.

"I had this friend when I was little," he said. "A girl. She lived on our street for two years. We were four and five. Or maybe five and six. Our mothers were friends so we played together. They used to take us to this park with trees just like this, maybe apple or something, I don't know. And we used to run through them, through the blossoms, in the spring. I remember her running ahead of me and wearing a dress. She had the strongest little legs. She took gymnastics."

"Cute," Kate said—bored by the story but attentive.

"Then she caught some sort of freak virus, the flu or meningitis or something. And she died. I remember my mom telling me. She came into my bedroom where I was playing and told me. I couldn't believe it. I couldn't believe it until we went to her funeral."

"Oh, Colin!" Kate stopped walking and pulled at him.

"I know."

"You never told me about her before."

"I haven't thought about her since I met you. Seriously."

She hugged him around the waist and pressed her face into his chest. He'd taken a shower at the apartment but still smelled of booze from the night before. They went to dinner. He got spaghetti carbonara and she got *zuppa di pesce*. They traded bites. They couldn't finish and took the rest home but forgot it in the car overnight.

IN SPITE OF their isolation and the ordinary quality of their days, something beautiful and mystical would persist for Kate about those years. She would recall, predominantly, a sense of having run away—to a bed and home shared with her wedded husband, but a place hanging about the fringes of life and civilization. Together, weekday mornings, they would drive to Stamford in the Jeep, Colin driving, Kate watching out the window at the sunlight striking patches of snow. They'd stop at the Dunkin' Donuts for coffee, and Kate remembered so distinctly the rows of frosted pastries, the Indian woman who served them, Colin in his big coat ordering coffee black with two sugars for himself, light and sweet for Kate, snow melting on his collar. Then the timed illuminated window, the pink light in the dark as Colin and she returned from Stamford in the Jeep, when the weather got cold and night came early, or on vaporous fall evenings, driving through a witches' brew of mist. She remembered the movies and the waitress with the bouffant. She recalled the train, those Fridays going into the city. She remembered standing with Colin by the doors and the rails, swaying and bumping into him, how sometimes they'd stand there for the whole trip, how she'd catch herself reflected in the dark glass. She remembered how he'd touched her and how much she'd wanted him to, how she'd run her hands over his face. How he'd rubbed her shoulders and hugged her, how she'd leaned against him. She remembered the way his glasses would steam and flash and his smile, which still possessed the roguish quality she'd loved. She remembered the slush and dirt of the train in winter, the houses built into the bay, the crowded stink of a bar in summer, the East Village waitresses with their hair done up in pencils. Then the last, late train home—the cars nearly empty and the windows giving back the overhead lights, Colin and she slumped against the ripped maroon seats—knees sprawling, hands linked, losing track of each other as they slept, separately dreaming.

5

KATE'S FATHER GETS TENURE and they paint the house dark red. The Andersons buy a VCR. Miles gains weight and loses teeth. Sebastian goes off to college. Kate's fifth-grade class begins a unit on Norway, and Kate stays up late in the living room reading the D'Aulaires' *Norse Gods and Giants.* She reads her book and her father reads his.

"What are you doing still up?" he asks. Knowing perfectly well. That she craves his attention, that she lives for him.

She rolls over on the hearth. "Not much."

"You like the book, huh?"

"Yes."

On his way to the kitchen to refresh his drink, he stops and examines the book. He points to the sepia illustration of Freya clasping her wonderful necklace to her bosom as she sleeps. "She looks like you."

Embarrassed, Kate says, "No, she doesn't. She's blond."

Miles has inherited their mother's freckles and dull, ashen hair. He's gotten their father's broad build and will eventually achieve his height. At six-three, Dennis has to duck through the side door, though the rest of the house with its high ceilings suits him. He does push-ups on the bedroom floor and chin-ups on a bar he's installed in the narrow back hall-way. Like a troll's, his footsteps disrupt the walls and floor-boards.

Kate has her mother's delicate, slanted features: her brief forehead, oval face, and soft chin; her mother's slender shoulders and small waist; her father's eyes and pale skin and coarse dark hair. "Beautiful," her father says, looking at her. He enjoys her appearance but, she senses, does not want her to grow into it. There seems to be something shameful, something basically desperate and humiliating and pleading about femininity in general and Kate's in particular. Her inferiority manifests itself in her mother's slavery to the household. As his eldest, for her to have been born a girl at all has hurt him in some way—has harmed him, weakened him. She's compromised him with her female body, her own general vulnerability and specific susceptibility to the elements of sex. Her disadvantage becomes his. His chaste love attached to her female body steals away some of his virility. She reads the Norse myths and the Greek myths, she reads *Little Women,* some Judy Blume, and she understands that her body will be hurt, damaged, and discarded. She understands that a boy maintains a certain strength and physical integrity but that when girls come into their reproductive capacities, everything changes; they and anyone who loves them—really loves them, for their minds and spirits—are liable. And that to maintain a certain dignity those people will need to love their girls less.

He asks Kate about her day; he does not ask Kate's mother about her day. He frames Kate's artwork and hangs it in his office. He praises her attention to detail, her good grades, her studious ways.

He takes her into the city. They leave the car for Edie and catch the eight fifty-two from Union Station. They shop on Fifth Avenue and he buys her a blue dress. He takes her ice-skating at Wollman Rink and to lunch at a café in Central Park. They eat shrimp cocktail and hamburgers and coffee ice cream in small glass bowls.

"I want to live in New York someday," Kate says. "When I'm grown-up. When I'm married."

"Oh, don't get married, Kate."

"Why not?" She picks at her nails. He hates this.

"Please don't do that."

"Fine." She returns to her ice cream. "Why not get married?"

"Well, get married if you really want to. Just don't have children. Parenthood is a terrible arrangement for women."

Sex is the only department in which he doesn't prefer Kate to her mother.

A screen breaks and a troop of moths invades Kate's room. She dances about, shrieking, sure one has found its way into her underpants before realizing the faint tickle is a stray bit of Scotch tape.

But still. She appears at her parents' door with a sleeping bag and her pillow.

"Your mother and I have a special relationship," her father says, sternly.

Her mother reclines on the bed with her drink and her biography. Uncommunicative, passive, remote. Shut off, suddenly, from Kate, from Miles and the chores and the once-lavender-now-red house.

He does not want Kate to become this sort of woman: a

wife. He anticipates better things for her. She understands that he hopes she'll somehow evade her sexuality, that she'll dodge the domestic, jealous, and promiscuous and remain purposeful and chaste. Anything less will hurt him, expose him, and generate shame: his and hers. Anything else will betray them both.

THE D'AULAIRES' ILLUSTRATIONS, while grotesque in their extremity of detail, achieve a splendid and peculiar gorgeousness, one that makes Kate want to dig her fingers into the pages, into the fantastic little creatures marking ends and beginnings of chapters (guarding, taunting, wrapped around capital letters), into Odin's eight-legged horse, into Sif's golden hair. Kate reads about Loki (prankster, entertainer, thief, liar); Freya, the sorrowful goddess of love, with her cats and crown of flowers; wise, one-eyed Odin; gentle Balder; short-tempered Thor; the many-headed trolls; the grouchy gnomes, hammering precious metals into valuable objects; the Norns, who spin the threads of life; the ice cow, who licks the first god into being from the salty brim of a pit; Odin's heroes, who fight every day for the fun of fighting, then pick up their severed limbs and put themselves back together; the Valkyries, warrior maidens.

Kate reads *Valkyrie* as *Valerie*, of which she knows three: in her class, Valerie Hamilton, Valerie ("Val") McCleary, and Valerie Mentz. Confusingly for the teachers, the Valeries form a trio of best friends. They hold hands in the hallway and giggle in the reading room. They give each other backrubs and play jacks and trade stickers. They crow when a teacher trips over a book bag, they stick pencils in their ears during math class, and, later, they unbutton their shirts to just below the bra in Mr. Mack's science section. Valerie Hamilton with her smooth blond ballerina bun; Val McCleary, a nail-biter, with blue eyes and a dark bob; Valerie Mentz with a carrot top and freckles and a crooked, broken nose (word is, her older brother punched her in the face for snapping the head off his Darth Vader figure). When Kate opens the book she sees the Valeries in helmets and braids. She internalizes the Valkyrie Valeries and they become her imaginary attendants, wayward spirits tracking her through her days, cheering and jeering at crucial moments.

Kate lies reading on her belly on the hearth, crossing her ankles in the air. Alone with her father, she feels herself to be as precious as Freya's necklace. She understands herself to be, for him, for now at least, generative and transforming: an invisible cloak, true love, a second, unanticipated chance.

He reads books by Richard Feynman: books on physical theory or autobiographies with cheeky titles. Sometimes he reads poetry. Sometimes novels and stories. He reads *Leaves of Grass.* He reads *Madame Bovary.* He reads *Ulysses* and *War and Peace* and *Dead Souls.*

"What's that about?" Kate asks, of the latter.

"The story I'm reading right now is about a man who gets separated from his nose."

"Weird."

"He sees his nose getting on a bus in a soldier's uniform. Or . . ." He skims back through the pages. "Never mind. Some sort of military attire. The idea is that he's become so estranged from his own life that his body parts move around Saint Petersburg without him. The modern world alienates him from his choices and actions."

"How . . . does it work?"

"Does what work?"

"Is the nose a big person-size nose wearing a regular-size uniform? Or is it a normal-size nose wearing a tiny uniform? Or a normal nose floating around on top of a regular-size uniform?"

"That last one, I'd say. How about you?"

"Me too. The nose floating around."

"Tell me about that." He points to the Norse myths.

"It's a lot like Greek mythology."

"How so?"

She looks through the table of contents. "There's a ruler god. Odin. Like Zeus. And eleven others. Thor is the god of war, like Ares. Freya is like Aphrodite, the goddess of love. But married to other people. The Norns are like the Fates. They spin the threads of life." She makes quote marks with her fingers. "The sun and the moon go on chariots around the earth. Balder is like Dionysus. Except Balder dies. He really dies; he doesn't come back to life. They all die, actually."

"The best stories always repeat themselves."

Eventually Kate finishes the book and her class finishes their unit. The school year ends. She gets her period and goes around untended to for nearly a week, hoping it will go away. The furtive smears recall 123 Livingston's fresh dark-red paint. Her mother finds her underpants in the laundry and confronts her and supplies her with feminine products and a book. Kate starts the sixth grade. She moves on to certain paperbacks, stealthily checked out from the school library, books with worn and yellow pages and dense, small type, the covers rubbed away at the corners, as if from much investigation, much handling. *Forever; Then Again, Maybe I Won't; My Dar-*

ling, My Hamburger; A Tree Grows in Brooklyn; Ode to Billy Joe.
The pages give off a faint odor: a musty, private smell. Kate
and Topher and other friends gather on weekends in built-
out basements. Here they play strip poker and kissing games:
I Never; In the Dark; Stop Signs; Rock, Paper, Kiss; Kiss
Around Town; Kiss or Dare; Kiss or Slap; Kiss and Push; Kissing Tag; Hide and Go Get It; Sixty Seconds in Heaven. Bras
become necessary. Edie takes Kate to Filene's Basement in the
Milford Mall. They hide her other developments from her
father.

DENNIS HAS A FRIEND with property in northwestern Connecticut. One Saturday morning in the fall he wakes Kate up
early and tells her to pack a bag. He hands her a cup of coffee
(half milk, three sugars), leaves a note for Edie, and stashes
Kate's bag and his own and a rifle in the trunk. They take
Route 8 north toward Waterbury.

The friend is a retired professor with family money. They
pull into the driveway of a big white house with balconies.
They eat pancakes and bacon with the friend and his wife,
who is several decades younger.

"So what do you think of this whole hunting thing?" the
friend asks Kate.

"Should be interesting."

"You don't mind killing Bambi?"

She pours more syrup on her pancake. "Someone has to do
it."

"You ever handled a gun before?"

"We do target shooting at my uncle's."

"She's an excellent shot," her father says.

"You have such nice posture," the wife—Mary—tells Kate. "So many girls your age slouch."

Everyone is focused on her, the way a gathering of adults will focus on a child. Kate enjoys the attention. She chews her bacon daintily. She is used to her father showing her off. For her mother, she is all need and worry, expanding like Alice in Wonderland, taking up space her mother (now home playing cards with boring Miles) once occupied. But for her father she is a luxury, a bonus.

They put their overnight bags in their respective rooms. Mary hands Kate and her father chocolate-chip cookies and a water bottle as they leave through the kitchen door. They get into an old Jeep missing a roof and doors and a backseat. The place where the backseat used to be is covered by a stained tarp. A hole gapes in the floor of the passenger side. Kate watches the matted grass rush below as they jolt through a field and then another downward-sloping field, the two divided by a low stone wall. Woods surround the second field, where Dennis brakes and kills the engine. They walk, Dennis carrying the gun, pointed down, and a bag that contains ammunition, binoculars, ear protectors. Kate carries the water and the cookies. Her father has changed from his tweedy academic clothes into mountain-man garb: green army pants, lace-up rubber-soled boots, a plaid flannel shirt. Twigs snap under his feet and wind tousles the grass. A breeze pushes around the wet bright leaves, and the life inside the forest quivers. Kate envisions sensitive English-speaking animals, as in a Disney movie or a children's book, crowded up to the very last front of trees, watching the girl and the man.

They arrive at a tree with twelve-inch lengths of wood nailed in increments to the trunk to create a makeshift ladder. Dennis ascends, rifle and bag slung over his shoulder. Kate follows and pulls herself through a wooden platform into a tree house, the kind she might, in other circumstances, decorate with curtains and a tea set.

They don the ear protectors. He has her practice holding and aiming the rifle. She kneels on one knee, the opposite foot on the platform.

"Hold the butt tight against your shoulder and look down the barrel. You see that little horseshoe. There. You want the tip of the barrel inside of it, between the two points. You want all that lined up. You want to know your surroundings. How deep the wood goes, what's beyond it, who lives next door. Last year maybe, up in Maine, this family had built a lean-to in somebody's woods and were living there. A bullet went right through the side of the house and into a crib."

She aims the gun at a tree. She lines the tip of the barrel up between the two ends of the horseshoe. "Seems too high," she says.

"They lined up?"

"Yup. But . . ."

"You can lie down if that's more comfortable."

She lies on her stomach. "That's better."

He lowers his voice. "Hey. There," he says. "See that?"

Something moves amid the trees. Leaves make a whispering sound. Branches crackle.

"Your shot," he says.

"I'm going to miss."

"You might. Not the end of the world."

He checks her hold on the gun. He clicks off the safety. "Line 'em up. Shoot. Now."

She snaps the trigger, a little thing that produces a gigantic noise. The bullet flies invisibly through the atmosphere, leaving no residue, very separate from its surroundings. Then the sound expands, softens, and loses focus. The sections of brown hide bound away.

"Did I hurt it?"

"No. You can hear if it hit."

"Sorry."

"Don't be."

"What happens if we get one?"

"Then we go back. You've got to clean the deer right away. Take out the organs. The sooner you do that the better the meat will taste."

"Gross."

"Well, it ain't for sissies."

They wait and wait and wait. They drink the water and eat the cookies.

"Let's try another spot," he says, finally.

She unwinds her tingling legs and goes first down the ladder and waits for Dennis at the bottom. Then as she follows him farther down the field she feels blood between her legs, warm and sudden. She keeps walking, squeezing her thighs together. This slows her down. Dennis glances back, frowning. "Everything okay?"

"Um, I kind of want to go back."

"To the house?"

"I have to go to the bathroom."

He points to a tree. She shuffles toward it and leans against

the trunk, out of his sight. She undoes her jeans and investi-
gates.

She hasn't yet learned to keep track. And some months she
doesn't get it at all. Other months, only for a day or two and
lightly. Now, though, the blood, or whatever it is, has soaked
through her underpants to the denim and smeared her inner
thighs.

She considers the fallen leaves an inch thick around her, the
moss growing against the trunk. Then she considers poison ivy
and bugs. She wedges her underpants into her crotch and ties
her sweatshirt around her waist. She rubs her finger on the
outside of her jeans. It comes back red and smelling of metal.
She hobbles up the incline to her father.

"I want to go back to the house," she tells him.

"What's the matter? You sick?"

"No. I just . . ." Too late, she realizes she should have said yes.

"We're just getting going here."

"I think maybe I am sick, actually."

"Now you're sick? What's going on?"

"I need something."

"What, you need what?"

"I need to lie down."

Mary is younger than her mother. She must still get it. If no,
or if she's gone out, there's toilet paper, tissue paper, a wash-
cloth. Enough to get her through the rest of the day if she
remains sedentary.

She crosses her legs. "I don't want to shoot Bambi after all."

"Well, you don't have to then. I will. You can keep me company."

"I really need you to drive me back right now." Her thighs
are soaked. Blood creeps into the cleft of her behind. "Please!"

"You upset about missing the shot? Don't feel bad. Takes a while. You'll get the hang of it. But in the meantime, pull yourself together. Be a sport about it. Move on."

"I have my *period*. I'm *bleeding*, I have to *go*, I need *stuff*."

Oh, shame! But. Never before has she managed to startle him. The rifle jerks at his side. His face twitches.

"Oh." He ducks his head in acknowledgment. "Of course."

They return to the truncated Jeep. He steers past the stone wall to the house and brakes in front of the garage.

"I have to go to the store."

"Think you could talk to Mary?"

Her original plan, but—

"She might already have what you need."

"Yeah. Okay."

She maneuvers out of her seat and swipes at the leather with her sweatshirt.

She finds Mary, who does in fact have what Kate needs. Dennis goes back out alone and bags a doe. They eat it that night, the four of them, with a side of mashed turnips. Kate and Dennis drive home in the morning with a cooler full of meat.

NOW HE SPENDS EVENINGS in his study instead of the living room. He asks Kate only occasionally about her day. He no longer insists on her beauty—it feels like he won't look at her directly. Maybe she isn't beautiful anymore; anyway, maybe she never was. She doesn't know. But the fault, the source of their estrangement, is hers; the problem rises directly from her flighty, supplicating body. Her father grows more interested in Miles, who, at age seven, comes up to Kate's shoulder and outweighs her by twenty pounds. Kate's family visits Galveston and the men and boys hunt and shoot at targets. Miles and Kate's father and uncle and cousins hunker down by the lake, her father in the army pants, her brother's plump backside squeezed into jeans and a KISS T-shirt. Kate lies on her side on the deck, doing homework. Over and over she answers the same question, losing her place every time a shot sounds, exploding down her ear canal like a handful of rocks.

6

KATE GOT A JOB in Yale's development office and now Colin and she commuted in opposite directions: she north on the train, he south in the Jeep. They earned money and saved it and spent it. They rearranged their bedroom and living room. They built additional bookshelves. They went on vacation. They attended weddings, wedding after wedding until everyone but Darcy was married. They celebrated their fourth anniversary. Then, over the subsequent year, something shifted between them. Some mechanism essential to their rapport began to shut down like a defective valve. Maybe it had been shutting down right from the beginning—maybe it had never been viable at all. To Kate, this development felt impersonal, unfortunate but arbitrary— hopelessly so, like a fatal car accident or illness. Still, she racked her brain for what she'd done wrong. Without contemplation or discussion, they rigged alternative structures, emergency conduits, makeshift constructions in the form of tense conversations that collapsed regularly under the stubborn accumulated weight of confined feeling.

She became finicky about sex, wanting it only occasionally. Her body began to feel like a recently tidied room she didn't want Colin to mess up. She flinched when he put his fingers in her vagina, then her hair. She found the tastes and the drips and the leaks newly objectionable and afterward she gargled twice or washed herself off.

Their sixth November as husband and wife, Kate's father fell on the street. He hit his nose, which bled so lividly that he drove himself to the Yale–New Haven emergency room. The staff conducted certain tests and directed him to an oncologist, who detected a glioblastoma tumor in the right temporal lobe of his brain. Kate's mother and father had split up when Kate was in college, after Dennis had carried on with one of his female graduate students. But even in divorce Edie remained his loyal concubine. Dennis informed her of his prognosis, and she notified Miles and Kate. Treatments were considered. But the cancer worsened immediately upon recognition, as if taking the diagnosis as a sort of prompt.

In December, Dennis Allison entered hospice. He called for his journals. Kate's mother transported them from his rented apartment. Soon, in spite of the journals, he would die. But he lay stubbornly reading them anyway.

Kate stayed with her mother for two weeks. Colin drove back and forth, visiting. "I could stay here with you," he said. "I could take time off."

"Don't do that. It's . . . I'm fine. It doesn't matter."

The temperature dropped and the days passed. Kate spent them at the hospice center, driving her father's car to and from Livingston Street. She sat in the visitor's chair in the antiseptic room, looking through magazines. He fidgeted in the mechanical bed, paging through his journals. She ate sandwiches from the cafeteria. She bought a pack of cigarettes, though she hadn't smoked since college, and stood outside the drab building on a drably developed street, smoking them. Miles came up from New York, where he now worked as a speechwriter for the mayor. He offered himself to their father upon his arrival, but Dennis pulled the covers over his head and grumbled, so Miles retreated to the waiting room, where he proceeded to sit for days, scanning the *New York Times* and talking on his cell phone. He'd dropped his baby fat after college finally, and now he appeared, if not ruggedly masculine, at least mature. Kate sat down next to him and offered him half a ham sandwich from the cafeteria. He took it and finished it in three bites. His glasses shone under the fluorescent lighting.

"I feel terrible that I'm not much help here," he said. "That you're dealing with everything."

"Don't worry. I can handle it." She patted his shoulder.

"Is he behaving himself?" Miles removed his glasses and cleaned them on his flannel shirt.

"He loves you. He wants you here. He's embarrassed for you to see him like this because you're the boy."

"You're too easy on him. After all that insanity."

"Oh, I don't know. I probably needed the discipline."

"You were just a kid."

"Whatever." Rolling the remains of her sandwich half into the paper bag, she wondered if Miles had a girlfriend, what music he listened to, if he still liked to brush his teeth in the shower.

That night Kate fell asleep in the visitor's chair over the December issue of *Martha Stewart Living*. She woke at three to beeping from the monitoring device. Her father sat up, beating his hands on the sheet, underneath which he appeared to have an erection. The Valeries snickered. The girls from the D'Aulaires: The Valerie Valkyries. Still Kate's attendant, incendiary spirits after all this time. Vanishing for years, emerging at critical junctures.

Dennis's mouth hung open. His tongue flailed. Clenched sounds came from his throat. Kate ran into the hall. She grabbed a passing nurse's arm and shook it inanely. The nurse hurried after her to the room but he'd checked out already, the sheet kicked off and the erection deflating.

The following morning Kate got a coffee at Dunkin' Donuts and caught an early train home to Bridgeport. A storm had threatened for days and finally snow was falling. She took a seat near the window. The car filled as they stopped in Milford and Stratford. Commuters read the paper or worked on their laptops, many leaving their big puffy coats on, some removing them and throwing them up onto the luggage rack. A graduate student scribbled something in a scientific journal. Kate looked out the window. The snow rushed toward the grimy glass. Bare trees reached, various nondescript specimens. She should know what they were called but she didn't. They spread their limbs longingly, bombarded by snow.

Her father would never see this—never see any of it again.

Factories and fences glided past—embankments, a car driving under a bridge, bulrushes, electrical wires and cables overreaching the tracks in complicated grids. Junkyards, machinery. Birches, pines, inlets. The smaller, less affluent houses clustered in the shadow of the train, colorful Christmas lights strung up around doors and porches. She held her coffee, light and sweet and very hot, in both hands and sipped at it. The highway erupted alongside the tracks at intervals. Nothing sounded in the car but the wheels, subdued, and coughs, and rustling coats. Heat came up from metal grids below the windows, against Kate's left leg and arm. There went a stadium, mysterious industrial structures, billboards and wrecked cars, graffiti messages on a concrete wall, brick buildings with boarded-up windows, ads for health clubs and Broadway shows, motorboats docked for winter, a maintenance crew in orange jackets, a discount car wash, housing projects, the signs for ferry parking and P. J. Murphy Moving & Storage. Across from her, the graduate student spread his long legs and shifted in his seat. His hair, cropped short, set off a handsome face. Snow piled up all around the tracks and on the wires and cables.

The Valeries spread their legs too. They slouched in their seats and got comfortable. They bumped their knees against those of the graduate student. They made lewd remarks about the size of his hands. Kate leaned her head against the grimy glass and watched him frown over the book.

She loved men—resented and abhorred them but adored them!—their big shoes, their loaded pockets, their consumption of space, their confounding sense of entitlement.

She could have called Colin to pick her up in the Jeep, but she didn't. She took a taxi from the train station to the apartment. Snow continued to fall and the taxi skidded on the road.

"On the left here," she said. She took out her wallet.

"You need your walk shoveled?"

"My husband will do it."

"You got a husband?"

"Yep."

"You don't look more than eighteen or nineteen."

The Valeries sneered. She tipped him an extra two bucks.

She stood in the entryway with her bag. The cold inside the apartment dug at her through her coat. Colin had prudently turned down the heat before work. It was she who left lights on, windows unlocked, cabinet doors open. She turned the thermostat up high, angered—but of course, he hadn't known she was coming home; he hadn't known to keep the apartment warm for her, didn't know she was here, didn't know anything.

Signs of his two weeks alone abounded. Cushions tossed off the couch. The television remote askew amid these cushions. The Xbox hooked up, wires sprawling. Her irrational irritation increased—playing his games when! But he didn't know, she hadn't told him, he would have stayed with her but she'd sent him away, why shouldn't he divert himself with Xbox?

In the kitchen, a cereal bowl and coffee mug sat beside the sink. She went into the bedroom and lay down on the unmade bed. This was the warmest room in the apartment. Years ago a fire had destroyed the back half of the house, which had then been rebuilt and properly insulated.

She made herself more coffee, added cream and sugar. White take-out cartons filled the fridge. Outside, the snow came down and down. She turned on the radio. A storm was mentioned. Yes, it did seem to be a storm. She saw a note in Colin's handwriting: *Humidifier, salt. Weekend?*

She stuck the note to the fridge with a magnet. What was she doing here? Who was he, this man she lived with, preoccupied with humidifiers?

She poured coffee into the sink and scrubbed out the pot with salt. She had no idea what to do with herself.

She kept the glass bowls and the barware and the wedding china in the latticework china closet, which occupied a corner of the dining room. She kept the beautiful but essentially useless bowls lined up in the back—things given by people who believed in her and Colin and their young marriage, were counting on them, had invested with these objects in their happy future. She reached into the back compartment and took out a Steuben bowl given to them by friends of Colin's parents. It was small and thick and heavy. On the rare occasions they entertained Kate filled it with salted almonds, which Colin and she and their guests would snack on over drinks.

She held the bowl and looked at it. She bounced it slightly in her hands, unsure of how to accomplish the task that suddenly seemed imperative.

She struck it, hesitantly, against the dining room table. The wood was soft, the glass strong. She wandered into the bedroom, where stood a marble-topped vanity, passed down to Kate from her grandmother. Kate cleared off the jewelry boxes and perfume, the clips and elastics, the makeup, piling it all on the bed, but the vanity trembled as she cleared it and its instability dismayed her suddenly. She walked all around the apartment, holding the bowl. She thought of the entryway. She knelt by the door. She struck the glass against the stone—timidly, then with confidence. The bowl came apart in two curved and feminine halves.

Now she felt worse. She'd ruined something she loved. She sat back on her knees and let out a little moan of regret. She gathered the glass into a plastic shopping bag. She cut her thumb, and the blood began to run alarmingly down her wrist and arm. She tied the glass in the shopping bag and threw the bag away and took out the trash. Then she wiped the blood from the cut and wrapped up her thumb.

Finished, she searched for something else to do. The snow had eased. As her driver had noted, the walk needed shoveling—she would shovel it. She put on a coat and boots and took the shovel from the entryway closet. She bent to lace her boots. The colorful flat-weave rug lay askew on the worn floorboards and in spite of everything it pleased her—the bright but faded colors and the droll designs. She marveled at interiors, charmingly arranged, with their strange power to comfort.

The snow gave way, swallowed her boots and dampened her jeans. She shoveled awkwardly, tossing the snow off to either side.

When Wes appeared from the side door with his own shovel she jumped. She'd forgotten about him, about everyone else.

"Well, look at you," he said.

She stopped and rested on her shovel.

"Everything well?"

"Fine," she said. "Same old, same old." The fib shamed her—she liked Wes.

"I'll finish this up."

"I don't mind."

"You've done a lot."

"My pleasure."

"You're just a little thing," he said approvingly.

Obediently, she went inside. She leaned the shovel against the wall. She stamped her feet.

She showered and washed her hair, washing the hospice and death taint out of it. She didn't want that smell associated with her anymore. Rudely, cruelly, she continued to live. She dressed in an old T-shirt, a short black jersey skirt, and socks pulled up to her knees. She tidied the living room, straightening the throw pillows, fanning magazines out on the coffee table. She lit a candle and made herself a scotch and water and got onto the couch and pulled a blanket over her body and turned on the television. She came across *It's a Wonderful Life* on TNT.

Outside it went dark. The timed pink lamp and the television screen lit the small room. Kate drank her drink and made another. The Jeep sounded in the driveway and its headlights caught the window. Then there was Colin's key in the door and a great stomping and rustling and banging. She saw him through the glass in his big coat.

"You're here." Colin paused in the door, surprised.

"I am."

"How is he?"

"He's conflicted. He's deciding whether to go to college or stay in Bedford Falls and run the Building and Loan."

Colin struggled briefly with irritation. Compassion overcame. "Not George Bailey. Your father."

"Dead. He died."

"What?" Colin dropped his coat on the floor. "Kate."

"What?"

"I'm so sorry."

"I know you are."

"I would have picked you up."

"I know. It doesn't matter. The storm."

Though of course she'd had no knowledge of the storm before finding herself in it. Now, though, it seemed as though she had—that the day, the last two weeks, in fact, had happened all at once, like a lucid dream.

"I would have come up there."

"It's okay. It wasn't a shock or anything. We knew how it was going to shake out. Right?"

"Why didn't you want me with you?" He removed his knit cap. Snow melted on his boots, darkening the welcome mat.

She understood that what Colin needed from her now were tears and collapse, something to establish her innate hysteria and consequent lack of sense. Then he would excuse her for shutting him out—he would console her, and the death, the whole question of her father, would be celebrated and put away. He waited there at the door, anticipating her outcry and his show of support.

"You know," she said. "Us Protestants."

He scratched the exposed section of his scalp. He noticed the scotch. Without removing his damp boots, he went to the kitchen and made himself the same drink. Then he threw himself into an armchair, legs spread out in that territorial male fashion, boots seeping into the rug. She didn't care. Maybe he wanted her to.

He questioned her about the death. Soberly, decently, tolerantly. As if her affairs came under his jurisdiction, his superior wisdom—all her emotional doings up for his consideration. He nodded. And she presented a report to him, obediently, albeit grudgingly. She unwound the parchment; she the surly messenger he—in his generosity! his tolerance!—chose once more to pardon.

Satisfied, he looked around and reviewed her other choices. The movie. The drink. The drink he could not condemn—he had partaken of the scotch himself—though for him a reasonable choice, for her a questionable one. The movie, though.

"Should you really be watching this?" he asked, quietly.

"Why shouldn't I watch it?"

"Just seems so sad."

"I want to feel sad."

"But—more than you already do?"

"I don't."

He frowned. He chewed on his lower lip. Puzzled, disappointed.

"Well. You hungry?"

"Nope."

"Not even a little?"

She raised her glass.

"You should eat something." Transforming, expertly, from disapproving father to fretting mother. He noticed her thumb. Gently, he seized her hand. "What happened?"

"I dropped a dish in the sink. At my mom's. Cut myself cleaning up."

He shook off his boots and headed to the kitchen. "How do lamb chops sound?" he called back. In her absence he had shopped, carried on, purchased lamb chops.

Cooking smells developed: onions, butter, meat. She sat in the dark with her drink. She breathed in the scented candle, the onions. She reviewed the death and hoarded it, squirreled it away in little bits and pieces.

The journals.

The sandwiches, the cigarettes, Miles.

The choking.

The terrible dying erection.

She put one piece here, another there.

Colin set the table in the small dining room, attached, as in so many similar urban New England homes, to the living room by an arch and columns. He set out the blue-and-yellow ceramic plates. He opened a bottle of wine and put out glasses. The film ending anyway, Clarence receiving his wings, Kate took the place Colin had prepared for her. He brought out lamb chops in a cast-iron pan and slid one onto her plate.

Bits of fat melted from meat and bone. She leaned over, put her nose into it. "Divine."

He had made Brussels sprouts as well, sautéed and chopped into a sort of hash. The butter and onion smell came from these. Colin sat and began to eat, occasionally glancing at her. She could not persuade herself, good as the food looked and smelled, to consume. She cut the fat from the chop and cut off a small piece, red at the center, and pushed the piece around in the vegetables. To eat on this day—tomorrow she would eat— seemed a betrayal of sorts.

Colin looked and looked at her. He ate faster and faster, the way he did when aggravated. "You're not going to eat it?" he asked, finally. "Any of it?"

She shook her head.

He looked at her sternly, as if he might force a bite of lamb or a forkful of sprouts down her throat.

"Okay, then," he said. He took her plate and ate her share as well. Then he gathered up the plates and utensils and brought them to the sink.

She stood also and helped him wrap and put things away: half an onion, two cooked chops, and the remaining sprouts. She rinsed the cast-iron pan and wiped it out. He swept and sprayed down counters. She washed plates and utensils. Outside the window over the sink, cars ground by slowly and snow glittered. Somewhere a boy shouted. The windows of neighboring houses emanated light. A man struggled down the street, hood up, trudging slowly, hopefully on.

Colin came up behind her and put a hand between her shoulder blades. Certain sensations tumbled about in her. She turned and pushed her head into his chest and reached for his zipper. He intercepted. "Don't." He removed her hand and squeezed it lightly.

She reached for him with the other hand.

"Stop."

"You kidding me?"

"I don't know; it just seems wrong."

"Well, then let go of me, please."

He did. She went for him again and got her hand past his belt and down his pants. He extracted her, took her by the elbows, and marched her to the kitchen table. "You're confused." He sat her in a chair. "I'll clean up the rest." He put his hand on her head. "You want more wine?"

She slouched in her chair. "Yes."

He poured the remaining Shiraz into her glass and took up the dishes.

"You don't want me," she said.

"Of course I do." He ran water into the Brussels sprouts pan. She put her head down on her arms. "So what did you do all day, anyway?" he asked.

"Shoveled the walk."

"Did you? The whole walk?" He looked out the window at her handiwork. "I noticed someone had done something."

"Well, Wes did some."

"You and Wes? Shoveled together?" He was teasing now. Her life one long hopeless antic.

"He took over. I went in." She lifted her head and swigged at the wine. "No. That's not what happened, actually. We did the walk together. Then the street. Together."

"Oh, yeah?"

"Then he told me he loves me. And has all this time! When we thought he loved Tara!"

"Ha."

"Then he told me I have a gorgeous ass."

"You're in shock."

"I told you, it's not a shock!"

Colin shut off the water and turned around. Kate continued.

"Right there in the snow, on the street. He said that. He said he lives each and every day to catch a glimpse of my ass. Anyway. I invited him in for hot chocolate." She paused, inventing. "No, wait. Then we went down to the basement to put the shovels away. Then he kissed me, right there against the dryer."

Colin crossed his arms across his chest.

"He laid down his coat. He picked me up and threw me down on it. Then he fucked my brains out."

"I get the idea."

"He didn't have anything so . . . he just came inside of me, no diaphragm, no nothing. Maybe we'll have another little Lucy."

"Okay, very funny."

"Afterward I helped him fold her laundry."

"You did, did you."

"She has the cutest little underpants! So small, you wouldn't believe they fit an actual talking thinking breathing walking person."

Little feet sounded above.

"Cheers." She lifted her glass toward the ceiling. "Wes! Wes! It was lovely, Wes!" she shouted.

"I think you're hysterical. Not funny hysterical, the other kind."

The footsteps paused.

"Wes, baby!"

"Stop it." Colin shook his head. He turned back to the sink. He set the Brussels sprouts pan to soak.

"Lucy, your dad is a spectacular fuck!"

Colin crossed the small room in two steps and pulled Kate up from her chair. She struggled away and dove below the table, laughing. He pulled her out by her waist, dragged her up, and marched her into the bathroom. He lifted her into the bathtub and turned on the shower.

She screamed. Cold water pummeled her face and shoulders. It ran into her mouth and quickly soaked her shirt and skirt. He shut down the tap and hauled her out. She shoved at his chest.

"Are you crying?" Colin took her chin in his right hand and looked intently at her.

Water from her hair ran down her face and neck.

"I didn't mean to make you cry. I just wanted you to snap out of it." He wrapped his arms around her and stroked her back. "Doesn't it feel good, though? Doesn't it?"

She nodded into his chest.

His hands went from her back to her waist. He kissed her mouth and pressed her against the wall and squeezed her breasts through the wet cotton of her shirt. He pushed up her skirt.

"I thought you didn't want to," she said.

"I do now, baby."

Above, Lucy banged out "Ode to Joy," then scraped back the piano bench and slammed the key top closed.

·   ·   ·

A WEEK LATER Kate dropped Colin at work and drove the
Jeep up to New Haven to collect her father's belongings. She
took the gun and the rack and all the journals. She tossed
the journals untidily into the middle seat and maneuvered the
antlers into the back. Then she hurtled back down I-95. At
home, she swept the piles of journals from the back of the car
into the snow and burned them.

7

WO YEARS LATER, another storm surrounding
the Bridgeport apartment, Kate and Colin sat up in
bed a little before midnight on a Wednesday. He read *Men's
Journal* and she read a novel. She reclined against a European
pillow and leaned the book against her pregnant stomach. Her
due date had come and gone. Every now and then, the baby
kicked and the book jumped.

He turned in her direction and scrutinized her before turning off his light. "Everything okay?"

"Yeah."

She was having pains, the same ones she'd been experienc-
ing, off and on, for several days. Braxton Hicks, the pregnancy
book said. She turned onto her side and tried to sleep. She
couldn't, though—the pain increased. Her rectal area felt tight.

"I think you're in labor," Colin said, also awake.

"No. Just indigestion, probably."

She couldn't see herself ever actually having the baby.

She got up and went to the bathroom and when she wiped
her front, the paper showed blood.

She went into the kitchen and called her obstetrician's
office and a few minutes later one of the midwives called her
back. She told Kate to wake up her husband and take a hot
shower and have a big glass of wine.

Colin went down into the basement for one of their nicer bottles. Kate took her shower and then she got into bed and drank the wine and breathed through the contractions. "Hello," she said to her glass of wine. "I'm back." Colin timed the contractions. They went from being eight to ten minutes apart to five to six minutes apart, where they stayed for a while. The midwife called to ask Kate if she wanted to meet her at the hospital to get checked, or if she wanted to wait and go into the office when it opened at eight-thirty. By now it was seven, so Kate said she'd wait. The midwife told her to eat something, even if she didn't feel like it, that she'd need the energy.

Colin brought her a scrambled egg and a piece of toast with butter and a cup of tea with milk and sugar. The tea tasted delicious—the egg she ate slowly, so that by the time she finished it had chilled completely. She took another hot shower. She stayed in a long time and bent against the wall when she had a contraction. Colin knocked on the door to say the office had just called and they were closing early, at ten, because of the storm. So Kate rushed to get ready and they got in the car. At the obstetrician's office, her water broke on the examining table. The midwife checked her and said that Kate was only three centimeters dilated, but that the labor would probably speed up now that her water had broken. They went home and waited. All afternoon, Kate tried to sleep between the contractions, which remained five to six minutes apart. She drank Gatorade, ginger ale, and water. In the living room, Colin watched a movie on television and ate pizza from the freezer. At six o'clock, Kate went out to watch with him. When the contractions hit she got on all fours on the couch and then got up and walked around.

Finally they called the hospital and another midwife told them to come in.

Colin collected Kate's things and they got back into the Jeep. She climbed into the backseat and curled up. She howled as the slowest person in the world ambled across the street. At the hospital, Colin went to park the car and an elderly male orderly took Kate up to Labor and Delivery. She stopped a few times for the contractions and leaned with her hands against the wall. A nurse met her in her room. She gave Kate the robes and got her settled and hooked her up to a monitor. The midwife came in and checked Kate's cervix and told her she was now eight centimeters dilated. Colin returned from the parking garage and Kate got into the shower again—a private shower attached to the room, with a little white plastic chair that she leaned over and put her hands on whenever a contraction came.

Then she was back in the bed, on her hands and knees, the television on, playing *Friends.* She held an ice cube in her hand and squeezed. She breathed like the birthing classes had taught her. She drank ginger ale and sucked on ice. The contractions came again and again. Kate felt as though she were being carried away by them. She hung on to the bed. The midwife checked her and said it was time to push.

She tried different positions: squatting with the squatting bar, on her hands and knees, on her back, "curled around the baby," the midwife kept saying. In this position Colin held one of her legs up and the nurse held the other one. Kate pushed through *ER* and then the local news.

"I want a C-section!" she cried.

"No, you don't," the midwife said.

"Just get this fucking thing out of me!"

Finally things picked up. During one of the pushes the midwife said, "I see a lot of dark hair!" She asked Kate if she wanted to look. She offered a mirror, which Kate refused. Colin looked, still holding Kate's leg. The midwife threw a towel over the squat bar and told Kate to push and pull herself up with the towel. She told Kate that the baby was crowning, and Kate felt a burning sensation around her vestibule and the pressure of a wall crashing down sideways inside of her. The head came out. Colin shouted. The midwife said, "Looks like a girl, from the face!" Then Kate had to stop pushing while they did something or other, and then the baby came out with just a few more pushes, and everyone surrounding Kate's nether regions was saying, "It's here, it's here," and the midwife said, "Get ready to hold your *daughter,*" and put the baby on Kate's chest. Kate put her hands around the baby's backside. Its sudden appearance shocked her. She, the baby, lay on Kate's bosom, naked and compact, moving and making noises. She looked around and she looked at Kate. Her eyes were bright and alert.

"Oh, my God." Kate looked around the room for Colin and found him next to her. "It's a real baby."

He cut the cord and Kate pushed the placenta out and they gave her a shot of Pitocin to shrink her uterus and the midwife got down between her legs and stitched her up. "Look at your stomach!" the nurse said. Kate looked down—her belly was sunken and empty and soft. She fed the baby. The nurse cleaned the baby and put her under the heat lamp. Colin called Kate's mother and put Kate on the phone. Her mother was beside herself, almost crying. She said, "I really wanted it to be a girl."

The orderly took everybody to the recovery floor. Kate

rode in the wheelchair and held the baby and Colin walked behind with Kate's things. Everyone in the hallways and elevators offered congratulations, just as if they'd been out there waiting all night.

A sandwich and a soda were delivered to her room. She didn't want the sandwich so Colin ate it. The nurse brought some graham crackers and peanut butter and Kate had those instead. The nurse gave Kate an ice pack and Motrin and Demerol and said she'd come in later to take her to the bathroom. Colin slept on the couch. The baby, now named Lila, went to the nursery. A different nurse brought her in to Kate in the middle of the night to be fed. At six Colin went home to sleep more comfortably. At eight they brought Lila in again and brought Kate breakfast and tea. Her mother called to say she was on her way. Kate took another shower and brushed her teeth and rinsed with mouthwash. She put on body and face lotion and brushed her hair. Naked, she felt her stomach, so amazingly pliable.

Her mother arrived and went straight over to Lila, who was lying in her clear plastic elevated bassinet. Edie wore her usual gray coat, which set off the gray in her hair—she appeared elderly, all of a sudden, standing there looking down at the fresh little infant, easily a grandmother.

Colin returned and plugged in the CD player. He put on the Goldberg Variations. A nurse poked her head in. "Y'all relaxing?"

"Yup," Colin said.

"Busy day yesterday."

The nurse vanished. "Busy for her," Colin said, indicating Lila.

"Maybe the busiest day of her life," Edie said.

"Well," Kate said, "busier than today. So that would be a yes."

"You know who just had a baby, Kate?" her mother said. "Rudy Anderson. Or, well, his wife did."

Kate's mother stayed until early evening; then she went to the Bridgeport apartment, where she would stay for the next ten days to do laundry and cook and help care for the baby until her daughter and son-in-law got the hang of it. Kate fed Lila and an orderly took her to the nursery for the night. Kate watched as Lila was wheeled out the door and down the hall in her clear plastic bassinet, until all she could see of her was the little pink hat. Then Kate turned on the television and ate the sandwich she'd saved from lunch. Now she was ravenous. She ate the sandwich and the little iceberg-lettuce hospital salad. She went to sleep. The nurse brought Lila to her in the middle of the night and left, leaving the door half-open. The sleepless white hallway dimly illuminated Kate's room and Lila was beautiful and clear-eyed at Kate's breast. The pink hat had come off and she looked up at Kate in the shallow light with her bright dark eyes and her dark mussed hair and her little blue T-shirt with the ends folded over her hands so she wouldn't scratch herself, a strange, extraterrestrial little creature, cross between radiant wood nymph and wrinkled gnome. Kate sat her up and burped her. Her jowly face and her patient, hunched back were suggestive of a grumpy old man's.

Lila left her pink hat that night, like a girl leaving a barrette at a boy's house after a hookup. Kate's mother appeared early the next morning. Lila had not yet come for her feeding. "Where is she?" Kate's mother asked.

Kate said, "In the nursery still." She pointed at the hat. "She left her hat," Kate said, and her mother laughed.

8

HEY BOUGHT A HOUSE in Fairfield, one stop farther south on the New Haven line, a three-bedroom, two-bath carriage house with low ceilings and latches on the doors. They bought a second car, that year's Subaru wagon. Darcy ended it with Jesse, lover of Indian food, and left New York for a job at the Getty Museum in Los Angeles. The recession of Colin's hair continued, as did the expansion of the bald spot at the back of his head. Kate cut her long hair to her shoulders. She lost weight and her breasts shrank a size from nursing.

They moved into the new house when Lila was an infant. The first few years as parents were happy ones. Again, it seemed as though everything was going to be all right, that something troubling had been put aside. Colin came home in time for Lila's bath and rolled up his sleeves and rinsed her hair with the removable showerhead and together they watched her tilt her face upward and stick out her tongue to catch the water, creases appearing in the plump back of her neck. Kate learned the song Colin had sung to Liam, the one about the man who lived in the moon. They read Lila board books, then picture books; they rolled her around the house in her high chair; they danced her in the air; they fed her puréed food out of tiny jars, jars Kate agonized over in the Stop & Shop: Would

Lila prefer Beef with Carrots or Chicken 'n' Dumplings (and *were* they dumplings? how *could* they be?) or Spaghetti Bolognese or Turkey with Rice?

THEY EMPLOYED A SITTER, Vanessa, to care for Lila at home. What they paid Vanessa was not all that much less than what Kate made. It therefore cost them about what it gave them for Kate to work, if one figured in the additional costs of dry cleaning, transportation, and the like. However, she factored in the money she would make after Lila went to school and the benefit to Lila's self-esteem to have a mother who worked. Vanessa did Lila's laundry and made the occasional run to Stop & Shop or BJ's. A woman named Beatrice came once a week to clean the house.

"We can afford it," Colin said. "She needs the money, right? We don't have to do it all ourselves."

Beatrice called for a comprehensive set of cleaning supplies and a special brand of vacuum. She required that the house be organized upon her arrival. When it wasn't she squirreled stray clothes and toys and objects away in unfathomable places. She accepted cash only as payment. Somehow Colin became separated from the details of this domestic activity and others, and a certain subtle fatigue developed and interfered with Kate's new, Lila-specific happiness. The fatigue was like a small rodent working its way through her brain. It was like a rat chewing away at all the essential connections that mobilized the labyrinthine gray matter of her mind. Lila of course brought about much of the fatigue, but the rest of it came from somewhere else, from something she and Colin had started on together and, with Lila, effected completely.

At the development office one afternoon she made a startling discovery. She had paused at the watercooler, where two coworkers, Joyce and Marcus, were discussing their respective law school ventures—hers in the past, his imminent.

"My household was in an uproar," Joyce said. "My kids were little then. Total chaos."

Both women looked at Marcus.

He shrugged. "I don't have a household."

Then Kate saw that she had one: a household. She had not known until that very moment. Like a rare glandular disorder, it had plagued her covertly. The groceries and the diapers. The lawn and the gutters. The furnace and the cleaning supplies and the recycling and the trash collection and the dishwasher and the running to the cash machine for Beatrice. Where the extra money went and where important things got lost, the cause of Kate's exhaustion and general dismay. Things to be bought and sorted and put and thrown or given away, a constant cascade of things tumbling in and out. She saw the secreted presence of it in her life, finally showing its face, like a troll in the attic. She saw the lack of it in Marcus's bland and aggressive chin, and she heard its damage in Joyce's flat, querulous tones.

Still, she kept her job at Yale Development a month past Lila's second birthday. Then three things happened.

The first thing: Vanessa got engaged and informed Kate that she'd be moving to New Jersey. Vanessa had taken Lila to the beach with her own friends instead of to the playground, to the mall instead of museums, had fed Lila Happy Meals instead of the healthy lunches Kate assembled and left in Tupperware in the fridge, but Lila loved 'Nessa, as she called her, and ran to her in the mornings. Kate interviewed a divinity student who did not like for little girls to play with trucks, a sweet Jamaican woman who didn't drive, and a charming former preschool teacher who wanted thirty dollars an hour.

The second thing: After the September 11 attacks, the Yale administration requested that the staff of the development office attend the Yale College graduation in the instance that an attack on the university and its freshly formed masters of the universe should occur, the idea being to surround the precious students with other, less valuable bodies. And as the development office was comprised mainly of women—young women in their twenties, pregnant women in their thirties, new mothers of babies and toddlers, forty-something mothers of teens—the strategy seemed, to Kate, decidedly ungallant of Yale. At the graduation, standing queasily in the hot sun with her arms crossed across tender breasts, she watched her father's old colleagues. Jack Auerbach, the graduate student from the Q Club (now a tenured professor), spotted her and offered a brief, masculine wave. The older professors (ensconced in the academic nucleus she and the other female bodies ostensibly safeguarded) surreptitiously picked their hoary noses.

And the third thing: Robin.

At home that evening, while Colin put Lila to bed, Kate took a pregnancy test. Colin found her crying in front of a *Seinfeld* rerun.

"I'm exhausted," she said. "And nauseous, all the damn time. And they threw us to the lions."

"Ivy League a-holes," Colin said. "Fuck 'em."

So she gave notice, completed her responsibilities, packed up her desk, and, soon enough, found herself at home with two children.

.   .   .

WITH ROBIN they became "a *real* family," as one person, then another remarked. The addition of Robin disproportionately increased their value as a unit in society. Until then they'd seemed to Kate mobile and reassuringly marginal, like a couple of careless teenagers carting their child around to restaurants and dinners on Saturday nights, taking the days as they came. Kate sensed something depressingly conventional in the transition; and now, like her mother, she sat up late sewing on buttons and paying bills. Colin, in pursuit of professional advancement, spent longer hours at work. The first time around they'd done the baby thing together—as a team—the bedtime, the burping, the changing. But with Robin, Colin quickly established his distance, and therefore his masculinity—threatened now, in this house of females. Kate's first night home from the hospital he said, "I don't have to get up, do I?"

"No," Kate said, startled. "I guess not."

"I mean now that you're not working. Right?"

So Kate woke alone to Robin's cries and sleepily nursed her and grudgingly burped and changed her and got her back to sleep and felt lonely doing so but supposed (as she'd been told by her fellow mothers) that she was lucky to feel lonely at all. As if his participation in Lila's infancy had been a favor to her—to Kate and, on some level, to Lila. And shamefully, she had felt it to be so, and even now, she felt anxiously and secretly that the responsibility and work of Lila belonged to her, even as she insisted on the logic of a shared effort.

She forgot relevant things at crucial times. She made a list of activities for a rainy day but forgot about it on rainy days, remembered it only on sunny ones. She forgot to apply sunscreen; she forgot to check her children for ticks. (She wrote a note in capital letters and taped it to a kitchen cabinet—*CHECK FOR TICKS!!!*) She forgot to pack Lila's library book on library day. She bought snow pants on sale in April for the following winter, then forgot about them until she came across them while hanging up the new ones. Toast went half-buttered, milk turned on the counter, to-do lists came down only half-tackled—frantic multitudinous lists addressing sundry aspects of life. For example:

Laundry
Electrician
Rug pad
Barry: storms, chair, garage
Rx
Résumé?
Cancel subscription
Pap smear
100 items, groups of 10 (a homework assignment)
Clip nails
Permission slip
Schedule wax
Ask about dreams!
Suicide

"Suicide?" said Colin.

"It's a group. I heard them on XMU."

"Well, it looks like you have suicide on your to-do list."

She considered going back to school, or to work, but put these thoughts away before even examining them thoroughly.

They had enough money—not heaps, but enough—and therefore any professional effort on her part, with kids this small, felt nearly recreational.

She learned from NPR that a dream deficit existed—that because families no longer gathered at the breakfast table and discussed their dreams, the dreams went unrecalled, creating a psychological void. So, dutifully, in the car on the way to school, Kate would ask her girls, "What did you dream?"

Sometimes they remembered—sometimes they didn't.

To get them going, she would relate her own dreams. Occasionally she remembered. Usually she made something up.

She moved from the house to school to the store as if through a series of tunnels, sometimes running into someone or other, sometimes an acquaintance busy with his or her own tunneling—but generally it seemed a clandestine business, this underground traveling, a myopic, itinerant concentration of self. Somewhere, in the center, a party was going on—Kate could hear it, smell it, and she turned corner after corner hoping to come across it but she never did. And, terrified by reports of cancer and girls getting their period at age eight, Kate drove from store to store in her tunnel collecting the correct defenses. The natural food co-op carried organic vegetables but no meat. The Stop & Shop carried the household essentials and organic produce, dried, jarred, and canned goods, but no organic juice boxes and organic or free-range chicken and meat only sometimes. The gourmet Italian market carried free-range chicken and meat but no organic vegetables and none of the household essentials.

However, regularly and amazingly, upon investigation of the fridge, there seemed to be nothing to eat.

The days ran sloppily together. An unwashed hamper of days.

There were occasions and distractions and routine. The girls were inevitable and wonderful but deeply problematic. They did adorable things like dance in diapers and underwear to Journey. Like hold earnest, private conversations with each other. Like offer their small faces in the dark for a kiss. They disrupted the night and consumed the day. Kate did what she could, taking demands and commands as they cropped up—in the car, in the bath, at mealtimes—she considered a limited future in the evenings after she cooked dinner and cleared up and gave the girls a bath and put them to bed and went around the downstairs picking up, removing, if diligent and successful, all trace of them.

And things had changed after Lila, after the regulation six weeks and then some, after the first vaguely painful postbaby round. It will take a while, the books had told her. But stay positive! Do your Kegels! Certainly, the area had taken a beating. Pain and swelling ebbed to divulge dulled nerves and laxity. But one night in May, feeling somewhat like herself again, Kate rubbed Colin's crotch through his boxer shorts, wriggled out of her underwear, and got onto her hands and knees. He got behind her and guided himself into her. He stroked her back. She flinched at his gentleness.

"Do that other thing," she said.

"What thing?"

"You know."

"Oh. That. Really?"

"You don't want to?"

"No, sure I do."

He hit her on the rear. He grabbed her hair. Then let go.

"This feels weird," he said.

"What do you mean?"

He ran a hand over her hair and smoothed it over her shoulders. "We have a baby now. A baby girl."

9

ROBIN BEGAN PRESCHOOL, Lila kindergarten. Kate extended her hours at the Rose Center: the women's and children's shelter where she'd volunteered since leaving Yale Development. Monday and Wednesday mornings she got the girls ready for school and dropped them off on her way to Bridgeport. On Tuesdays, Thursdays, and Fridays, she got the girls ready and Colin dropped them. Then the empty house affected the silence of a freshly abandoned crime scene, so while Kate drank coffee and ate toast she listened to Martha Stewart on the satellite radio. Tuesday was "Everyday Food" with Sandy Gluck. Thursday was "Cat Chat" with Tracie Hotchner. Kate didn't own a cat and didn't particularly like cats, but she listened anyway because she found the shows, the station, and the whole idea of Martha deeply reassuring. Divorce! Insider trading! Public disgrace! Jail! And yet on and on she went, dispensing ideas and advice, chuckling over Sandy's segment on gorgeous gourds, validating domestic concerns both crucial and superfluous, developing an industry she'd practically invented. Kate now knew more about cats—their habits and temperament and physiology—than she'd ever imagined she might. There were amazing stories of cats' heroism. One little girl's cat stood outside her bedroom door and meowed as her stepfather sexually abused her. Another cat fetched a neighbor when its owner went into anaphylactic shock. Tracie spoke scathingly of people who abused and tortured their cats, of couples who became pregnant and threw their cats out onto the street. (And Kate recalled Moira and Alice, the Great Dane.) The people who ran the animal shelters were like wardens, a guest once said, in that they grew fond of their charges and then sometimes had to kill them—once again, a clear case of the privileged asking the less so to do their dirty work.

A WEEK INTO THE SCHOOL YEAR, Colin and the girls still asleep, Kate stripped off her nightshirt and stood before the full-length master bedroom mirror. A bruise flowered over her left knee. Another colored her thigh. Another darkened her hip where she'd collided with the marble-topped kitchen island. She rarely recalled specific accidents. The bruises seemed simply to appear, as if erupting from within.

She pulled on yoga pants and a T-shirt and woke the girls.

"Is it a weekend, Mommy?"

"No. We're getting ready for school, remember?"

"Can we watch TV?"

"Did you brush your teeth?"

"We want *Dragon Tales,*" Lila said.

"After your teeth. A little."

They followed her downstairs. She spread an old tablecloth on the floor in front of the television.

"Can I have tea, please," Lila said.

"May I."

"May I have tea."

"May I have tea, please."

So tedious it was!

"May I please have tea!"

"Don't shout," Kate said. "Yes. You may please have tea. I mean, you may have tea. I will make you tea."

"Tea too!" Robin shouted. "Tea for me!"

"Robin, don't shout. You may have tea too."

"Hey, why didn't she have to say 'please' and 'may,' " Lila said.

Kate headed for the kitchen, pretending she hadn't heard.

She prepared chamomile tea and tiny bagels. While the water boiled and the bagels toasted she stood at the pantry window and watched a confused raccoon crouch beneath the neighbor's dormant lilac. She served the tea and bagels on a tray on the floor cloth. She gathered clean clothes. She hung the pajamas over the banister. She laid sneaker sandals before the back door. She climbed back upstairs to the bedroom and shook Colin by the shoulder. "You're going to be late again."

He sat up and reached for his water glass. "We're in the window."

"Lila's supposed to be there at eight-fifteen. You leave the *house* at eight-fifteen."

"We're not late."

"It is physically impossible for you to make it to Wintergreen in negative one minute."

"We are In The Window."

"There *is* no window. It's an *eight-fifteen* drop-off. Why don't I just take them today."

"I like taking my daughters to school."

"Well, get up then!"

"We are not the Last Ones There," he said. "Those Swedes. The architect. With the chubby wife. They're the Last Ones."

"You mean the Later Than Us Ones."

"Yeah. That."

"Oh, well, that's all fine then!"

Back downstairs, this time stomping. Something had happened in her absence to *Dragon Tales* and the girls were crying, the screen gone to static. "What, guys? What is it?" Had she paid the cable bill? She knelt to investigate.

"Robin did it. She turned it off. Bad baby!" Lila smacked her sister on the shoulder.

"Lila, no hitting, no *hitting*!"

As usual, the girls had refused to spend the entire night in their beds and had crawled into Colin and Kate's around two a.m. and, after sharp words between the parents, been allowed to stay.

Rounding back into the kitchen she found Colin at the table, brandishing a spoon over his Wheaties.

"Why is it," she said, "that we wait on them? It used to be children who were slaves. Now we're the slaves."

"Ha, ha. So true."

"I'm just going to take them, okay? They're ready."

"But—"

"Guys! Let's go!"

The girls ran in and swarmed over Colin—sampling his Wheaties, sipping his coffee. Somehow Lila had donned a pink tutu over her pants. Kate herded them down the back steps. She strapped them into their booster seats and started the car and took the highway to downtown Fairfield.

"Don't you look pretty." Maggie, Lila's teacher and a retired ballerina, clasped her hands.

Didn't Maggie know one wasn't supposed to say that? Lila would hear it and learn to feel proud.

Lila twirled. "I want to be a ballerina when I grow up."

"Wonderful!"

"I'm going to be world-famous."

"Being famous is difficult," Kate said. "Especially world-famous."

Lila stared at her. Robin wandered away and wedged herself into a cubby.

"The important thing," Kate said, "is not to be famous, but to do something you love to do." She looked at Maggie—she couldn't help feeling proud of such an appropriate response. It was her role, she understood, to gently temper such fantasies.

What would they lead to, ever?

But Maggie was frowning slightly and looking back and forth from Kate to Lila.

"Is that your dream?" Maggie asked.

"Yes."

"It's great to have dreams like that."

Had that been Maggie's dream, to be a famous ballerina? Did she consider herself a dancer still? Was she resigned to teaching kindergarten, or did she wish she'd been world-famous?

Lila ran off to the sand table. Kate pulled Robin from the cubby. She dropped Robin at preschool and, in the cheery low-ceilinged hallway, encountered Mave Silverman, the mother of Robin's best classroom buddy, and Brooke Williams, who lived in a pink mansion down the road from Kate and Colin with her five strawberry-blond children and a blond, handsome husband who favored pink shirts and ties. Trey, the husband, suffered from an eye tic, the family's one flaw. For years Kate had assumed he was winking at her, that the two of them shared a special camaraderie, and she'd consequently become fond of him. However, after she spotted him winking into his beer at the club, she registered his winking at everyone and everything—but the fondness stayed, not so easily displaced.

"It's been way too long," Brooke said, hugging Kate.

The truth was, they saw each other at drop-off and pickup often. But Kate said, "I know," and hugged back.

Years ago she'd participated in a book club with both Brooke and Mave. But the club had broken up after Brooke, the informal director, delivered her third child.

"Do you want to come over for coffee?" Brooke asked. "Mave's coming over for coffee."

"And then I'm going to use her Pilates machine," Mave said.

"And then she's going to use my Pilates machine," Brooke said.

"Oh, jeez," Kate said. "I probably shouldn't."

She didn't want to.

"Oh, come on, it's right on your way."

"Hmmm . . . I have to go to the store. . . ." She didn't want to stop at Brooke's for coffee and Pilates, but if she didn't spend some time with Brooke and Mave now they would insist on it later. "Okay. Yeah, I can swing it."

They got into their respective cars and got onto I-95 and pulled up in the driveway of the pink house. They entered through the ubiquitous mudroom: a row of hooks for coats, some sort of dull tile, and a colorful framed Toulouse-Lautrec print, artfully incongruous. They sat in Brooke's stylishly outfitted kitchen, around the stainless-steel (to match the appliances) table from Pottery Barn. Children's art, housed in chunky black frames, hung about the purple-painted walls. Five green ceramic plates, bearing handprints of ascending sizes, climbed a defunct but ornamental brick chimney. A carved walking stick beautified the western wainscoting.

"How's the crew?" Kate asked.

Brooke rolled her eyes as if five children were a condition that had been thrust upon her instead of something she'd actively sought. Surely they allowed themselves birth control, if desired? How else had they conveniently avoided children before marriage?

"All those kids you have. I can barely get through the day with one. Weekends kill me—snow days, holidays." Mave shook her head. "Awful. I'm an awful mother."

"Oh, stop with that awful-mother business." Brooke took plates and cups down from the sleek white cupboard. "I think a whole bunch of kids is easier than two. There's sort of this group mentality. They all just fall in line. They play with each other. They entertain each other. They do." She started coffee and sliced up some sort of tea cake and put the slices on a plate. "So when are you going to have another baby, Mave?"

"I'm practically forty," Mave said. "Besides, I have no desire to go around smelling like Preparation H for a month. And I just lost my baby weight, four years later. Kind of absurd that something, I mean parenting, that makes you so physically exhausted doesn't just burn the pounds right off. Sometimes it takes me over an hour just to get Hannah out the door in the morning."

"I struggle with that too," Brooke said. "You have to tell them ten times. Shoes on. Et cetera, et cetera."

"Do your kids fight?" Kate asked. "What do you do about it?"

"A little. I ignore it; it works itself out."

"You're smart." Mave reached for a piece of cake.

"I can't do that," Kate said. "I can't stand it—the whining, the biting, the hitting. I panic. I feel like they'll kill each other if I don't intervene."

"They won't. They just want attention. If they know you're going to work it out for them they won't do it themselves."

"But what if one of them bullies the other one? What if they feel abandoned?"

Brooke shrugged. How Kate envied her. How she wanted and didn't want.

"Oh, look," said Mave, suddenly distracted. "European animal crackers! So cute!"

Brooke got up and poured the coffee and took the animal crackers down from the shelf.

"How do they compare to Nabisco?" Mave asked.

"Try one." Brooke pushed the bag in her direction. "These are more vanilla-y, I think. And with Nabisco you get wild animals; I mean exotic animals, what you'd see in a zoo. These are domestic animals, farm animals. Cows, dogs, cats. Sheep. Horses."

"You did a great job with the framing in here," Mave said.

Mave had an MFA in studio art. She taught part-time at the University of Bridgeport.

"Pottery Barn," Brooke said.

"I went down to the basement for a bottle of wine the other day," Mave said. "And I saw all this work I did maybe ten years ago, when I was in grad school and right after, this whole gouache series. God. And not like they were so great or anything, but I thought, Shouldn't I still be doing this?" She stirred sugar into her coffee. "I don't know. Probably not."

"Of course you should be," Brooke said encouragingly.

"Just seems like, with the kid, there's always something else, something more pressing."

"You should do it on the weekends," Brooke said. "Get Dan to babysit and get back into it."

"Babysit?" Kate reached for another animal cracker. "She's his kid too, right?"

Mave laughed. "Allegedly."

Something moved suddenly in the corner of the room. Kate jumped. Mave shrieked.

"Sorry," Brooke said. She got up again. "That's just Artoo."

A foot-high replica of the robot sidekick from *Star Wars* ground its mechanical limbs by the mudroom door.

"He responds to voices. Watch this." She stood in front of the toy with her hands on her hips. "Artoo! Walk, Artoo!"

"I think he's stuck," Kate said.

With her foot, Brooke nudged him over a divergence in the floorboards. "Artoo! Walk! Artoo!"

The robot marched forward.

"No wonder your kids fall in line," Mave said.

"Stop, Artoo!" He stopped. Brooke leaped toward him and switched something in his back. "They always leave him on," she said. "Then this happens. They left him on and they left him in our bedroom once. He started up in the middle of the night while we were having sex."

"Wow," Mave said, "sex."

"You don't have sex?"

"I do, we do, but not middle-of-the-night sex. Just regular scheduled sex."

"What a shame." Brooke looked at Kate.

"Not scheduled," Kate said. "But he gives me a backrub and I give him sex. Basically, it's a trade."

"Does Dan know how you feel about your sex life?" Brooke asked Mave.

"Dan? He knows nothing. I could have a lover, for all he knows." She raised her chin and cast her eyes upward. To an imaginary lover, she said, "Meet me at Yankee Donut."

"It feels like homework," Kate said.

"Exactly like that." Mave snapped her fingers.

"Oh, come on." Brooke poured more coffee all around. "Try some new positions or something. Trey and I do. All the time."

"Fantastic," Mave said. "Wow, am I happy to have that information. No, but seriously, good for you. And Trey. What a stud. And on that note, I should take off. I have to teach a class today at some point; can you believe it?"

"Good for *you,*" Kate said.

Brooke said, "I do not miss going into an office."

"I sometimes miss it," Kate said.

"I'm just not cut out for it, I swear. I'd so much rather do what I do." Brooke looked around her beautiful kitchen.

"What *do* you do, Brooke?" Mave put her elbows on the table and leaned forward. Then: "Just teasing."

"I manage the household," Brooke said. "And I consume. I support the economy! I'm a consumer. That's what I do. No, really," she said, "it's like running a small business."

"It must be challenging," Mave said, "managing a staff of six."

"I know I'm copping out in a way, but it's fun. Being home with the kids. Why not just . . ." Brooke shrugged. "It's totally personal. It's a personal choice."

"Ideally," Mave said.

"It's only fun if you have money, though," Kate said. "And have someone to do all the crap. Laundry, cleaning the house, et cetera."

"I guess."

"And," Kate said, "do you really feel right about not being out there? In the workplace, in society? I mean, I don't; I don't feel right about it. I feel like I'm causing, I don't know, women to lose ground. Or something."

"I *am* in society, though," Brooke said. "I *have* a job. Raising five responsible citizens. That's my job."

"Five little consumers?" Mave said.

"Yup."

"But don't you feel like you've given up power, in a way?" Kate asked. "Being financially dependent?"

"I don't think of it like that. It's a collaborative effort. A business. It's like, I'm the director and Trey is the producer. Or . . ." Brooke thought for a moment. "I'm the developer and he's the bank. The kids, they're the project. So I get developers' fees, in exchange for my contribution and my work. But I'm in charge. And Trey respects that."

"So you work for him?" Mave said.

"I think what she's saying is he's where she gets her funding," Kate said. "I see what you mean, Brooke."

"I'm being a bitch," Mave said. "Sorry. I'll stop. I really have to go anyway." She stood up.

"The Pilates machine!" Brooke cried.

"Shit!"

"Stay just a few more minutes?"

"Next time. Next time Pilates."

Mave departed and Brooke looked hopefully at Kate.

"I don't think I'm in the mood for Pilates," Kate said. "I'm sorry. This cake is really good, though." She took another piece. "What about sleeping? Your kids. How do they sleep?"

"They sleep well."

Of course—of course they slept well.

"Don't get me wrong. I worked at it," Brooke said. "It wasn't magic or anything. You have to get them when they're babies. Discipline. No eye contact after seven p.m. No playing after six p.m. No sleeping in the bed."

"Oh, God, they sleep in our bed every night. Or I in theirs."

"It's what works for you. That's what matters."

"It works okay for me. Not for Colin."

Kate suspected that his aversion to the kids in the bed was linked to the fact that their presence canceled out his already extremely small chance of getting spontaneously laid. But she loved them warmly next to her; she wrapped her limbs around their heated small soft ones; she let Robin, then Lila into the bed. She couldn't or wouldn't say no. She'd make room and hold them, open her eyes in the dark. Considering the years ahead, the years with Colin and her growing detachment from their physical relationship, she'd feel, mawkishly but sincerely, that this, the contraband snuggling with her girls, was to be her last experience of bodily love—of physical intimacy—on this earth.

And he—Colin—wanted to take even that from her!

"So what happens?"

"They run out of their rooms. I walk them back. They run out again. I walk them back and sit with them for a while. I go back to bed. They run out again. Like those toys. Weebles. Weebles wobble but they don't fall down. I give up and make room in the bed. Then Colin makes a fuss."

"Bedtime?"

"The same. Eventually they fall asleep in their beds, knowing of course that they'll come into ours later. I just never know if they *will* fall asleep in the first place. They know that. They can feel that."

"Act confident. Be strong."

"But what do I do? When they run out?"

"Walk them back."

"That's what I do!"

"Even if you have to do it one hundred times."

"Really? That seems . . . I don't know. Wrong."

"It's not easy. For a while I had to hold Taylor down in her bed."

Taylor was Lila's age. "Hold her down?"

"That's right. In her bed."

"Wow."

"The rule is, they're in bed. They don't have to sleep so long as they stay in bed."

"That's a good rule."

"Madison reads. He loves Harry Potter, of course. Taylor too. She reads. Now it's fine. She stays in bed. Maybe you feel like it's selfish, wanting them to go to bed, but it's not. They need it. They need the sleep, and you and Colin need your time together. When we moved to this house, Madison ran out of his room again and again and again. So I set up camp outside his room. I had dinner in his bathroom for a week. When he tried to run out, I'd hold the door shut. For a week, dinner on the bathroom floor."

"Jeez."

Maybe if the kids slept, she would be able to pull herself together, lose the insidious sense of time constantly running out. Colin would make a killing and she would want him the way she once had, without inhibition and grudges. She knew one had nothing to do with the other, but a goal felt useful, generative. She could see it. She could! A happy future, children who slept through the night!

"So maybe," said Kate, "maybe I should put a lock on the door. Or something."

"A lock?"

"So they don't run out. So, I don't know, I don't have to stand there, holding the door shut. In the middle of the night. And also, I can't hold both doors closed at once."

"*Lock* them in their rooms." Brooke sipped her coffee and put it down. "No."

"But—"

Brooke held up a hand. She gazed down at her coffee, as if receiving insight from its lovely chemistry of tastes. "You do not lock them in their rooms. Ever. If you do that, which again you shouldn't ever do, they will think of their room as a bad place, somewhere they don't want to be. The room is supposed to be a happy place."

"But—you said you held Taylor down in her bed."

"That's different," Brooke said, somehow knowing. "Don't you see how it's different?"

Kate didn't. She crumbled a bit of tea cake between her thumb and index finger. It was only ten-thirty in the morning and already she had shot down her daughter's special dream of world fame and contemplated jailing her children in their rooms. Confined to bed, confined to room, what was the difference? But if Brooke said it was different it must be so. Kate wanted to understand—she wanted to know without being told. She could follow directions and revise and correct but she wanted to know the formulas and to understand them, their application in various situations and which ones to use when.

"Have you guys seen a therapist?" Brooke asked. "You and Colin?"

"No—about the sleeping? The kids?"

"You might want to think about it. When parents are stressed out the kids pick up on it. Which is probably, ironically, making the whole sleeping thing worse."

"Hmm."

Of course, the bedtime struggles were beside the point.

"Do you two do date night?"

"We do fight night. Every Saturday. After the kids are finally in bed we order takeout and fight."

"Trey and I go out to a movie or dinner or an art opening or something every Friday."

"We used to see movies. We used to go into the city. Not since the kids."

"You should. You should get a sitter and get out. You have to get away from the little ones once in a while, the two of you together."

"Well, that's what they say, but . . ."

"You might surprise yourself."

"A surprise would be nice."

"We went."

"Where, to the city?"

"No, to therapy."

"You and *Trey*?"

"Yup. After Taylor. I stopped wanting to sleep with him."

"Well. That's normal. Especially after a baby." *Was* it? "I think the guys just really need to get over it."

"So bad for the marriage, though. I mean, a man is entitled to have sex with his wife, right? And if you're not enjoying it, well, he can tell. I know it can be hard to get in the mood. But you can't just shut him out sexually."

"No?"

"No."

"You mean sex is part of the deal."

"No, I mean, well . . . yes."

"Did it help? The therapy?"

"It *did*. It helped me feel . . . that I had some control, I guess, so I didn't have to control Trey by withholding sex."

"Is that how he felt? That you were trying to control him?"

"Well, I was."

"Hmm." Kate stood and transported her cup and plate to the sink. She opened the dishwasher.

"Oh, don't do that. I'll do that."

"You sure?"

"Leave it."

"Thanks so much, Brooke. I should probably get going."

"I'll give you the number. Just so you have it." Brooke wrote on a pink Post-it.

"One more thing to do." Kate took the Post-it anyway.

"Don't feel obliged. You have the number if you want it."

"I know. Thanks." She looked at Brooke's tidy handwriting. "I'll probably leave this in my car and find it in a year."

But she folded the Post-it into a rectangle and stuck it in her wallet. Driving home, she felt buoyed, connected. Brooke and Trey had been to therapy. Mave kept paintings in her basement. If Kate wanted, she could make ceramic plates with the girls' handprints and hang them on her kitchen wall. Then all might be well.

On arrival home, however, disorder prevailed. There it was—the dried-out Play-Doh, the Lincoln Logs, the lipstick-smeared Ariel head, the Woodkins, the Webkinz, the puzzle pieces, the stuffed animals that surely screwed and reproduced in their baskets, the cottage-cheese cup overturned on the rug. Nothing had shifted since she'd left in the clean crisp light of early morning. She felt almost let down, as if she'd expected the rooms to clean and organize themselves in her absence. Last year Beatrice had moved away and now they employed Portia, who demanded less preparatory organization, but still, how could the poor woman work in such conditions?

That night, after putting the girls to bed, after Kate had eaten a sandwich standing at the kitchen counter and Colin had eaten a larger version of the same sandwich in front of the Patriots game, she began, listlessly, to pick up.

"What we should do here," she said, "is no more birthday parties."

"Birthday parties?"

"You know. Kids' birthday parties. The Children's Museum. Creative Arts, Gymboree."

"It's nice for kids to see their friends," he said, somewhat piously.

But he got up off the couch and began to help her. He

tossed Lincoln Logs into a basket. He tossed the Woodkins in after, ignoring the plastic organizing sheath. Then he paused in his efforts, picked the week-old *New York Times* sports section pages she'd used for crafts off the floor, and started to read an article.

"The presents," she said. "The cake. The pizza. The party bags. The boring other parents. The inevitable, eventual barfing. They invite us and we invite them and the toys and the junk . . ."

"I think a kid should have a birthday party," Colin said. He rustled the newspaper and folded it.

"Well. Why don't you plan Robin's?"

He tossed the paper askew onto the coffee table, just cleared of children's toys.

"Yeah. Okay," he said. He walked away, toward the kitchen.

"So—you'll plan Robin's party? Is that what you're saying?" she called after his broad, indifferent back, his smooth-shaven neck, his thinning crown. She rounded the corner into the kitchen.

"Fine." He opened a sleeve of chocolate-chip cookies and held it out to her. "No big deal."

"Oh," she said grimly, taking a cookie, "you'll see. You'll see it all. It's not over when it's over, you know. Then you still have the thank-you notes."

"Book the museum, get a cake from Stop & Shop, call it a day. Forget the notes."

"You can't do that!"

"You want 'em, you write 'em."

"But why is it always us!" she cried. "The women! Why do *we* have to do it!"

"Because chicks like that stuff. You included."

"Do not."

"Then what's up with the Martha Stewart habit?"

She turned away and poured herself more wine. "I read Martha for the recipes."

"Kate. I said I'd do it."

"Yes, but—so, you're doing me this big favor."

"No favors. I don't mind."

"You're not going to do it," she said. "You're going to wait till the last minute and then you're not going to do it."

He folded up the cookies and returned them to the cabinet and went back to the game. She followed him.

"So you're not going to help me after all," she said. She indicated the still-disheveled downstairs.

He shifted his pose and again fixed his eyes on the screen. "Let's do it later."

"When?"

"Tomorrow or something?"

"Okay. But will you remind me? I need you to initiate it, okay?" She moved in order to more completely block the game. "I can't ask you again. I don't want to be that person."

"It's the Patriots. Please."

"What if you don't? Remind me? Then what?"

"Then Beatrice will do it or something."

Colin refused to remember the subtleties of the respective housekeepers' names, as if he could not be expected to absorb a matter so trivial; and as if his insistence on his own igno-rance, his failure to keep track, further and necessarily empha-sized his superior status in the life of the household.

"There are just too many toys," Kate said.

"So get rid of them. Tell the girls to choose ten things they really want—"

"Ten! Look at all this stuff!"

"—or fifteen or twenty and we'll give the rest away."

"*We'll* give it away? Okay. Let's see. So *I* put all the little bits and pieces together and clean the sticky off. But who wants it?"

"Take them to work with you," Colin said reasonably. "Take them to the ladies at the center."

This actually seemed like a good plan.

But she picked up the Ariel head. "The parties, the presents, all the plastic crap. Remember *Santa Comes to Little House*? Mr. Edwards? Swimming the creek with the presents on his head? One cake. One penny. One tin cup."

"What are you talking about?"

"Never mind." She stepped away from the football and returned to the living room and began to sort the toys into four piles: miscellaneous, throw out, give away, put away. She attempted to put companion objects together in their rightful manner. Into the garbage bag went toast crusts, stray Cheerios, a cracked sippy cup, doll parts, torn playing cards, a Tupperware container that had once held water for paint—she should recycle it she but couldn't face it, not right now—she could not face one more task.

Colin appeared in the doorframe. "Okay," he said. "Here I am. Jets thirty-eight, Patriots thirty-one."

Warm air blew from a vent. On the coffee table, the newspaper crackled where he'd left it. She spotted it and seized it. "Oh, you're more effing trouble than you're worth!"

He turned around and shut off the television and headed upstairs.

"I'm sorry," she called after him. "Colin, I'm sorry; I didn't mean that."

He disappeared into their bedroom.

She neatened the kitchen and prepped the coffee and assembled the girls' lunches. Then she picked up a vase that had been sitting by the side of the pantry sink for a month, since a late-summer cookout—not a wedding vase, not valuable, just one that had been delivered, with flowers, perhaps when Lila was born. She had not yet found the energy to clean it and put it away. It waited, gourd-shaped, for handling. Residual fauna hung inside and soft green mold coated the bottom.

She lifted it and smashed it in the sink.

SHE SAT UP in the middle of the night.

"We should see somebody, Colin," she said.

"Huh?"

"A counselor. We should see a marriage counselor. Brooke and Trey did it. Brooke gave me a number."

" 'S too late," he said drowsily.

The Valeries woke and pushed against her slumbering organs, his words reaching them. They dug their nails into her liver.

"No, Colin. Please don't say that. If you say it you'll make it true."

"Kate . . ."

"You make your own reality. Things don't have to be like this."

"Just let me sleep."

She slept and dreamed of a whole other room in the house, a room that existed in a parallel universe only she could enter. The room sucked energy from the rest of the house and accumulated filth that contaminated the communal air. The vents needed cleaning, the windows excavating. Bracken and bird excrement and wasps' nests filled that elusive spot between storm and pane. Dust rolled wraithlike along baseboards. Busy spiders hung from beams, and cracks extended where molding died into the plaster. There was something rotting in that room, something someone had partaken of and forgotten to put away. Someone had stored pad thai under the bed. Someone had left plates of pasta below sheaves of unpaid bills and unsorted bank statements—spaghetti and sauce growing green like houseplants. Everything Kate had ever lost was in that room: every sock, every earring, every beloved object—a bracelet given to her by her bridesmaids, Lila's first clipped curl, an ironically signed copy of her father's last book. There could be found the dark-eyed elf babies her children had once been. Her love for Colin was in that room as well. Here the Valeries loafed and lingered, depressed and muted by domesticity, bickering and gaining weight, grubby and grumpy in ill-fitting tunics, their hair gone to nests.

And unloved objects also filled the room: every misplaced toy, every last whatsit and whosit, every puzzle piece. Every manual to every confounding appliance and electronic device. These items magnetized and merged to create hybrid creatures that claimed her as their manufacturer, her neglect having given them life. They chattered horribly among themselves of her daily doings and at night slunk into her bedroom and sat on her face.

She woke suddenly in the hopeful light of morning.

"Not a sound from them," Colin said. He stared at the ceiling, his arms crossed behind his neck.

"They were exhausted."

"Aren't we all. Can't sleep in, though."

"Me neither."

She got up and went down to the kitchen and poured two mugs of coffee. She carried the mugs upstairs and put one on Colin's bedside table.

She said, "If it's too late now, well, when wasn't it?"

"What?"

"You don't remember?"

"Yeah, okay."

"Okay what?"

He leaned up against one of the big pillows and sipped the coffee. "The idea bothers me. But we could. See someone."

"Really?" She shifted to her side, facing him, and rested her head on her hand. "That's good. I think it might be good. Maybe we just need a little help."

"But what's wrong? What do we need help with? I'm not sure I understand."

"I don't either. But something is, right? Something feels wrong. Something we might be able to figure out." She reached over and slipped a hand under his shirt and rubbed his abdomen. "I don't know, maybe—"

He rolled on top of her. She parted her knees. Aroused for once.

"Do it quick," she said. "The girls. It's almost seven."

She grabbed a pillow and maneuvered it under her behind. Sweat dripped from his shoulders onto hers. His breath, coffee-scented, covered her face.

She clutched his biceps. "Oh, Colin. That feels good."

He finished fast. As directed. She heard the soft bump of the girls' bedroom door and two sets of running feet. She watched the knob of her own closed door begin to twist frantically. The small hands pushed and grabbed and the knob expressed their struggle. Outside a straggling bird twittered in the spare branches of a copper beech. The door opened and the girls fell over each other into the room. They ran to Kate's side of the bed. She caught Robin under her armpits and hauled her up: a small fish. Then Lila, a bigger fish. She kissed their faces all over—their little noses, their soft full cheeks, their pliable mouths. She pulled them lecherously close to her. Colin got up and headed for the bathroom. Kate heard his urine hitting the water.

Robin pushed at Kate's shoulder. "Get up. You smelly bed sleeper."

"Ouch, baby. Don't push Mommy."

Robin pushed her again, harder.

"Robin. It's not nice." She slid her hand down the girl's back. Water rushed through walls as Colin started the shower.

Lila grabbed *The Marvelous Land of Oz* from Kate's nightstand and curled up on the sex pillow and began to read. Robin crawled under the bed and surfaced with a dusty coconut shell. Once the shell had contained coconut sorbet, served to Robin at their favorite local restaurant, and the girls had insisted on taking the shell home and rinsing it and keeping it. Now it held rotten petals gathered from the park. Robin picked the petals one by one from the shell and inserted them into Kate's underpants (reclaimed and faintly damp). Colin returned from the bathroom in a towel and watched, curiously.

"You're letting her do that?" he said.

"I guess I am."

"Huh." He bent from his waist to touch his toes. His joints cracked. His bald spot glared balefully at her, a dull stubborn eye. Robin sang at her task. "Downstairs, kids," he said. He gathered them up, one under each arm, and carried them away. Kate visited the bathroom. When she sat, petals fell from her crotch.

10

T HE WEATHER COOLED. Kate took the girls for haircuts and dental exams. She tucked the girls under a blanket on the couch in front of their morning show and made tea and warmed their undershirts in the microwave.

She made a phone call to the number Brooke had given her and left a message. The therapist—Dr. Levy—called back and left a message. She called him again. Finally they connected and scheduled an appointment. On a Tuesday, Kate and Colin sat in a small, overheated office in what had once been a residential building. A framed photograph hung behind the therapist's head—a door, adobe-style, and through it a desert, New Mexico maybe? Kate wondered if Dr. Levy had hung it there to inspire or signify insight.

"What brings you here?" he asked quietly.

They looked at each other. Colin shifted on the couch. Silence.

Dr. Levy tried again. "Are you fighting? Are you stuck on something?"

She should tell him about her dream, the messy room. She should tell him about the Valeries and how they tormented her. She should tell him about the Valeries in her body and the rat in her head.

"Is it sex?"

Last night, once again, the kids had ended up in their bed. Kate and Colin had gone out into the hallway to fight. Now she felt crabby and drowsy. She'd taken two Excedrin before heading to the appointment but her head still ached. The rat chewed. It chewed and chewed, meticulously, at the very center of her brain.

"Are you considering a separation?"

"That's not even on the table at all," Colin said.

Kate played with the magazine she'd carried in from the waiting room. She flipped through the pages and rolled the magazine into a tube. "No. Not that. Things are just wrong," she said. "And we don't know how to fix them."

She looked at Colin. He looked at her. She looked at Dr. Levy.

"Has that been your experience?" he asked.

Colin seemed unsure. He nodded, then grimaced.

"We can't really separate," Kate said.

"Why not? What's your feeling about that?" Dr. Levy shifted toward her in his chair. His expression revealed no tendency toward either of them. He spoke with a slight lisp, a special inflection, in a serious but animated tone. Kate wondered about his sexual orientation.

"We have two children. It's not what I want for them."

Dr. Levy raised his eyebrows sympathetically.

"And now?"

"Well, I guess it's just . . ." She shrugged. "We're here, aren't we?"

Dr. Levy looked at Colin. Colin also shrugged. With his larger frame, he outshrugged her.

"We're here," he said.

Kate could feel her face starting to flush in the radiator heat. But happily, the Excedrin was taking effect. "Do you mind if I open the window?" She looked from one man to the other. She stood and shoved it open. Old construction, it rose reluctantly, spitting lead. She sat. "It's just not something I want, anyway. A separation."

"Is that fear talking?"

"I guess."

"It's limiting. Living in fear."

"But sometimes I have a fantasy about it. About . . . leaving."

"Whoa, whoa," Colin said. "You do?"

"It's just silly."

"Tell me about the fantasy," Dr. Levy said.

"Well . . . it's absurd." But the poor fellow needed something from at least one of them, something to work with. So she continued. "There's this book I read to our kids, about an elephant: a little girl elephant and her mom. *Ella the Elegant Elephant*. They live on this island and the mom runs a pastry shop. We don't even know what happened to the dad."

"Deadbeat," Colin said.

"So I think about something along those lines. I imagine running away with the girls and living somewhere just *different,* on an *island* or the *city* or *Europe*—"

"Europe!" Colin shouted.

Levy held up his hand.

"And just baking a lot and happily ever after."

"A compelling scenario," Dr. Levy said.

"This isn't how it was supposed to turn out for us," she said.

"Why not? How were . . . things supposed to go?"

"Well. We were so crazy about each other once. At the beginning."

The doctor nodded. They were like children, she thought, Colin and she, quarreling children called into the principal's office. They sat facing him together, guilty as charged.

"It was such a happy thing," she said.

Colin's cheeks flushed over his tie. She worried about him, there on the other side of the overheated office. Who was he, anyway? What did he want from her, from himself? He sat reddening over the tie, the one she'd somehow put him in, while she failed him in ways she did not understand, in ways he could not articulate. She had not even wanted him to take this job, the one that had driven him into the suit—she'd wanted New York, downtown, bohemia! But he'd insisted, driven by his sense of responsibility and propriety, insisted on their life as it was.

And likewise she could see but not describe the ways in which he cheated her and silenced her, the way he stopped up all exits, the way he stubbornly denied her and testified against her. Once, back in the Bridgeport apartment, Andie had thought him a lawyer. And yes, he seemed—hatefully—like a lawyer.

The chewing began again. The Valeries at her gut, the rat at her brain.

"Let's backtrack a bit," the doctor said. "Tell me about your-selves."

So, in turn, they told him, silently correcting and critiquing each other's stories. Kate heard Colin sigh as she expressed her wish for less housework, more fun.

"Tell me about your children," Levy said. "What are they like?"

Kate described Lila and Robin. Colin joined in with details

and anecdotes. They became a team again, suddenly—comic, in sync.

Then they divided.

"If you had to, what would you say you want from each other?"

"I guess . . . I want him to understand me. That sounds like a cop-out, but I do."

"Colin?"

"I want her to be happy. I want her to be fun again. I want her to blow me in the car, like the old days."

"Really, Colin?" Kate wrapped her arms across her chest, embarrassed. She avoided eye contact with Levy. "Is that really, actually what you want?"

"Yes. Yes, it is."

"What do you hope for your girls?" the doctor asked.

Colin looked at the ceiling and frowned.

Kate said, "That question always makes me sad. But if I have to answer it, well, I hope they're gay."

She did. As she said it, she knew it.

Both men stared.

"Men bully women. I don't want that for them."

"I—" Colin said.

Dr. Levy held up a finger. "Do you feel bullied, Kate?"

"Yes."

"And that's my fault, of course," Colin said.

"How? In what way? Can you tell us?"

"No." Kate fanned herself. She looked up at the drop ceiling. Strips of aluminum divided the squares. "I can't explain how. But I see it at work all the time. I mean, where I volunteer."

Dr. Levy nodded. His expression flattened—too many matters at once. "Okay. Let's come back to the job later. For now, tell me, just quickly, about your family life. What are your routines?"

"Routines?" Colin said.

"What do you do in the evenings?"

Colin said, "Sometimes she puts them to bed. Sometimes I do."

"Do you eat dinner together? As a family?"

They had agreed early on—soon after Robin's first birthday—that for now they could not endure the chaos of family dinners: the mashed potatoes on heads and noses, the jumping in and out of laps, the constant imperious demands for juice bread salt napkin, the nipping from plates, the shrieking and crying. They couldn't enjoy the experience; nor could they agree on the division of labor in such circumstances.

"I get home on the late side," Colin said.

"Weekends?"

"Sometimes we all go out to dinner on the weekends," Kate said. "Just to the Japanese place or the bar and grill, something simple. And during the day, well, sometimes we go strawberry or apple picking or whatever."

"Mornings? I'm just trying to get a sense of your family dynamic."

Kate said, "We get up and I get them to school."

"I usually take them to school."

"I get them ready. You drop them off. Late."

"Robin's not late." Robin's preschool began at nine.

"Well. Congratulations."

Dr. Levy looked intently from one face to the other, as if watching a bird dive to and fro, a bird trapped inside the tiny hot room. Kate played with the magazine in her lap. She tore out a page and folded it into a fan. Colin frowned at her.

"You make them late. You do. You don't care that they're late. Or that Lila's late. Whatever. You care more about your fucking shaving and primping and Wheaties or fucking whatever than you do about them." She paused, and edited. "Being late."

"Okay." Dr. Levy leaned forward in his chair. She'd excited him—this pleased her. "A more productive way to talk, when it comes to this sort of miscommunication, is to use *I* instead of *you*. For example: 'When the kids are late to school, I feel frustrated and angry, as I make an effort to get them ready and feel it's important for them to be on time.' " He sat back. "And they should be on time for school, no?"

Colin nodded dubiously—unsure, it seemed, whether he was incriminating himself with agreement. Kate experienced a certain brief sensation of triumph.

"And you, Colin, could say: 'I feel angry when you approach me about the children's punctuality. It makes me feel . . .' " He looked at Colin and raised his hands. "Colin, how does it make you feel?"

"Angry." Was he mocking Dr. Levy?

"And then you could say to each other, 'So what is this about?' " He looked from Kate to Colin, from Colin to Kate. They stared at the floor, naughty children. "Try it," Dr. Levy said. "Try that approach. Try, when expressing yourselves, to focus on yourself, not on the other person—on your own feelings, not what the other person has 'done.' Instead of saying, 'You did this, you're doing that, you're acting like this,' say, 'I feel this, I feel that.' "

"I don't mean to be a jerk, but that sounds kind of precious to me," Colin said.

The radiator banged. Kate fanned herself in silent agreement.

"Try it now," the doctor said. "Kate. Do you think you can express yourself to Colin in such a way?"

"I guess I could give it a shot."

"Wonderful," Colin said.

Dr. Levy watched the darting bird.

Kate said, "When Colin doesn't contribute to the household it makes me feel . . . really mad."

"The household?" Colin raised an eyebrow.

"I mean," Kate said, "I spend my day—like, a whole day every week, which is not so terrible but he doesn't do it—running all over town shopping for organic this, free-range and hormone-free that. . . ."

"And then there's nothing to eat. Nothing to eat, ever, in our house."

"That's not *true*. And why don't *you* shop for food once in a while. Do you think it just magically appears on the shelves?"

"No."

"That's right. Someone has to shop for it. Go to the store."

"Someone does."

"You think I don't spend half my life at the fucking store?"

"I also spend time at the store."

The one item that motivated Colin to shop was toilet paper. It had become her habit to remove the final few existing rolls and hide them for her own personal use and that of the children in hopes he would be driven to the store. The strategy worked, for the most part, but he did a shoddy job with the list, bringing home Fig Newtons instead of Fig New-mans, whole milk instead of one-percent, Zest instead of Dove.

"Talk to Brooke," he said. "She's always got good stuff around. Those noodles. That chicken salad."

"Brooke has an au pair. And a housekeeper every day."

The implication being: If he delivered on his end—the economic—she would deliver on hers—the domestic.

"At any rate," Kate said, "so I go running around. . . . Stop & Shop has the produce, right, and the whole organic section, but not the meat and the chicken, not always, at least, and not the juice boxes, so I have to go to Thyme and Season for the juice boxes . . . but then they don't have chicken or meat so I have to go to Dominic's for that . . . and so on and so on."

"And this is why we need a Whole Foods right here, in Fairfield," Colin announced.

"Really? And Whole Foods would change my life? Our lives?"

"It might!"

"There's a Whole Foods in Westport," Dr. Levy offered.

Kate stared at him, betrayed.

"Okay. Well, Whole Foods is expensive, for one," she said. "Colin? And I'm sure it comes with its own set of problems that we don't even understand yet."

"You're a pessimist," Colin said.

"And when I finish shopping it's time to pick up the girls and then by the time I get it all home and get the kids and the groceries out of the car and break up the fight and unpack the groceries, then it's time to make dinner . . . and then I do, and

I make extra, for their lunches, or the next day, or whatever, but the more I make the more Colin eats! And he pouts if I tell him I've spent all this time shopping and making it for the kids!"

"Because that makes me feel like you don't think of me as part of the family."

"Oh, Colin, and that, *that* in and of itself . . . just because your mother spent every minute of her life stocking the fridge and feeding you doesn't mean I'm under any obligation to *take care* of you. . . . As part of 'the family,' you should be helping me. . . . They're your kids too!"

"Fuck, woman . . ."

Dr. Levy held up a hand to each. Then he motioned to Kate to move forward. "Back to the girls and their food. What's that about?"

"Well, that's it, sort of . . ."

"Something about it, I sense, is very distressing to you. Causing you deep anxiety."

"Yes. I suppose."

"For example. Why go to all that trouble?"

"Be*cause*"—and she sat up straight in her chair—"just because of everything you *read*, about girls getting their periods at eight years old, because of all the hormones . . . you don't want *that* to happen! And then, of course, there's cancer, and child obesity, and et cetera."

"Well—let's focus on the former concern. Let's say it did. Your girls got their periods early. Whether or not diet is the real culprit is debatable, I believe. But, that aside. Let's say you fed your girls regular—meaning, paradoxically maybe, not organic, not free-range, not hormone- and engineering-free—food, and 'that' did happen to them. Would it be the worst thing in the world? And perhaps more important, would it be your fault?"

"Well, yes! And his too, okay? But not as much, because he doesn't take any responsibility in the first place. For stuff like that. For anything that's not . . . completely obvious and in the moment. And the thing is, if it were just me, if I were a single mom or something, it—their puberty, that is—wouldn't feel so threatening. Though, of course, for an eight-year-old to wear a tampon, or a sanitary pad even, is not age-appropriate. But it's like, I worry because of him"—and this was just occurring to her, just hitting her, and saying it, articulating it, she knew it to be true!—"because, it's like . . . I want to protect him . . . I feel responsible or something."

The men looked at her, over their ties and collars.

"You're not making sense," Colin said.

"She makes sense to me," Dr. Levy said.

"And it all just feels bad, like I need to do something about it, to stop it!"

Now both men looked perplexed. Kate herself felt perplexed. What did she mean?

"Let's give Colin a chance to talk," Dr. Levy said. "Colin, what are your thoughts? Do you share Kate's anxiety in this matter?"

"I mean, you know. I want to be a good father to them. So—well, besides all the obvious reasons, such as I'm crazy about them, so they don't run around, fucking around . . ."

"Fucking around?" Kate glanced at Dr. Levy—would he allow the interruption? "What do you mean by that?"

"You know. Fooling around, sex, blow jobs."

"And what's wrong with blow jobs? *You* like blow jobs."

"Getting them!"

"Well, someone has to give them."

She knew what he meant. But she wanted him to say it.

"You know what I mean," he said.

"So it's fine for me to give them but not for your daughters to give them."

"It's just . . . It's degrading, I guess."

"Okay for me to do it, though."

"That's different."

"A guy going down on a woman, is that degrading? If you had a son, would it bother you to think about that?"

"Fuck, no!"

"But that's the problem!"

"They're my little girls."

Dr. Levy, the crossing guard, held up his hand. "Time's up. Look, I believe in looking at what's going on inside, but also in experimenting with what's on the outside. I'm sensing a lot of separateness here. Do you do things together alone? Do you have a regular night out? A date night, if you will?"

"We have fight night," Colin said.

Kate laughed.

Dr. Levy looked from one to the other, sharply. "Good," he said.

11

*S*o COLIN BOOKED A TABLE at an Italian restaurant in South Norwalk and Kate called Portia—and, finding her busy, called Bella Hertzberg, junior at Fairfield Warde and lifeguard at the club. Kate gave the girls dinner (chicken tenders, string cheese, baby carrots), and at seven Bella arrived in a hot-pink T-shirt displaying the Go-Go's in pastel relief, towel clad and turban headed. Below, hotter-pink glittery script read, *We Got the Beat*. The T-shirt had been purchased at Target, Kate knew, because she owned the same one, though after two babies she did not fill it out quite as exuberantly.

Kate let her inside and gave her a thumbs-up. "Have a boy over if you want," she said. "My lips are sealed."

Bella regarded her dispassionately. "I would never do that." She looked around the entryway and sucked in her ribs. "I'm super-responsible."

Lila and Robin ran from the den where Kate had installed them and accosted Bella's voluptuous person. Lila took hold of the pink T-shirt and pulled Bella toward the den while Robin pushed her by the rear, a hand on each cheek.

They vanished. Bella's voice rang over the television: "I love, love, love Hannah Montana!"

Kate returned to the bedroom and finished blow-drying her hair. She put on black lace panties and a matching bra.

Colin would see the evening as an occasion for sex. As he should. Her defect, this impulse toward evasion, and its significance evaded her in turn. But the other morning had gone all right. Maybe things would get better. And Mave felt apathy too. Maybe sex mattered less than Kate suspected—maybe she could fake desire for Colin and that would be enough. She wanted the girls to thrive. She wanted her dream: a happy family.

She put on high-heeled boots, dark blue jeans, a gauzy top printed with pink roses, and a pink velvet scarf Colin had given her. She attached rhinestone chandelier earrings and applied lipstick. She negotiated the stairs in her heels and stuck her head into the den. The three girls huddled on the couch, Robin's hand below Bella's T-shirt, Lila's head on Bella's lap.

"Will you give them a bath?" Kate asked. "Will you unload the dishwasher?"

"No prob."

Colin's headlights flashed in back and the engine shut off.

"Who is it!" Lila shrieked.

"Just Daddy. He's picking me up."

Colin appeared in the door. His eyes registered them all, then concentrated not on Kate, or Lila, or Robin, but on Bella: specifically, on Bella's jaunty breasts below the glittering Gs and Os, then her abdomen, against which Robin's small hand roamed, under the thin soft cotton. The girls laughed over *Hannah Montana*. Bella flipped her hair. She licked her lips. She crossed her legs up on the couch, and her breasts—a life of their own!—shimmied and settled.

"Have I met her before?" Colin asked in the car.

"Bella. From the pool."

"The Hertzbergs' kid?"

"Yup." Kate reached forward and fiddled with the radio.

"She's developed a lot," he said earnestly.

"Yes. I saw you noticing her developments."

"Well, that shirt . . ."

"Guess what? I have the same shirt."

"So wear it!"

"I wear it all the time."

"You're too skinny."

"Oh, I don't care."

They parked outside the restaurant. They sat across from each other and shared a bottle of Chianti. He ordered spaghetti Bolognese and she ordered angel-hair pasta with basil and tomato sauce. They stuck to safe topics at first: a potential kitchen renovation, holiday plans. He seemed tired, pouring her Chianti and winding pasta around his fork—his blue eyes flat, his skin dull. She took inventory of his best features: nice nose, strong chin, high cheekbones. He really was a good-looking man—why couldn't she appreciate this, or anything about him?

He took his glasses off and rubbed them on his shirt to clean them. He sighed over his spaghetti.

"What?"

"Just this account I'm working on."

"You'll win 'em over, I'm sure."

"And Sheila might quit." Sheila was his assistant. "She's getting married. She's twenty-eight. She wants to have kids; I know because I've heard all about it. Her fiancé just got promoted. He's at Merrill. She's right in that sweet spot."

"Well . . . so if she quits, so what? You hire someone else."

"A hassle, though. To train a whole new person."

She tried to amuse him. "I heard the cutest thing the other day."

"What?"

"At Wintergreen. These two little twin boys were walking with their nanny, not old enough for kindergarten . . . they must have been picking up a sibling. One of the boys says to the other little boy, 'When we were a baby . . .' "

"Huh?"

"Don't you get it? As if they were, had been the same baby."

"Oh. Yeah, I get it."

"Are you grudging me my moment of whimsy?"

"That is cute," he said. "I get it. 'When we were a baby.' "

"Just trying to cheer you up."

"Cheer me up at home." He took her hand across the table. She attempted a smile. Something unpleasant nagged at her, something besides fear of her own sexual indifference.

She ate little of her angel hair and got the leftovers wrapped to go. She put the container in the backseat. She flipped through radio stations and came across a Miley Cyrus song. "Oh, God," she said.

"What?"

"Miley. Hannah Montana."

The unpleasant thing took shape. She changed the station, then turned the radio off and frowned at the dark road ahead. "So. Bella," she said.

"Bella?"

"Hertzberg. From the pool."

"Right. The sitter."

"The thing is, it's just inappropriate to stare like that in front of your daughters."

"Robin's with me. She had her hand up the kid's shirt."

"I mean, what kind of a message are you sending . . . how are they going to feel about their developing bodies if their dad tromps around drooling over the teenage sitter?"

"I don't know. How *will* they feel?"

"It's hard enough as it is. Developing girls are self-conscious enough as it is. If they see you staring at *her* they're going to worry about you staring at *them*."

"I cannot even begin to tell you how effed-up that is."

"Well, it is!"

"That you said that, is what I mean."

"I'm not saying you *would* be! Of course not!"

"But to even put that out there—"

"I wouldn't say it to them. I said it to you."

"Yeah, well, you shouldn't even say it to me. You shouldn't even have that thought."

"Oh, Colin. Are you really such a shrinking violet?"

"Of all the messed-up, offensive . . . Look, I'm driving, here."

"I'm just going to call you Violet from now on."

"I admit it. I was looking at the kid's rack. I'm a man; that's what we're wired to do."

"Oh, yuck!"

"But that's obviously completely different from looking at my very own daughter."

"Bella is an underage girl. A child."

"As a matter of fact, if anyone, you know, down the road, ever looks at Lila or Robin like that I'll crack his skull."

He was hateful, hurtful on so many levels, too many to understand all at once!

"As if they need to be protected or something."

"And why? What is the problem with that?"

"So many things . . ."

"Tell me one."

"If they were boys you wouldn't worry, right, about women or girls checking them out."

"Christ, no!"

". . . but with girls, you do, you worry, you see them as so vulnerable. . . ."

"Well, they are vulnerable. Women are more vulnerable."

"We're not! We live longer! We survive infancy at a higher ratio . . . rate . . . whatever!"

"That's not what I mean."

"What do you mean?"

"*Sexually* vulnerable."

"Sexually vulnerable how? How?"

"Like, I don't know, some kid could . . ."

"Have sex with them?"

"What is wrong with you?"

"Are you going to freak out when they get their periods?"

"Of course not . . ."

"Yes, you are! I know you are!"

"I have no intention of freaking out."

"They aren't *property*!"

"They're my little girls, okay? So just leave them out of it."

"I wish I could. I would love to leave them out of it."

"They're going to be fine. We're providing them with a wholesome environment. Fairfield is a good place to raise kids."

She rolled down the window. Papers blew about the interior of the car.

"Kate . . ."

"I need the air."

They pulled up in front of the house. He shut off the engine and sat silently behind the wheel, hands by his sides.

How sad he looked—how she tormented him!

"I just don't understand what you're so angry about," he said eventually.

"I'm not sure I do either. It's hard to explain. But I am."

"I'm going inside," he said. He got out of the car and retrieved her leftovers from the backseat.

She sat up and pushed her hair from her face. "Can't we just figure this out?"

"No. Not now. I have to end this conversation."

"Oh, fine! Go on, end it!"

He walked around the front and leaned into her window, one hand on the roof of the car, the other holding the take-out container. "Thanks for a lovely evening."

"Fuck off! Go drool on your girlfriend's tits!"

He thrust the take-out container through the window and opened it over her head. Then he shouted incoherently and hurled the empty Styrofoam to the ground and thundered into the house.

Angel hair sat on her shoulders and lap. It dangled from her ears. She watched Bella leave and bike up the street. She hoped that Colin had paid her the correct amount, because if not and Bella had been too shy to tell him, Kate would need to amend the discrepancy, a nuisance. She sat in the car until the lights went out downstairs and on in their bedroom window. She began to shiver. The angel hair chilled and coagulated on her scalp and skin. Kate looked at herself in the rearview mirror and laughed. She pulled pasta from her head and shoulders and from the steering wheel, where it hung in long sauce-flecked strands. She gathered it and dropped it out the window. She got out of the car, moving slowly in the grip of what felt like pain but was probably just the cold.

She walked toward the house, a capsule of warmth in the chilly night—illuminated in spots, the kitchen and master bedroom windows sweetly radiant. She stopped midway up the walk and looked at where she lived. The yellow light filled her with obscure longing. As a teenager, returning home late from the Andersons, she might pause outside 123 Livingston Street with a similar longing, and a similar yen for combat. Her lips sore from kissing. The altercation yet to occur.

Her bedroom light went out. The Valeries pulled their knees to their chests and moaned.

KATE AND COLIN DIDN'T SPEAK until the following Tuesday. Then, after putting the kids to bed, Colin approached her with the Royal Garden menu: a conciliatory gesture. "Chinese?" She took the menu from his outstretched hand. The decorative photos of featured dishes resembled double homicides. She read quickly through anyway. Peking Duck. Baby Ginger Chicken. Szechuan Triple. Crispy Walnut Shrimp. Red-Hot Spicy Shrimp. Velvet Triple. Happy Family.

Even Royal Garden was mocking her!

She handed back the menu. "Just order me whatever. Please."

"We could share the duck."

"Okay. Great. The duck." She giggled.

"What?"

" 'Duck' is a funny word."

The food came and they ate. They leaned into each other

on the couch, watching *ER*. The hospital was decorated for Halloween and some of the doctors and nurses wore costumes.

"Are we going to tell Levy about the date night?" Colin asked.

"Do you want to?"

"Not really."

"He won't approve."

"No. He won't like it."

"What do you think he'd say?"

"I don't know." Colin put his arm around her. "Should we keep seeing him? If we do and we don't tell him it's weird."

"We have to tell him, then."

"What if he wants us to separate? He's all into that."

"He was just asking."

"Right," Colin said.

"You don't want that, do you?"

"Me? No, I don't want that."

"Me neither. The girls. I'm afraid they'd miss it. The family. Miss us."

"I'm afraid of that too."

"They're our biggest fans." She put her head on his shoulder. "And we love each other."

"We do," he said, with some regret. He rubbed her forearm. They watched the show.

"Abby's drinking again, huh?" Colin said.

"For a while now."

The remains of the Peking duck sat on the coffee table.

"I'll put this stuff away," Colin said. He dislodged himself and got up.

"You want help?"

"No. I'm good."

"You want me to pause it?" she called after him.

"S'okay," he called back.

She paused the show anyway. It wasn't the same without him.

12

HE ROSE CENTER, where Kate ran workshops on developing and maintaining a budget, provided shelter for women "in transition," which meant battered women running from their husbands or boyfriends and homes. The shelter housed these women and attempted to orient them. Some ended up moving in with their relatives. Some found jobs and apartments or rooms in a house of employment. Some returned to their husbands or boyfriends.

On Tuesday, Kate gathered toys to bring to work with her, as Colin had suggested. Toys in general, though, weren't needed as much as other items: warm plus-size clothing, gently worn shoes, toasters, microwaves, pots and pans, towels, bedding, clean mattresses, sofas, kitchen or dining tables, chairs, household supplies, spare tires, life skills, jobs, child care, health insurance.

On Wednesday, Kate delivered the toys to the shelter. She pulled up into the parking lot and opened the back of the station wagon. A toddler with rotting teeth ran up to the car and tried to climb in amid the bags of toys. Kate carried the bags into the office. She'd made cinnamon rolls and picked up a thermos of coffee, and these she carried to the radiator- and foot-scented provisional classroom. The women clustered around the snack table.

On the brown faces, the bruises showed up dark purple and black. On the white faces, the bruises came out blue when fresh, or a lighter but still lurid purple. They became yellow as they aged, or puce, or brown.

The funny thing was, the women would remark on Kate's bruises.

"You have lot of black and blue."

"Fuckin' A!"

"That's some ugly shit."

"Jee—zus!"

Today pale faces outnumbered dark faces. One woman wore a cast on her right wrist. Another sported burn marks up and down her arms, another a half smile of stitches from the corner of her actual mouth.

It was the kind of group that made Kate feel as if, by associating herself with a man, by participating in the socioeconomic template of cohabiting opposite-sex partners, she was perpetuating a terrible conspiracy. It was the kind of group that made her feel like moving back in with Darcy—or, like the elephant mother in *Ella the Elegant Elephant,* relocating to a sparsely populated, mountainous island and opening a pastry shop. On the other hand, there to Kate's right sat Cherry, one half of a lesbian couple. Cherry's girlfriend had killed Cherry's cat by trapping him in the dryer and turning it on. When Cherry confronted her, the girlfriend punched her in the face and broke her nose. Then she threw Cherry down on the ground and kicked her repeatedly in the teeth. The girlfriend, Cherry told Kate, lispingly, had flipped out last spring after her abusive father died. She'd never knocked Cherry around before, but now beatings were routinely administered, as if the girlfriend, Louise, were in some fashion honoring her father's legacy. Cherry was working toward a master's in psychology at Fairfield University, and, employing her own life in an empirical manner, she deconstructed Louise's behavior in the common room over *Full House* reruns.

And once, rumor had it, a man whose wife had beaten him with a tire iron had knocked on the door of the office, bleeding from his head. Ruby, the director, had driven him to the emergency room and directed him to the Christian Service Center.

They settled into the chairs with their sweets. A new girl sat by herself in the otherwise empty front row. She had pushed her hands into her lap and passed on the rolls when Kate set them out. One side of her face was white and European-looking. The other looked as though someone had dragged her across gravel by her ankles.

She resembled a Picasso, or a yin and a yang, or maybe a black-and-white cookie.

As usual, Kate went around the room with names. The girl gave hers: Eva. When she said her name, her hand went to the damaged side of her face and hovered about it.

Many of the women were ten years younger than Kate but looked ten years older. Rough living, poor diet—many smoked; many under- or overate. Alcohol was not allowed on the premises, though like boarding school kids, sometimes the women sneaked it in. The age range spread from the teen years to very late middle age, with the highest percentage in the twenties and thirties. Several were pregnant. When Kate looked at the pregnant ones, she wanted to shake them or slap them, or maybe shake and slap herself—she wanted to do something, but she had no idea what, so she just continued to lecture and write on a dry-erase board in primary colors. Some of the women were taking notes. Others sat sullenly with arms crossed, snapping gum, as if waiting for Kate to deliver the information directly to their brains. Children wandered in and out of the room, distracting their mothers from the task at hand and their own possible financial security.

Pregnant Brittany was sleeping and leaning against the covered radiator.

"Somebody—Cherise—will you please wake Brittany up? Give her a shake or something?"

"Aww, she's tired."

Kate walked over and snapped into the air by Brittany's ear.

The pregnant ones, especially, often tried to sleep. The class was optional, Kate reminded them, and if they wanted to nap they should go upstairs and do that. Still they returned and leaned their heads against the wall or down on their arms on the desk, as if dreaming, precariously, that the information would seep into them regardless of attention paid, would infiltrate them like the polluted New England air, the exhaust and smoke and by-products of industry, and that all they needed to do was remain still and passively accept, let Kate do her thing the way their men had done theirs, leading to the girls' and women's current delicate conditions.

Brittany jerked awake. The women murmured. Kate tried to appear strict and schoolmarmish.

"Brittany, this hour isn't going to help you if you sleep."

"I know, Katie, I know." The kid rubbed her eyes and nodded. She'd resided at the Rose Center for a couple of months last year. She'd moved out, but now, in the wake of another disastrous relationship, she was back.

"Have some coffee."

"Coffee's bad for the baby!"

"Oh, not so bad."

"The book says!"

The shelter possessed a copy of *What to Expect When You're Expecting,* a tome Kate had bought then discarded during her own first pregnancy, finding the book silly at best, misogynistic at worst.

"A cup or two is fine. A cup or two a day is fine. Hell, ten cups a day is probably fine."

"I don't like coffee," Brittany said.

"Don't listen to that stupid book. Listen to me. And get yourself some coffee."

Brittany pursed her lips. Then, so challenged, she got up and fixed herself a cup of three parts cream and sugar, one part coffee.

After class Kate collected her books and notes and rubbed off the dry-erase board. She turned to see Eva at the snack table, biting into a roll. She had lovely teeth, Kate noted.

"You settling in okay?" Kate asked.

Eva started and coughed over her pastry.

A list of the stages these women allegedly experienced hung on the office bulletin board, right below a warning letter from Public Works:

> Stage 1) Running Scared (She jumps at the doorbell or the phone.)
>
> Stage 2) Depression (With no immediate crisis to filter

emotions, she experiences loneliness and grief. She
considers returning to her abuser.)

Stage 3) Moving On (She makes constructive decisions
and gets on with her life.)

"Sorry," Kate said. She touched her hand lightly to Eva's
shoulder. She wished she could wipe the ugly markings from
the girl's face.

"Yes, I like it," Eva said. "Bed is comfortable. People nice."

The girls and women slept and napped in several large
rooms in an arrangement that recalled the Madeline series, the
twelve little girls in two straight lines (on excursions, breaking
bread, brushing teeth, going to bed). The kids shared beds or
got their own next to their mothers. Cribs occupied the north
wall. Kate had donated the girls' old one and collected others
from Brooke and Mave and the like. Books, as well as toys,
abounded, and while the books were not partaken of quite as
much as the common room television, sometimes, curled up
in bed in their dormitory in the daytime, the women read to
their kids. Sometimes a group would hang around the dorm
together, the kids off playing—then domestic battles were
described and raunchy stories were told.

Eva chewed and covered her mouth politely. "I am supposed to be on diet."

"These aren't so bad."

She could say something about how Eva didn't need to be
on a diet, but if it helped the kid to worry about her weight, if
it provided a distraction, so be it.

"Yes?" Tears jumped into Eva's black eye and her good one.
"It is so, so good."

.   .   .

AT TWO-THIRTY Kate picked up a coffee for herself and a bagel for the kids and got back on the highway. She found a Springsteen song on the radio—a song from *The River*, a song about driving—and turned it up. In his songs the men were always driving. The story concerned the man, the person behind the wheel, and the women just ran across porches or rode shotgun. But Kate felt included by the songs anyway. She drove to Robin's preschool, then to Lila's kindergarten classroom. Lila thrust toward Kate a ceramic dragonlike creature with an endearingly gloomy expression on its long, crooked, polka-dotted face. Kate took it, admiring, exclaiming, looked into its face, turned it this way and that. "I love it, baby girl. Does it have a name?"

"Love Monster." Lila skipped ahead.

"Fabulous."

"Can we get our costumes today?"

"Not today. Soon, though."

"I'm going to be a witch. A witch with a green face."

"I thought you were going to be a fairy."

"I changed my mind."

"What are you going to be, Rob? Still a dragon?"

"Nothing!"

When they reached the car, Robin refused to attach her seat belt. Kate reached in—leaning, straining—and, holding her child down in the booster, forced on the belt. Robin screamed, "Pinch you!" She pinched Kate's arms, already riddled with tiny bruises.

"Time out for that," Kate prescribed, wearily. "Time out the second we get home."

The pediatrician had recommended *1-2-3 Magic,* a popular book on disciplining children. Kate had read it cover to cover, then applied the method as prescribed. Colin had glanced through the book and also taken up the method, but he'd bastardized it, Kate felt—giving them "three" immediately, dropping the matter after "two" though the bad behavior persisted—until the system became compromised and was no longer effective. Since last spring, Robin's behavior had taken a particularly dreadful turn and Kate had reinstalled time-outs, but the newer, compromised version. Now she too went straight to the time-out, skipping the warnings but applying the formula for punishment: a minute in exile for each year of the child's age.

Over the summer the playroom door had stuck when closed, so Kate could essentially trap Robin in that room. Now, as the atmosphere cooled and dried, the wood shrank under its influence and Robin was able to open the door and come shrieking out, rendering Kate impotent and unable to administer punishment unless she stood there, holding the door closed, for the full agonizing four minutes. On one of her multitudinous lists were instructions to call a locksmith.

She held her daughter down and clicked the seat belt closed again. There was something demeaning about the ducking in and ducking out, the bending and the stooping. Maybe here lay the appeal of the SUV: The slight lift, the reaching up instead of down to buckle the child rid the act of some of its struggle, its tedium, and its degradation. Extracting herself from the backseat, she whacked her head on the metal doorframe. She cursed and held her head. "Are you okay, Mommy?" Lila leaned anxiously forward to investigate.

"Thanks, baby girl. I'm okay."

She got into the driver's seat.

Lila leaned back and buckled herself up, gazing warily at her naughty sister. Kate started the engine. Something clicked behind her.

"Mommy, Robin took her seat belt off again."

"Goddamn it."

"She has it off."

"Put your belt back on, Robin."

"No, I'm not going to do that any day."

"Robin. Do you want *two* time-outs?"

"Hmpfh."

Oh, she could slap the girl silly!

"Robin, you know Mommy will get arrested. Don't you? The police will arrest Mommy and put her in jail."

"What kind of jail?" Lila asked.

Kate turned to wink at her older daughter. Lila nodded, unsure.

"I want you to put it on," Robin said.

"I just did. Twice. You put it back on yourself."

"I'll do it," Lila said.

"No. I want Mommy to do it."

"Fine. Fine fine fine fine fine." Kate got out, slammed her door shut, opened Robin's, reattached the seat belt. She got back in and slammed the door again. Another click. She began to breathe rapidly. Heat assaulted her face and neck. A vision surged up—of shaking Robin, of whacking her across the face—an urge toward something that felt, in this demented moment, like justice.

"Do not," she said. "Do not tell me that was your seat belt."

"She took it off, Mommy!" Lila cried. "She took it off again!"

Kate pulled out and drove.

"Mommy, Mommy! Her seat belt's off!"

"Thank you, Lila, honey. You know what, though? That's her problem now."

"Oh, Mommy! She needs it; she needs it on!"

"Oh, Lila, you're so sweet." She pulled over. "Robin, do you know that if we get into a car accident you will be killed?"

Silence.

"You will be killed; you will die. Die!"

More silence, then scuffling sounds. Kate turned off the engine.

"She's trying to put it on," Lila said.

"Can you help her, sweetie? Can you?"

"Yes, I can. I will." More sounds. "There." Lila whispered tenderly to her sister, "There you go, just like that."

They sat for a moment by the side of the road, all three troubled and spent. Then, "Okay," Kate said. She turned the key in the ignition.

Finding Black Rock Avenue congested, she detoured through the arts district. They drove down Linden Street. A sculpture had been installed outside the music school: a zigzag steel construction topped by a glowing, metallic red ball.

The girls noticed it and clamored for it. "Can we stop, Mommy?" Lila asked.

"Not today."

"When?"

"Some other day."

"You always say that about stuff."

"I want to touch it!" Robin pounded on the back of Kate's seat.

Kate experienced an illogical fury at the perpetrators of the installation. "There's no parking right now. It's just not a good place to pull over."

"But—"

"Shut up!" Kate shrieked.

At home, she ushered and coaxed them out of the car. She unloaded two backpacks, two drippy lunch bags, several days' worth of art projects, school notices, her purse, tossed-off jackets, a fork, her stainless-steel coffee cup, and Love Monster, which she handed to Lila. "Carry this, please." Then, "Come on," she said to Robin. She talked them up the back steps and into the house. "Move your bodies, up the steps."

How much longer could she continue, could she stand it: the serving and directing, the resulting, absurd sense of abuse, the constant tiny negotiations of space? On the landing, as Kate dropped the stuff and bent over to collect her keys from her purse, Robin kicked her in the behind.

"Time-out," she said. As she said it, she remembered the earlier sentence. "Time-out for you."

She punted it all inside—the backpacks, the lunch packs, the notices, the jackets, the art—and carried Robin, screaming and struggling, to the playroom. She slammed the door and ran away in the hopes it might hold this time. But she heard Robin's feet on the stairs, her voice. "You stinky girl! Mommy, you're a stinky girl!"

Kate took Lila's hand and led her elder daughter to the master bathroom. She locked the door and they sat against it, their knees up.

"Why are we hiding?"

"If she won't take a time-out, we'll take one from her."

Lila nodded. A seriousness and calm set over her face, that of a difficult justice implemented.

"I'm mean, aren't I?"

"No, Mommy." Lila leaned her head on Kate's shoulder. "You're the best mommy."

Robin sniffed them out. She banged on the door, pulled and twisted at the knob. "Be nice to me!" she cried. "Mommy, be nice to me!"

Kate took her own arm skin between her fingers and pinched it. The Valeries scraped at her heart. *Be nice to her,* they said. Four times Kate counted to sixty. Lila counted also. When Kate opened the door, onto Robin, onto the light, Robin held a board book: *Owl Babies.* Her mouth turned down in a cry; her nose receded and became small. She stretched out her arms. Kate picked her up. Robin's short muscular legs arched in preparation and seized Kate's waist.

Kate found a place for Love Monster on the pantry shelf alongside the sock puppets, the wooden ships, the papier-mâché cat and the cardboard-towel-tube dog. She brought the satellite radio into the bedroom and for the remainder of the afternoon, in relative peace, they listened to the Disney station and read books and played cards on the bed. At six Kate, Lila, and Robin sat at the kitchen table while the girls ate their dinner (fish fingers, mashed potatoes, and canned peas). Kate opened and sampled a bottle of South African merlot.

"Plates to the sink, guys!" she cried.

Then upstairs for a bath. Naked and smooth as seals, their wet dark hair clinging to their biggish heads, the girls appeared younger, babyish—their bodies plumper, their eyes and cheeks rounder, their skin brand-spanking-new. Kate shampooed their hair and washed behind their ears. She loved it, loved touching them, washing them, sliding soapy hands over their slick skin; she experienced an almost erotic pleasure in this handling of someone smaller and softer than she. She admired their bald little vaginas, so frank and adorable, so much personality in those neat cleft triangles! Robin's squat and short, Lila's longer and somehow thoughtful-looking.

She rinsed their hair. Both tilted their heads back; both stuck their tongues out, catching the water.

Later, the girls in bed and asleep, Kate stretched out on the sofa and put her feet in Colin's lap.

"Cherry's taking my class," she told him.

"The dyke?"

"Oh, Colin. Yes."

" 'Dyke' is okay these days."

"She thinks that the girlfriend freaked out because her father died. That Louise—Louise?—is transferring her father's violence onto Cherry."

"Right. Maybe it's not because of her father, though, per se. Or maybe yes, but genetic rather than behavioral—I mean, nature over nurture. So she's violent all on her own, not because of the father."

"Doubt it."

"For once, just once, can we not blame men for all the problems of the world? What about that other guy, with the tire iron?"

"You have to admit that usually—"

"Yeah, but in this case, let's say it is nurture over nature then. What about the abusive men who were beaten up by their fathers? Why can't we let them off the hook? I mean, not that anyone should be let off the hook, but . . . when we hear about a man beating up a woman we say, 'What a bastard,' not, 'Well, he must have had an abusive father.' "

"Well, I'm sure he did. I'm sure they all did!"

"But when a woman does it you rush to trace the behavior back to a man and stop when you get there."

"Well . . . okay. Look. I see what I see, that's all."

He squeezed her feet and forwarded through the commercials to the next segment of *ER*.

"Amazing this show is still going," she said. "It's, like, prehistoric."

He paused the screen. "So what happened today?"

A report, was that what he wanted? She curled her toes away from his fingers. How she hated the part of her job that involved the dutiful relaying of the day, the girls' moods and activities and doings.

But then she wanted, of course, to tell him, to tell him everything, or at least everything good, to share with him the girls in their bath and the adorableness of Love Monster!

"Robin had a tantrum. We played cards. Lila brought home an art project. You should check it out. In the pantry."

"Uh-huh. What else?"

Was that not enough? What did he want from her?

"Well, that's it."

He nodded and pressed play. A gory operation ensued.

"Rub my feet, will you?"

He dug his thumbs into the tender spot above her heel.

"Oh . . . that feels nice."

"Maybe all this is normal," he said.

"You mean maybe all married couples are secretly miserable?"

"*Are* you miserable?"

"Maybe. Possibly. Not sure."

He massaged vigorously. "Me neither."

"Everyone pretends to be so happy. Maybe they *are* happy."

"Who knows."

"You know what I was thinking about before? That J. D. Salinger story, 'Uncle Wiggily in Connecticut.' I think just because of Brooke, you know, two women talking. In Connecticut. I mean, Brooke and I of course were having coffee, not martinis or whatever. I don't think she even drinks."

"She's constantly pregnant."

"Like Brooke and I would ever have that conversation anyway. The dead lover-soldier. The boss, the affair. The little girl, the imaginary friend."

"The brass ring."

"No. That's *The Catcher in the Rye.* Anyway, that Uncle Wiggily story always appealed to me so much, when I was younger, I mean. Why? They're so unhappy, those two. But I love how they sit around having drinks all day, and the storm, and the way the girl replaces the dead imaginary boyfriend with a new imaginary boyfriend, just the way her mom replaced the man she loved with the girl's father. What's his name? Begins with an L. I'm not unhappy like that but I wish I were. It's like, I want to be. Is that weird?"

"Yes." He held the remote in one hand expectantly. With the other he rubbed her right ankle.

"Go ahead."

He pressed play.

They finished *ER.* Kate made lunches for the next day and Colin shut out the lights and they went upstairs. He checked in on the girls before Kate did, as always.

"What are they doing?" she asked him.

She would ask and he would make something up. This had been their ritual since Lila's infancy.

"They're doing a blow-by-blow reenactment of that amputation scene."

"Oh, yeah? Who's who?"

"Lila is Abby Lockhart. Robin is Rocket Romano. Chicken Dance Elmo is the patient."

"Goodness. I'll have to see this for myself."

She crept in and kissed their soft, serious foreheads and cheeks. She washed her face and Colin wandered in and out of the bathroom, brushing his teeth, looking curiously at the photographs taken during that first optimistic year with Lila—so many of them!—all hung in careful arrangements on the bedroom wall. And a few of Robin too, hastily added. Poor neglected girl, sad little second child.

He spit. He flossed.

She applied Oil of Olay eye lotion and then Pond's everywhere but the area between her brows. There she applied an expensive cream discovered and purchased through the Bliss website, a cream that dried on contact and, according to Bliss, paralyzed the skin as Botox did in order to soften and stave off frown lines. Kate leaned into the mirror. She shook the bottle in her right hand and tapped on the cream.

"What's that all about, again?" Colin asked.

"It's supposed to stop frown lines. By freezing my face. My expression. See? Look. It dries. It's drying. You wear it in your sleep and it keeps you from frowning so you don't get lines."

"But you don't frown in your sleep."

"Don't I?"

"Nope."

"Well. I don't know then." Kate leaned into the mirror and poked at the substance hardening between her brows. "A hundred bucks for this stuff. What a racket. I might as well just ask you to come in my face."

"Free of charge."

She curled up on her side in bed to read her book. But he pressed up against her from behind and put a hand on her breast. All that week and the previous one she'd avoided sex. She'd relied on her usual strategies: going to bed and getting up early, falling asleep in the girls' room, picking a fight, referring to fatigue, wearing a special pink faux-silk nightie, a garment that would have enticed had it not been given to Kate by her mother-in-law (as she reminded Colin if need arose). But it had found its way into the wash, she'd replaced it with an old T-shirt, and now Colin was groping her, running his hand up and down her waist and over her hip.

She counted back the days to their last sexual encounter. Not yet two weeks. Two weeks was her deadline. But only a few days shy. She turned down the page and put the book aside and turned around. With great effort she suppressed her physical indifference to him. Poor man. He didn't deserve such apathy.

How sick she was over it all—how she wanted to love him again.

She put her arms around his neck and closed her eyes.

He rolled on top of her and pulled at her underpants. She bent one leg and he slid them over her foot. She maneuvered her pillow under her rear. He nudged her thighs apart and pushed himself through her dryness. She watched the serious, intent look of him inserting himself into her, tongue protruding slightly and clenched between his teeth—his habitual expression of sexual entry. With the same expression he played video games and had aimed purées toward his infant daughters' mouths.

Once engaged, her capitulating body loosened and dampened. He supported himself on his forearms and pounded away. She made appreciative sounds and lifted her pelvis and contracted her muscles, hoping to facilitate the process. She felt his face close to hers.

"Does that feel good?" he asked.

"Yes, yes."

It did feel good—physically, it did. But mysteriously, the pleasure restricted itself to a specific area of her body, and she still didn't want him. The pleasurable sensation was like a piece of information that had little to do with her. It was like one of those dye tablets, the kind that came in kits for coloring Easter eggs, one that wouldn't dissolve even when submerged in a tub full of hot water. Something had gone wrong—since the old days, when the tablet would melt and turn the water deep colors.

Why, why did he insist on wanting her—and why couldn't she get the same pleasure out of it he still seemed to get? He reached for it and there it was, a simple normal satisfaction that eluded her.

Activity ceased and he lay heavily on top of her. She shifted irritably. On her way to the bathroom, to wash herself clean of him, her right foot struck the satellite radio contraption. She sank and clutched her toe. She rocked back and forth on the floor. "Ouch. Ouch, ouch."

"Let me see." Naked, he bent to examine her foot. He touched the injury: the loose skin flap, the blood. "Hang on." He fetched and applied peroxide, Neosporin, a Band-Aid. He kissed the doctored toe.

"Poor Uncle Wiggily," he said. "Poor, poor Uncle Wiggily."

13

THE FOLLOWING EVENING, after Colin's celebrated return from the office, Kate got between the girls on the parental bed with *Norse Gods and Giants,* now titled *D'Aulaires' Book of Norse Myths*—a brand-new copy, purchased by Kate several weeks earlier while she disposed of time between the shelter and school pickup. She skipped the introduction and began with "Chapter One: The First Gods and Giants." She read, "Early in the morning of time there was no sand, no grass, no lapping wave. There was no earth, no sun, no moon, no stars."

There was a pit of fire and one of water and one, in between, of chaos. The frost giant, Ymir, and an enormous ice cow emerged eventually from this pit. The giant lived off the cow, drinking from her udder, and the cow sustained herself by licking the salt-crusted brim of the pit.

"Why is it salty?" Lila asked.

"I don't know why. Maybe—I don't know; it's like the ocean."

"What are udders?"

"They're like the cow's nipples."

"Did we drink from your *nimples*?" Robin asked. She already knew the devastating answer.

"Yes, yes, you did; you know you did."

Both girls screamed exuberantly.

"Hey, no teasing."

They screamed louder and drummed their legs on the bed.

"Enough, guys, enough. Do you want me to read or not?"

They shushed each other and settled down.

Ymir slept, and two more giants, a male and a female, were born from his damp, warm armpit and a six-headed troll from his rank, sweaty feet. The ice cow, now with nine mouths to feed, licked vigorously at the salt rim, and under her industrious tongue a head formed, then a whole beautiful man.

"Who is he?" Lila asked.

"He is . . ." She skimmed ahead. "The grandfather to the Norse gods. So that's how it began," she said. "And now," she said, segueing to Maurice Sendak, "let the wild rumpus start!" She grabbed the girls' solid thighs and squeezed. They giggled and wriggled away.

Colin walked in and stood at the end of the bed in a T-shirt and striped boxer shorts and observed the three females he lived with. He waited for a break in the commotion and asked, "Who wants to brush their teeth?"

"I brushed mine!" Lila cried.

"Did you floss?" Kate asked.

"Yes!"

"Good girl."

"Robin? You?" Colin pointed at his younger daughter.

"She didn't," Lila said.

"I'll take her." He lifted Robin from the bed and carried her off.

Lila turned to Kate. "Mommy?"

"Yes, baby girl."

"There's this girl, Leonora, in ballet? She's a fifth grader, I think."

"Does she go to Wintergreen?"

"I think so."

"Leonora. Is she the one with the long black hair? The one who played Drosselmeyer?"

"Yes."

"Then yes. She's at Wintergreen."

"I like her so much."

"Are you two friends?"

"I haven't ever talked to her. I just like to look at her."

"Well, you should! Talk to her."

"I don't know what to talk to her about."

"Ballet? School?"

"I love her face. I love how she stands. On ballet days I think about her and then I get so excited to see her."

"That probably has something to do with how you feel about ballet. But that's very sweet. That you like her so much."

"It's funny."

"It's called a crush."

"Mommy, did you ever feel this way about anybody?"

"Well. About Daddy, at one point."

"You did?"

"Yes, Daddy. You know, I felt romantic about Daddy once. That's why people get married; they feel romantic about each other. So Daddy and I, we did too; we felt romantic about each other."

Visibly, Lila struggled with this notion. Robin and Colin returned with clean teeth and Colin swept the kids off to bed.

"Lila likes a girl," Kate said later. They were cleaning up the kitchen, carefully carrying out their allotted tasks: Kate the dishwasher and the sink and the dishes in it, Colin the counters and the putting away of items in cabinets and fridge and depositing of other items beside the sink.

"*Likes* likes?"

"I think so."

"Well, maybe your dream will come true."

"My dream?"

"Of lesbian daughters."

"Well. She also likes Floyd from Dr. Teeth and the Electric Mayhem."

"*What?*"

"The Muppets. Floyd? The saxophone player? Hat, gold tooth?"

Then, the kitchen cleaned up and lunch packed and clothes and boots and coats laid out, Kate sat up in bed, paying bills on her laptop. Colin walked in and out of the bedroom, brushing and flossing his teeth.

"It's just that I don't want them to be like me," she said. "With the whole gay thing. I don't want them to turn out like me."

He frowned and went into the bathroom and spit. He returned, wiping his face with a hand towel.

"But why don't you want them to be like you?" he asked patiently. "What's wrong with you?"

She shook her head. "Do *you* want them to be like me?"

"No, I guess not."

"Touché."

"But not like me either." He sat next to her on the bed and rubbed her shoulder. "You know. I wish they could stay like they are."

"I feel like we should do family dinners," Kate said.

"Family dinners?"

"Like Dr. Levy asked about."

"Oh. Right."

"Other people do it, and it's probably good for the kids."

"I get home so late."

"I don't know, maybe once a week or something we could try it?"

"I guess. But we love our kids and we communicate with them anyway. Just because everyone else does something doesn't mean we have to."

"I know, I know. But. I bet they would really like it."

"Okay. Well, sure. One night a week, family dinner, why not."

"I just want them to be happy," she said.

He kissed her hair. "I'm going to go check on them."

She shut down her laptop and closed it and put it on her night table. When Colin came back she asked, "What are they doing?"

"They're singing the pivotal Laurey and Curly duet from *Oklahoma!*"

"Ha, ha. No, really. What are they doing? Are they comfortable? Are they each still in their own bed? Are they snoring?"

"They're talking. Holding a meeting. They're talking about you. They're saying that you're the best mommy in the world."

14

S̶O THEY GATHERED for a Family Dinner. Kate made pork chops and applesauce and salad and green beans and mashed butternut squash. "Couldn't we just have spaghetti or something? Does it have to be so elaborate?" Colin eyed her warily, as if she might transfer to him her own special infectious extravagance.

"Spaghetti? Really?"

"Oh, right. Right. I wasn't . . . Okay. No spaghetti. No angel hair. No pasta at all." He put his hands on her shoulders and stared into her face. Impatiently, she let him. "You are a really beautiful woman," he said solemnly.

She kissed him—she didn't feel like throwing down but she didn't hate the compliment either. "Thanks. Thank you."

He unloaded the dishwasher while she set the dining room table. She carried the food out and he rounded up the girls and led them to their seats. Robin dropped her tiny cut-up bits of pork one by one onto the rug. Lila made a design with them on her plate. Colin ate swiftly, spearing another bite before swallowing his current one, tucking the first into the corner of his mouth to make room. Dinner lasted twenty minutes. Released, the girls ran to the couch in the den, where they negotiated bitterly over whose turn it was to choose the show. It was Lila's night, Lila claimed, but no one could back her up—so Robin, thrower of tantrums, got her *Super Why!* "Dumb baby show," Lila cried, and pushed Robin off the couch.

Kate slid dishes into the empty dishwasher, pans into the sink. She poured herself another glass of wine. She heard Colin soothing in the next room. She scrubbed the pan, rushing, eager to join her children before their show. Lila would settle down and enjoy the baby show. Kate would sit between the girls and put her arms around their warm pliable bodies— this, her happiest time of day—a transgression, not something she'd admit to Brooke or Mave, but true.

Colin walked in and out of the kitchen, snorting and clearing his sinuses. He carried out the trash and sorted the recycling. He brought in firewood. He kicked the door shut and open. The cold air crept below her shirt. She felt, acutely, the heavy presence of him. His footsteps, each one, seemed to steal something from her, seemed to nudge her into a smaller and more compromised psychological space. Finished with his chores, he opened the corner cabinet and took something down. He rustled, rodentlike, in a plastic sleeve. She heard the munching and crunching of wafer, a disruptive accompaniment to the low running of water. His big sounds displaced her—his small sounds invaded her. He swallowed and spoke.

"Do you want this on?"

She turned, looked over her shoulder, understood that he meant the oven.

She had left it on again. Shutting it off was the last step, the one she often forgot when she cooked or baked or reheated. And Colin, instead of turning it off himself—because clearly, clearly she was through with it!—would notice and ask, as if in reproach.

Of course she did not want it on.

"No," she said. "Thanks."

He shut it off. He put a hand to his chest. "Do you have a Zantac by any chance? I'm out."

"I have Prilosec."

"Can you spare one?"

"It doesn't work right away. You have to keep taking it. But sure, okay." She reached into the medicine cabinet.

Once they had traded bodily fluids and childhood memories. Now they begrudged each other heartburn medication.

She dropped the pill into his outstretched hand and returned the bottle to the shelf. From the den she heard the *Super Why!* finale.

"I'll get them up," he said.

Internally, she lamented and cursed. He herded them up the stairs. She followed, drying her hands on her jeans. Colin got the girls into the master bedroom, then wandered away, mumbling something about the cable bill. Kate got onto the parental bed between her daughters and broke out *D'Aulaires.* Loki stole Sif's golden hair and then replaced it, in atonement, with real gold. He stole Freya's necklace. Thor attended a banquet dressed as a woman but gave himself away with his tremendous appetite.

"Okay," Kate said. "Teeth." Lila brushed her teeth quickly and got involved in her own book. Robin darted around the bedroom clutching her SpongeBob toothbrush, giggling.

"Robin, don't run with that." Kate didn't care, really, what Robin did with the toothbrush, so long as she eventually brushed her teeth, but she knew what she was supposed to say: no, no, and no. Robin removed her freshly applied pajamas and ran in circles, naked but for her underpants.

"You're lucky you're cute, Robin." Kate stepped toward her, stopped, crossed her arms across her chest, and sighed. Kate heard the computer booting up in Colin's study, then the sounds of *Grand Theft Auto*.

"Okay, Robin. Now." Kate lunged toward the girl and seized the toothbrush. "Should I brush them or do you want to do it yourself?"

Robin pouted and pointed to Kate.

"Okay. Climb on the bed then."

Robin climbed on and lay back against the European pillow. Kate bent over her with the brush. "Open your mouth, please."

Robin clamped her lips shut.

"Open, please. Open. Open sesame."

Robin clamped harder.

"Do you want to do it?"

The heavy head shook. The curls bounced.

"Open your mouth, please. I'm going to count to ten." She counted. Robin's lips vanished into the fold of her mouth. From Colin's study, computerized explosions sounded.

"Okay," Kate said. "Okay, that's it." Fury, with Robin its most available object, welled in her chest. She let it; she let it come over her—like an intestinal or sexual eruption, it insisted on its own release.

"Goddamn it!" she shouted in a voice several octaves lower than her speaking voice. With this voice she seized the paternal role—yes, she wanted to frighten, to bully, to intimidate!

She covered Robin's nose with her hand. She pulled at the soft chin, pried the lips open. She forced the brush past the flattened lips and onto the tiny teeth. Robin began to scream.

Colin appeared in the doorway. Kate finished and rolled away from Robin and shook off the brush. "I think I got them all."

"Don't you think you're being a little rough with her?" Colin said.

Lila crept toward him.

"Couldn't you just let it go?"

"Let it go!" Kate cried. She sat up. "Well, if I let it go tonight then how about tomorrow night? And the next? How about we just ditch brushing teeth altogether? Fuck Dr. Reed! Or rather, how about *you* explain to him and that dental hygienist bitch Danielle when their teeth rot and fall out?"

He picked Robin up and took Lila's hand. "I'll get them to bed."

Kate put the D'Aulaires book away. She brushed her own teeth. Colin returned, girl-free. She said, "I hate when you wander away like that." She recalled Dr. Levy. "No. When you wander away like that, it makes me feel ... shitty." She searched for a better word. "Abandoned."

SHE SAT UP against the European pillow, reading *Martha Stewart Living.* She read about how to make candy critters from marshmallows, licorice, and gumdrops. She read about how to make spiderweb eggs and swamp sangria and witch cupcakes with sugar-cone hats. Colin went to check on the girls. Upon his return she asked, "What are they doing?"

"They're line dancing to 'Achy Breaky Heart.' " He got into bed and scooted up close to her. "I'll rub your back if you want," he said.

"I have my period."

"I'm sorry about before. You're right. I shouldn't disappear like that."

"It's okay. I'm sorry I lost my shit."

He put his hand up her nightshirt and held her breast. He played with her nipple, rolled it between his index finger and thumb. Her nipple hardened—so promiscuous it was.

"No, no, no. I'm bleeding. And I've got to go to sleep."

"I just want to feel close to you."

"You can spoon me while I read Martha."

"Okay. Whatever." He wrapped his arms around her. A compelling odor rose from his armpits.

"You know what's amazing? That smells are made up of molecules. Just like things. Um, right?"

"Huh." He squeezed her. "It's been a while," he said.

She felt his erection against her hip. She closed her eyes. She listened to the highway—still a constant sound, though less intense than in Bridgeport. She thought of the train, a mnemonic for intimacy. The blue-and-maroon seats, the crushed paper cups, the wrecked buildings and stations and waterfront towns jolting by outside the filthy windows. Her mind strayed to actual mnemonics and her old kitchen, Livingston Street, the refrigerator and the lists: *Virgins Are Rare, Eli the Ice Man, When You Catch German Measles Remain Between Blankets.*

She reached down and put her hand on him. He rolled on his back and pulled her on top of him and nudged at her shoulders, lightly enough for her to ignore if she wanted to. But unexpectedly inspired, she wriggled down his torso. When had she last spent time down here? Not since the spring. She recalled a night of debauchery: a party at the club to celebrate the renovated squash courts, a torrent of dirty martinis and her subsequent generosity later in bed, and, the following morning, mascara on her pillow and a horrific taste on her tongue.

She hesitated, her nose in his crotch, her hair mingling with his slightly larger-than-average penis.

"Please," he said. "Just for a minute."

"Okay. A minute. Five minutes."

"Okay."

"And I don't want you to come in my mouth, okay? I really don't feel like it."

"Okay, baby. Deal."

She put her left hand around his scrotum and her right at the base of his shaft and ran her tongue around the tip. She worked on him with the right hand while she sucked: less demanding than using her throat, and he never knew the difference. His testicles contracted under her hand.

He grabbed her hair. "I'm going to come."

She pulled off. His ejaculate hit her in the face and neck.

"Oh, Colin!" She sat up on her knees. "Goddamn it."

"Sorry!" He threw her his T-shirt. She swiped at herself.

"What the fuck?"

"You said not your mouth."

"That doesn't mean my *face*."

"Well, what did you want me to do with it?"

"Just, I don't know, catch it or something."

"Hey. Free goop for your frown lines."

"Don't laugh, Colin; this isn't funny. I'm taking a shower. And you're not invited."

She washed her hair and let the hot water run over her

body for an environmentally negligent length of time. Back in bed, clean nightshirt and hair in a towel, she prodded Colin, whose face was obscured by *Men's Journal.*

"That made me feel . . . disrespected."

"I'm sorry." His arm shot out and found her shoulder. "I'm really sorry."

"*Do* you respect me?"

"Of course!"

"Really?"

"Well." He contemplated. "Actually, I assume I do, but I guess . . . I don't know."

Could he respect her and do *that* at the same time? Was that possible; was that ever possible?

"Do *you* respect *me?*" he asked.

"I don't know if I do. I don't know either. Not like I used to."

He put the *Men's Journal* aside and lay back and closed his eyes. "I think . . . I think I actually respect you more than I used to."

"Really? Why?"

"You're a great mother. You have an irrepressible spirit."

"But that doesn't make you feel the way I used to make you feel."

"No. Not exactly."

"So we should go back to that then," she said. "When I respected you and you didn't respect me. That was better."

"What?" Amazingly, he'd nodded off since his last utterance.

"Never mind. Sleep. Go to sleep."

15

I T IS A WINTER AFTERNOON, a Saturday. The day that things change between Kate and her father. The day things happen between Kate and the boy next door. A day that will last, to some incalculable degree, for the rest of her life.

Dennis has announced a driving lesson. "She's too young," Edie Allison says as her husband grabs the keys. She stands at the counter, kneading bread dough.

He says, "Not in Texas she's not."

"We live in Connecticut. Remember, Professor?"

But she says this to their backs. Kate follows the professor out the kitchen door. She sits in the driver's seat and he turns the key in the ignition. As the car warms up he reviews: accelerator, brake, blinker, side- and rearview mirrors, hands at ten and two o'clock.

"Now," he says. "Signal." She tries to put the car into drive. "Foot on the brake," he says. She pulls out from the curb. A passing station wagon honks. "Blind spot," he says.

She slams on the brake. The car juts into the empty road.

"Okay. Let's try this again. Check your mirrors. Then glance over your shoulder—"

"Which one?"

"Well, depends. On where you want to go. Now, for instance. We're pulling out to the right, so check your mirrors, then look over your right shoulder. See? That spot right alongside the car."

They drive slowly around and around the block. Winter has trashed the whimsically colored houses: salt and dirt and water deposits dull the paint; a storm door hangs loose; a porch railing has lost integral parts. A squirrel runs the length of a telephone cable. A dog chases a ball in the park. A crow flies, cawing, across the opaque white sky.

"Keep your eyes on the road," Kate's father says. "If you look at the scenery, you'll end up in the scenery."

They turn into the Wilbur Cross High School parking lot and he has her back into a space. He has her make a three-point turn. She performs quite respectably until they call it a day and she pulls up to the curb and directly into the blue government-issue mailbox. Her father gets out and looks. In the front yard, Miles is climbing the copper beech, pudge hanging out from under his down jacket. Kate sees the dent in the blue box. In her father's expression, she sees that the fender is dented too. She puts on the emergency brake and takes the key from the ignition and leans her head against the steering wheel, accidentally honking the horn. Her father gets back into the passenger seat and checks around and takes the key. "No big deal," he says. But he feels sorry, she can tell, sorry for her. The sorry feeling is icky and heavy in the car, cagey and creepy like slime under a rock, unpleasant and interfering as a dental exam. Both want to rid themselves and each other of it. They can't move on until they do.

She picks at her nails. "I saw it; I was just worrying about that squirrel."

"What squirrel?" He watches her fingers.

"The squirrel in the road."

"Squirrels will get out of the way," he says. "So will birds."

"The mailbox is too close to the street."

"Please don't do that." He pulls her hands apart.

"I can do it if I want." She resumes the picking.

"Look," Dennis says. "At Miles. Climbing that tree. Isn't that nice, Kate?"

She turns to look, hooking her elbow over the back of the seat.

It *is* nice. Miles jams a foot against the trunk and pulls himself to a higher branch, struggling a little with his excess weight. Still, he strikes Kate as unencumbered somehow.

"He's leaned out a lot, hasn't he?" her father says.

"I don't know."

He has. And Kate has developed further, as if Miles's extra pounds have fallen off and landed on her in all the right places.

"He's really growing up. You'll be giving *him* driving lessons before we know it."

"Yeah, if he can fit behind the wheel."

"Don't be like that. He's your brother."

Miles is three-quarters of the way up the tree.

"Look at him go," Dennis says.

"I hope he falls," Kate says. She turns back to the wheel. "And breaks his neck."

Dennis grabs Kate's arm and stares at her. Then smacks her flat-handed across the face.

DURING THE DRIVING LESSON, Kate's mother has been baking bread. Oatmeal, buttermilk, anadama. She has brought out the old loaf pans, kneaded dough in the big yellow bowl. The kitchen is warm and fragrant. Kate runs through it on her way from the car and up to the bathroom. She splashes cold water on her face. She hears the car pull away from the curb. Back downstairs, she smears the fresh bread with butter and crams it into her mouth. She has slice after slice of bread. The butter, which has been sitting out anyway, melts into the spongy nooks and crevices.

She calls Topher. They have homework in common, a science assignment. Also, they've become an item. They stop after school at Clark's for milk shakes and pizza. They nuzzle in the reading room between classes. He sits on the couch— she stretches out and recites her Latin and lodges her head in his lap. He sighs and fidgets. She encourages his excitement by flipping up her skirt and pulling at her tights and twisting her head this way and that. They've graduated from kissing games to real makeout sessions. They make out in the climber in the playground and on the swings, her straddling him. They fool around in basements and rec rooms: his hand under her shirt, her hand at his crotch, rubbing at the cloth. His friends look at her knowingly, lewdly. Her friends call her names and she insults them back—they do this the way girls do, as if challenging the future name-calling their indiscretions will bring, as if beating the guys to the punch:

Easy Access.

Loose Lips.

Jizface.

Sometimes she feels as though she loves Topher. But still she suspects that her real affection concerns the house and the Anderson-slash-D'Amato family, the whole rambunctious swept-away feeling of all of them together, the televised sports, the sitcoms, the wrestling, the whacking off. She has tender and intense feelings for Topher. But she has them also for Nick and Bobby (both away at college now), for Sebastian and for Rudy, certainly for Rudy.

AFTER DINNER, which Kate and Miles and Edie eat at the kitchen table and Dennis eats alone in his study, Kate walks next door with her backpack and books and a loaf of bread for Ella Anderson. The Andersons have finished dinner and are moving on to dessert. Kate pulls up a chair and partakes. She flirts with Sebastian, with Rudy, with Mr. Anderson. She describes the day's lesson, including the mailbox but leaving out the bad feelings and the slap. She's surprised that the Andersons can't tell anyway, can't see fingers like a brand across her face.

"And then, bam!" she says.

Everyone laughs, even Ella Anderson. Rudy leans back in his chair. He crumples his napkin and throws it onto his plate. His hair, almost black, several shades darker than Topher's, sticks up in cowlicks all over his scalp, and reminds Kate of his swarthy testicles. Ella Anderson gathers up his plate and the others.

Then, with their books, Kate and Topher go up to Topher's room. They take out the assignment they've been charged with: blowing up a balloon with a banana. Supposedly, the decomposition of the banana will inflate the balloon. Bacteria will flock to the rotting fruit, multiply by eating the banana, and, while processing the food, release gas that fills the balloon with sweetly rancid air.

"This is charming," Kate says, mashing the banana in a small bowl.

Topher clears debris off the radiator. They must place the banana mush and balloon in a warm sunny spot and note the balloon's progress over the course of a week. Kate scoops the mashed banana into a glass juice bottle and Topher fits the neck of the balloon over the bottle top and moves both to the radiator, adjacent to a window.

That done, they begin to make out. There are the usual maneuvers: his hand up her shirt, hers against his zipper. His bed sits under the window, a plain melamine rectangle— there is something military about his room, the sparseness and squareness of it, as there is about his brothers' rooms: the empty bureau tops, the neat corners and swept floors and frugal lighting, the plain colors and overall lack of adornment. A draft comes in through the window. They find their way under the covers. The sheets are worn and soft with a *Peanuts* motif. Her tights come off, her short corduroy skirt.

"Wait," she says.

"What?"

"Don't." She pulls the skirt back on.

Topher gets out of bed. He goes to his closet and returns with a magazine. She untangles herself from the sheets and sits up also, crossing her legs.

He hands her the magazine: this month's *Cosmopolitan.* "You wanna try something?"

"Oh, God." She holds the magazine at arm's length, between thumb and index finger. "Did you . . ."

"Nope. Today's mail."

"You stole it out of the mail? Your poor mom."

"Check out page thirty-four."

She muddles her way through makeup and perfume ads to the page. " 'Fellatio 101.' Oh, please."

"Come on, read it."

" 'Step One. Hydrate! A lubricated mouth interior will get things off to a steamy start. Swig from a glass of water before going down on your guy.' " She looks at Topher. "Oh, man."

"Keep going."

" 'Step Two. Position.' Blah, blah, blah."

"Hey!"

" 'Step Three: Execution. Run your tongue around the tip of his penis for a minute or so. Lick up and down the sides. Tease him by licking his inner thighs and his testicles. Put one hand on him and make a ring with your thumb and forefinger. Attach the ring to your lips—' " She breaks off. She waves the magazine in Topher's direction, also, surreptitiously, fanning herself—she is blushing. "Attach it? Like with duct tape? Masking tape? Elmer's? Staples?"

Topher pantomimes a full-body shudder. He grabs his crotch and rolls off the bed and lies on the floor.

"Not you, me!" she cries. "It's me they're saying should staple my fingers to my lips! For your enjoyment!"

"Oh, well, okay then . . ." He raises himself on his elbows. "Go on."

" 'With your palm and remaining fingers, grip the skin of the penis as you might while pleasuring him manually. Move your hand up and down in tandem with your mouth.' "

"SAT word. Tandem."

Rudy is deep into prepping for the SATs. Vocabulary lists flap under refrigerator magnets, drift off counters and tables, wilt on bathroom and mudroom walls. Unlike his brothers and unlike Kate, Rudy struggles in school, and therefore all this effort is unlikely to yield meaningful results. When he has a paper he sits at the kitchen table, slowly typing under the basket-shaped overhead light. Sometimes tutors sit with him there. They bend their sleek ponytailed heads toward him with tender concentration, their soft voices speaking of precalculus, the Civil War, the atria and ventricles of the heart.

"Poor Rudy," Kate says.

"Just keep reading."

She wiggles her behind on the mattress. She uncrosses her legs and recrosses them the opposite way. " 'The ring will mean greater friction for him and less work for you. Don't be shy about putting a little spit and slobber into it. Move your tongue constantly in a back-and-forth or circular motion around the tip of the penis.' Wow." She looks up. "This is like one of those patting-your-head-and-rubbing-your-stomach-at-the-same-time kind of things."

"I can do that," Topher says. He does it.

" 'Conclusion: To Swallow or Not to Swallow?' Oh, yuck." She closes the magazine and tosses it onto the floor.

"What music should we listen to?"

"You've got to be kidding me. No way."

"Rudy and Karen Baker did it. I mean she did it. To him."

"They're juniors!"

"Yeah, well. It sounds complicated."

"I'm just not interested."

"You'd be stumped the second you got down there."

He knows—and he knows she knows he knows—that she likes a challenge. "I don't want my number on the boys' bathroom walls." But she retrieves the magazine and opens it to page thirty-four and reads the remaining paragraphs to herself. Then, standing: "I'll be right back."

"Where are you going?"

"I'm thirsty."

"Really? Stay here." He looks at her meaningfully, delighted and alarmed. "I'll get the water."

"Don't get all excited. I'm actually thirsty. And. I have to pee. Right back."

She walks down the hall to the second-floor bathroom. At this point, she might as well. Her father's slap has woken her up—or something—brought her to her senses, or maybe the opposite. Everything feels different. She has no idea what she'll do back in Topher's room but one variable is leading to another, faster and faster, and extreme measures seem suddenly available.

Rudy's door is open. He's lying on his bed with a book, wearing jeans and a Whitney Hall T-shirt, listening to Bob Dylan. She stops outside. "Hey," she says.

He looks up, miserably, from his studying. "Hey."

She puts her hand against the doorframe and leans into the room.

"Do you have a test?"

He gestures toward his flash cards. "SATs."

"Did you know the SATs were developed by a racist?"

"Where'd you hear that?"

"My dad."

"No shit." The misery gripping his face loosens a little.

"So if you don't do well, don't feel bad. A racist. He wanted to keep black people out of colleges. It wasn't a secret or anything either. He said as much. He admitted it!"

"Your dad is smart," Rudy said. "He's, like, the smartest person I've ever met."

"Yup. He's writing an essay on Richard Feynman."

"The guy who invented the atomic bomb?"

"Yeah. Except he didn't know what he was doing. That's what my dad's writing about."

"Yeah? Well, then, what the hell did he *think* he was doing?"

"Something for the government, he just didn't know what."

"Something for the government. If you say so."

"It's true." She lets go of the door. She swings into the room and over to the bed. He shifts, makes room for her.

"How's Delaney?" Rudy asks. Janey Delaney is the ninth-grade homeroom and English teacher.

"We're reading *Beowulf.*"

"It's a drag, huh?"

"Also short stories. We just read, um, 'Bartleby the Scrivener'?"

"Any good?"

"All I remember is it has the word 'erections' in it. Like, in the story it means buildings? But my friend Suzanne circled it. And we were laughing and Ms. D. sent us out into the hall."

"Bad girl," Rudy says. He pushes his flash cards aside. He leans back against the headboard.

She looks right at him, into his bloodshot eyes. "Are you high?"

"A little."

"Can I have some?"

"We'd have to go outside. To the garage. And I don't feel like getting up right now. And anyway, you're way too young."

"I am not."

"You ever smoked before?"

"No. People I hang out with do, though."

"Topher?"

"No, no."

"Well. Do it with them then. I don't want to be responsible for your first joint."

She picks up a flash card. "Dearth."

"Fuck. No clue."

"Lack of. Scarcity of. *Paucity* of." She takes the pile of cards into her lap. She sits with one leg folded on the bed, the other hanging off and kicking at the floor. "Tremulous."

"Unsteady."

"Perilous."

"Dangerous."

"Esoteric."

"Obscure."

"Cryptic."

"Esoteric!"

"Now you quiz me." She passes him the cards. "If I win you have to . . . you have to do my laundry for a month."

"A fucking month?"

"That's right."

"And if I win? My mom already does my laundry."

"If you win . . ." The Valeries are alert, listening, beginning to jig like popping corn. "If you win I have to kiss you."

"Like *kiss* kiss me?"

"Yes, exactly."

"You ever done that?"

"Of course. With your brother. And Lev Santiago."

Rudy shakes his head to imply no knowledge of Lev Santiago, another inconsequential ninth grader.

"And I've gone to second base too. With your brother."

"You like doing that?"

"What?"

"Making out."

"Yes! It's my favorite thing to do."

"But. You're like a little sister to me."

Topher is waiting, wondering. Where could she be? They hear feet in the hall and his voice getting closer: "Kate! Kate!"

She rolls off the far side of the bed, spilling the flash cards. She lies on the carpet, in the narrow space between the side of the bed and the wall. She registers scuff marks on the baseboard, an outlet, a hardened gym sock, which she picks up and clutches to her chest. Rudy's bed, like Topher's, is a block of melamine with a pullout trundle below.

"You seen Kate?"

"Not since dinner."

Topher's footsteps recede. She hears Rudy get up and close the door and lock it.

She slips back onto the bed, holding the sock.

"You don't want to touch that," Rudy says.

"No?"

"I whacked off in it." He takes it from her and tosses it into the hamper. He gathers the flash cards. "Okay. Let's see how you do."

Topher, meanwhile, scours the house, his feet going this way and that. Down the stairs. Through the kitchen. All around the first floor, which, like Kate's first floor, is a perfect square, each room leading into another.

She knows all the words but deliberately gets four wrong.

"So," Rudy says.

"So."

"So now . . ." He points to her and then to himself. "Right?"

"I thought I was your little sister."

"Kiss me. Kiss me, Kate." He crosses his arms behind his head and lies back against the mess of pillows.

She sits up on her knees. She crawls across the mattress and leans over him.

He seizes her neck and slides his other hand under her shirt, then under her pink cotton bra. He pulls her face against his, pushes his lips into hers, gets his tongue into her mouth. They kiss like that all through a long song about a girl named Louise. Then, boldly, she climbs on top of him and sits astride his lower abdomen.

His excitement is nothing like Topher's. Where Topher's is spastic and disorganized, Rudy's is purposeful. Her idea, this encounter, but quickly he takes over. His hands on her hips, he moves her back and forth, pulling her against him. He gets her shirt off and sucks at her left nipple. This is startling but pleasant. He flips her onto her back and rolls on top of her. One hand holds hers above her head, and, while he French-kisses her mouth and neck, the other is busy with his fly.

He takes her hand and directs it down there and closes it around him. She holds the bare supple appendage in her hand and squeezes lightly; she recalls the Durham Fair, to which her mother takes Miles and her every summer, and how once, years ago, they stood around in a crowd in the shade of a striped tent watching a monkey juggle two cucumbers, how afterward the monkey man came right up to Kate and chose her and put the live monkey into her arms. Rudy's anatomy—a live thing suddenly in her charge—reminds her of the monkey, who, finding himself in a strange girl's embrace, turned his head to the side and fidgeted and climbed up on her shoulder and sucked his protuberant lips.

Rudy keeps his hand over hers, showing her how to do it. She knows a little from watching him in the bathroom. But he wants her to hold him more tightly than seems comfortable.

"Doesn't that hurt?"

"No. No."

She tugs the skin up and down and rubs her thumb around the end.

He pulls aside her underpants and puts a finger inside of her. This is divine. She forgets to move her hand.

"Shh," he whispers. She opens her eyes. He's smiling down at her. He kisses her face. "Shh. You like that, don't you?"

When it starts to hurt she goes to work on him again. "What do you want me to do?"

"That's really good. What you're doing."

"Like this?"

"Yeah. Unless . . ."

"Unless?"

"Unless you want to . . ." He looks in her face and glances down at himself. "Do that other thing."

"*What* thing?" For all she knows—she suspects there's much she doesn't know—it's something too dirty for even *Cosmo* to address.

"That thing with your mouth."

"Oh. That thing."

"You ever done that?"

"Umm . . . well, once . . ."

"Don't lie. You haven't."

"No. I haven't."

"I'll help you out."

"I mean, I know a little."

"You'll catch on. You're a smart kid."

He rolls on his back and pulls her on top of him. She puts her hands on his chest and pushes up the Whitney Hall T-shirt. Sweet little black hairs sprout around his nipples and in a line down his abdomen. He strokes her hips. His hair is in disarray, black cowlicks everywhere. She combs it with her fingers.

"I feel like if I do that you'll tell everybody."

"Fuck, no!"

"What if you're lying? What if you do?"

"I wouldn't. No way."

She is willing to experiment. Now she wants to see. And she trusts Rudy. More, in fact, than she does Topher.

But she sits up on her knees and puts her hands on his chest. From his window she can see her own house and a light in Miles's bedroom, where he is most likely reading Tintin comics and eating Fritos by the handful. Whether or not her father should have slapped her seems debatable, but certainly she should never have said such a thing about her brother, poor chubby little Miles; she deserved something along the lines of a slap; that much she knows.

"It's weird," she says. "I feel like I'm still in the car."

"I know what you mean."

"I backed into a space and did a three-point turn."

"Girls suck at driving. We're afraid when you drive."

"Not me."

"Didn't you just tell us a whole story about how you ran into the mailbox?"

"Yes, but okay, so I forgot to pay attention for like half a second."

"Half a second can take lives when you're behind the wheel," he says gravely.

"Well, I'm just a beginner." Through Rudy's thin curtains she sees Miles cross his room. "I can see my brother," she says. "That means he can see us."

Rudy unwinds the pull on the aluminum shade installed behind the curtain. The shade falls with a clatter.

"I should go home."

He moves her hand back down. His thing, wet at the tip, twitches under her palm. His eyes reel with lust. He wants her—her in particular, not a magazine, not his right hand.

The Valeries murmur encouragement. She recounts the steps. Position—check.

She slides down his abdomen.

"Wait," she says. "Water."

Swiftly, he hands her a glass. She drinks. Musty tap water, the same as runs through her pipes next door. Then back down. She holds him at the root. She kneels between his legs. Her hair falls over his pelvis. She runs her tongue around the tip.

"Oh, fuck," Rudy says.

From the Valeries, shrieks of glee.

The album ends. The record crackles; the arm lifts and settles.

"You've got some mouth on you, little sister."

Outside, in the house, Topher perseveres. Up and down the stairs he travels, through the first- and second-floor rooms and hallways, opening closets and knocking on doors. Over and over he calls her name, seeking her, his fairy-tale companion lost in the woods.

"Kate! Kate! Kate!"

16

RIVING NORTH to the Rose Center, Kate glimpsed signs for the Home Depot she used to frequent, the dangerous diner, the steakhouse, the Showcase Cinemas. She registered a scattering of titles, films she'd never heard of and would most likely never see. The generic nature of these titles frightened her, titles that years ago would have elicited a happy jolt of recognition—the word arrangements basic but relentlessly opaque. Andie and Brice had vanished, never to be heard from again. Sometimes Kate worried that Andie had died from her mysterious illness. Wes had moved out soon after Kate and Colin had—Kate had run into him once, at an Exxon station along 95. Lucy would be into her teens by now. Possibly living in Oregon, with the woman who used to be her mother.

Kate got off the highway and drove past the granite yards, the fierce fenced dogs, the tied sneakers looped over telephone wires.

She taught her class. Brittany dozed against the radiator, but Eva was absent. Kate looked for her afterward and found her in the common room, reading *The Kreutzer Sonata,* or rather, *Kreytserova Sonata.*

"I missed you in class today," Kate said. She sat down beside Eva on the grubby couch.

Eva shrugged. "Is hard for me."

"Could I make it easier? What, what about it?"

"English, very hard."

"What's this about?" Kate indicated the book.

"Man kills his wife."

"Oh, dear."

Eva smiled, exposing her pretty teeth. On the floor at her feet her son, a toddler, played with oversize LEGOs. In his full pale cheeks and perfect lips and teeth he resembled his mother—in his blue eyes and coarse nose, somebody else, a blue-eyed man who had fucked the boy's mother, then dragged her by her ankles across the driveway. A tremendous unease, an anxiety, hung about the boy on the floor—to Kate, even the way he seized the LEGOs and forced one onto another, the exact same way Robin did, appeared ominous.

"It's good? You like it? You like the book?"

"Oh, yes." Eva paused, as if pursuing some exquisite insight, or at least its English expression. It eluded her and she said, "Yes, yes. Very good."

"I tried to read *War and Peace* but I couldn't get into it. I've read *Anna Karenina* twice, though. The first time in school. The second time for my book club."

"Yes, me too. In school too."

"But the last time I read it I didn't like it as much. Basically because the Levin–Kitty relationship really bothered me."

Three other women, one of them pregnant, dozed in front of the television. The common room smelled, not unpleasantly, of chicken soup—better, at least, than feet and radiators.

Eva had finally stopped jumping at the doorbell and the phone. The dramatic effect of her Picasso face had lessened. The scratches had contracted and the bruising had dulled to an advanced state of yellow and puce. Kate gestured toward it. "Any word on him?"

"He wants to see Ivan." Eva looked at the boy. "He speaks with my family. My aunt. He will want to take him, to keep him."

"Don't worry. Even if he took it to court . . . you're the mother and he's, you know." Wife beater. Monster.

It was often the case that these men went after their sons, not their daughters, as if their boys were phallic extensions of themselves.

"He miss him."

"Ivan? Misses his dad?"

"Yes. And me too."

"You miss him?"

"Yes."

On the wall over her bed, below a poster of Jon Bon Jovi, Eva had taped a photograph of her little family, in summer, at a crowded Connecticut beach. Eva wore a sexy flowered bikini, maybe one size too small. She held Ivan, who held a plastic bucket and pail, on one hip. The husband posed with a muscled arm around her shoulders. He looked brutishly out with his blue eyes. Eva, smiling, appeared genuinely happy.

The guy did, at least, have a nice body.

"I miss him," Eva said again. She looked at her son.

"What did you like about him? Can you say?"

Eva shook her head.

"Okay. Well, what didn't you like about him? Barring the obvious?"

"He tells me I am fat."

She reached for a cookie, then withdrew her hand. She

reached again. She took a cookie and looked at it and put it in her lap.

"My aunt says he is with girl," Eva said. She bit into the cookie. "Young girl." She examined the cookie again. "I must stop. I must to smoke but I have no cigarettes." She looked hopefully at Kate. "You smoke?"

"No, sorry. Sometimes. Once in a while."

How young could the girlfriend be? Eva wasn't more than twenty-two.

"I hope she's okay," Kate said.

"If I meet her, I will spit on her," Eva said.

"You'll find another guy, Eva. You're young too. Very, very young."

Would she? And, if so, was there more than a middling chance that any man she chose would deviate extremely from Nikolai? If she did meet someone else, what would she go through with him?

"It is good, all this"—and Eva waved her hand to signify the room—"but men hit their women, their children, is not so strange. Nikolai, his father hit him. My father, his father beat him with belt. Mother too."

"He beat his mother with his belt? Your grandfather? Or his wife?"

"No. My father mother. She beat him. With husband's belt."

"Did your father hit you?"

"No." She chewed. "My father have stroke."

"Your mother?"

"She is gentle person." Eva reached for another cookie.

Kate took one also. "When I was in the fifth grade? In school? We, my class, had this whole secret code for whoever had gotten their period. If you'd had your period, you were oatmeal. If you hadn't you were chocolate chip."

"And you were? Which cookie?"

"I was oatmeal. I got it that year. But I lied; I said I was chocolate chip. I was embarrassed." She finished the cookie and wiped her fingers on her jeans. "It fits, doesn't it, the oatmeal and chocolate chip. Like, oatmeal is sort of earthy. Womanly. You think of grains and harvest, fertility symbols. And chocolate chip is innocent, childlike."

Eva looked at Kate with some puzzlement. But she offered: "When I have period Nikolai wants me take out trash. I have this, you know, heavy flow? He does not like to smell."

The house line rang. The pregnant woman started in her sleep.

"And you do it? You take out the trash when you have your period?"

"Yes, yes."

Kate found herself obliged to indicate what was wrong about this but reluctant to do so directly. So she said, "My father, when he found out I had my period, he told my mother to tell me not to use the downstairs bathroom when I had it—or theirs, or my brother's."

"You had own bathroom?" Eva's eyes widened. "Everyone own bathroom?"

"Oh, well . . . I had my own, yeah. My parents. My brother. Then, one downstairs." This wasn't the point she'd wanted to make. "What I mean is, it seems cruel of Nikolai to make such a song and dance out of your period."

"Song? Dance?"

"To act disgusted by it. You know?"

"Except for"—and she touched her healing face—"only he slap me. Is okay."

"Only!"

"In families, people hit each other, is so normal. For me, and . . ." Again, she indicated the room, the television, Ivan, the three women. "Not for you. For people like you, is different."

Kate shook her head. She took a second cookie and, instead of eating it, began to pick it apart over a napkin. "Eva, these things happen to . . . happen with all kinds of people."

"If he and girl have family, I cannot stand it." Eva took a third cookie. "Tomorrow, diet."

LATER, Kate bathed the girls and washed their hair. Colin returned from the office and dried them off and got them into pajamas and in front of their show. Kate opened the fridge and looked inside. Colin came up behind her and closed the door from under her hand.

"Family dinner," she said.

"I'm beat. We can't scratch it this week?"

"I went to the store."

"Thank you."

She showered and dressed in her softest jeans, one of Colin's old shirts, and beaded mesh slippers from the Chinese dollar store. Back downstairs, she put water on to boil. Colin, finding her, raised and knotted his eyebrows.

"I set the table," she said. "I'm making spaghetti. And we won't throw it at each other. Okay?"

17

KATE RAN into Jack Auerbach at a gallery opening, a group show in which Mave had a piece. Colin stayed home with the girls and Kate drove up to New Haven alone. She avoided 95 with its menacing trucks and took the Merritt Parkway, lovely this time of year, edged by oaks and maples, their leaves flinging color at the cars. How predictably enchanting it was, but still, she passed through enchanted. She got off the Merritt and drove toward downtown.

She parked and entered the gallery. Guests milled in appreciative stances—necks angled, plastic cups of wine at the ready. A blond girl in a bikini top worked her way through the crowd, handing out nude Barbie dolls to the men. Kate looked around for Mave and Dan. No trace, or of anyone else Kate knew. She took the everlasting plastic cup of white wine from the card-table bar and began her viewing. There was a life-size dress with a slim bodice made of bubble wrap and a giant flowing skirt made of Target bags. There was a tinfoil bull hanging piñata-style from the ceiling. There was a man in a glass case, kneeling and drenched in honey—another man stood behind him and stuck tiny mirrored tiles to the first man and took them off and stuck them back on again. There was a Barbie doll dressed in a skirt made of a Dunkin' Donuts napkin and a tube top made of an empty Sweet'N Low packet. She held a purse constructed from an empty white real sugar packet and a red stirring straw, bent to form a handle, and she held a parasol made from a cup sleeve and another red straw. There was a bank of metal drawers. On top sat a yellow legal pad and a pen. A printed sign instructed the viewer to read a secret and write a secret.

Kate opened one drawer, then another, then another:

Once I stole money from my grandmother.

When I was fourteen I dumped my best friend. We used to play with dolls together. I told her she wasn't cool and I didn't want to be friends with her anymore.

I have herpes.

Bulimia has ruined my life.

Tomorrow I'm buying a gun.

There was a painting of a couple making love on a pink bedspread, the man looking at the woman, the woman looking at herself in the mirror. Not at the man, not at them together, but at herself—one could tell—the man was just context for her, his rough textures accentuating her soft ones. There was a papier-mâché-and-cardboard tunnel that some of the younger guests were crawling through. There was a diorama of what seemed to be a gang bang. A tiny blond celluloid girl-doll lay on her back on the floor of a miniature replica of a boy's room, her skirt up, smiling. A boy-doll lay on top of her. Other boy-dolls clustered around, some thrusting their pale bent arms in the air. Some of the boy-dolls had originally been girl-dolls—Kate could tell by their bodies and faces—but the artist had cropped their hair and dressed them accordingly.

She registered a man next to her, also scrutinizing the gang bang. Somewhat older—familiar. Dark hair graying a bit. Crooked teeth.

Jack Auerbach. Her father's grad student from years ago.

She tapped him on the shoulder. "Jack. Hi. Hi, there." She pointed to her chest. "Kate. Dennis's daughter."

"Kate! Right. Of course!"

"Funny!"

"You visiting your mom?"

"Sort of. Yes. How are you? Still at Yale?"

"Yep. Still there. We miss your dad."

"I do too." Sometimes she actually did.

"You were married, as I recall."

"I was. Am. Still am."

"And what does your husband do? Remind me."

"Finance. And I'm home with the kids," she added quickly.

"Kids. How many?"

"Two. Two girls."

"Hard to believe." He looked at her.

She folded her arms to her chest, her index finger inside the plastic cup. "What? Why?"

"I don't know. When we met, when I met your dad, *you* were a little girl."

"Well, you couldn't have been all that much older." A fruit fly sauntered by and fell into her wine. She fished it out with her pinkie finger. "Anyway. You?"

"No kids. Not married. I was but it didn't work out."

She nodded sympathetically.

"Or rather, it was what it was. Now it's over. I kind of hate the whole vocabulary of breakups, don't you? 'It wasn't meant to be,' et cetera—as if it never was at all unless you end up dying together, and only then if death ends the marriage is the relationship viable."

He'd hung onto most of his dark brown hair. The skin of his face had the geological look that men got after a certain point, that Colin was getting—as if the road from his chin to his hairline would be rough, as if a tiny earthbound insect might need a walking stick and a bottle of water to make its way.

"I don't think I ever met your wife."

"We weren't married all that long. She's at Harvard now. Married again, kids, et cetera. Well," he said, "that's great, that you're still married. That it's, ah, working out."

She laughed. She rolled her eyes. "We'll see!" She looked down into her empty plastic cup. Boldly, he took it from her.

"Refill?"

"Sure. Yes, thanks."

"You seen everything?"

"I was going to go over there." She pointed.

He went to the bar, she to the other side of the gallery, where guests wrote secrets on slips of paper and dropped them into a box and a girl in a tunic and tight jeans tacked the slips to the wall.

I had a nose job, one read.

I fake orgasms.

I cheat on my taxes.

I ate six thousand calories today. I feel like shit.

I am a happily married man with a son and daughter but my wife no longer sleeps with me and sometimes I have this daydream that my best friend and I go on a fishing trip and we end up watching some porn on his laptop and then we suck each other off. I don't think I'm gay but the dream still makes me horny.

I have been in the closet for twenty years.

I hate my life so much sometimes.

I have a gambling addiction. I have lost over twenty-five thousand dollars. If I tell my wife she'll leave me.

I want to bring home a young beautiful girl with big breasts and watch her have sex with my husband.

I pick my nose when I'm alone in my car.

I am a successful businessman and I own property and a truck but I have been addicted to crack for fourteen years.

Once I ordered a Mac. They sent me two and charged me for one. I called but got disconnected. So I kept them both.

I don't recycle.

Once my dog licked my leg under my skirt and got an erection and I took him into the bathroom and jerked him off.

And so on.

"Which is yours?" Jack held out the wine. She took it.

"Nope. I mean, I haven't done one. Have you?"

"Yeah, but I'm not telling you which it is."

"Oh, my. That bad, huh?"

"It is bad."

"Not the one about the dog."

"No, not that." The tunic girl swung by them and reached up with her paper and tacks. "So you get up here often?"

"Time to time."

"How is your mother? And your brother?"

"She's good. Still in the old house. And Miles—he's in New York. Working for the mayor. Running the city!" She laughed.

Fruit flies hung about Jack's head—something about him in particular, or his red wine maybe, seemed to be attracting them. He brushed them off and they scattered, then reattached themselves. She recalled his shaggy hair at the Q Club, the butter in the shape of a star. Now here he was, standing in front of her, flicking flies from his face.

One settled on his temple and she reached forward instinctively and brushed it away. Then, immediately embarrassed by the intimacy of the gesture, she looked down into her wine. "I really shouldn't drink this, actually," she said. "I'm driving. I should probably actually take off."

He filched a slip of paper from the secret girl. "Well, if you're up here again," he said, "or if I'm down there for some reason, we could have coffee or a drink or something." He wrote on the paper and handed it to Kate. "Get in touch."

She dropped the paper into her bag. There was something about his voice. A hoarse, craggy quality that matched his face. She wanted to stay. But she'd already announced her departure.

"Great to see you," he said.

"Yes! Likewise! You too!"

18

ALLOWEEN HIJACKED the neighborhood. Pumpkins adorned front steps and artificial cobwebs draped bushes. Witches and skeletons hung from trees, their limbs shaking in the wind. After sundown, cauldrons glowed with demonic red lights, withered arms hanging over the sides. Kate and Lila and Robin attended a Halloween party at the club. Robin went as a princess, Lila as a witch. The face painter gave Robin red cheeks and a pink bow mouth and painted Lila's face green. Kate took them out back to the club playground and pushed them on the swings. Lila asked repeatedly, "Is it still green?" as if afraid the paint might fly off midswing.

The last weekend in October the family drove to Litchfield County to pick pumpkins. Kate had planned the trip for the previous weekend but the car had acted up and Robin had run a fever. The sun had shone all Saturday and Sunday as happy families frolicked in hay, stuffed scarecrows, and photographed themselves against blue sky and orange leaves. But on Tuesday a high wind swept through the state and snatched the leaves from the trees. The temperature dropped. Now Kate and Colin and the girls stood shivering under a curved gray drum in a dirt parking lot beside farmland.

"We could have just gone to Bishop's," Colin said. He had

waited in the car, reading the paper, while the females struggled with bathroom, shoes, coats, snacks, books, toys, hair.
"Maybe I just shouldn't go," he'd said, when they finally materialized in the station wagon. "Maybe I should stay home, get
some work done."

"This is an adventure," Kate said. She took Robin's hand
and started toward an open barn. Other families greeted them
there, other stragglers lining up for doughnuts and cider.
"Look," Kate said. "Doughnuts!" Conceiving of appealing
activities, then generating enthusiasm for said activities, in
spite of whiners (Robin) and naysayers (Colin), seemed an
implicit component of her job as mother and wife. A horse
stamped and switched its tail. Pigs rutted behind a fence. Goats
looked anxiously over boards, their funny ears at attention,
their funny faces so human.

Lila went right up to the fence. "Those pigs don't smell,"
she said.

"Maybe it's too cold." Kate took out her wallet. "Do you
guys want doughnuts?"

Then they stood by the goat pen with their cider and coffee and doughnuts, not quite knowing what came next. They
stood close together, as if enclosed in a gray capsule. On Route
44 a lone car passed. Kate felt responsible for their near isolation in this dull landscape. She looked about, hoping to reas-
sure herself with the sight of other people. A mom and a dad,
two girls, and a boy knocked shoulders by the bonfire. The
comfort of their company quickly gave way to pain as she felt
herself to be separate from them, that most enviable of entities,
a happy family. The mother she envied most, of course—neat
bobbed hair, a gray coat, and pink gloves. Enthusiasm would

come naturally to this woman, as would calm, as would peace of mind. Kate wanted to walk into the woman's reality, taking her own family along, to own it or be owned by it.

An assemblage of ducks and geese quacked by. Robin ran after them. They sped up and raised their voices, then escaped under a fence.

"They're talking about Robin," Lila said.

"Should we get going?" Colin swigged his coffee. "Or maybe we should just buy a couple pumpkins and call it a day."

Kate said, "I'll find out." She walked toward the barn and inquired after the pumpkins. They must journey to the field, by foot or wagon. She returned. "There's a wagon," she said. "Or we can walk."

Colin groaned.

"Oh, fie on you, naysayer!" she cried.

Lila sidled back to the pigs. "They smell, Mommy," she said. "Now they smell."

"They must have heard us," Kate said. "They must have forgotten to put their smell on this morning. They heard us and they put it on."

Kate's family and the happy family waited for the wagon. Lila's and Robin's hands flushed red around their cider—their bare little hands—it hurt Kate to see it.

Colin noticed too. "Doesn't anyone have gloves?" he asked.

Kate set down her coffee and searched her own pockets, then, getting to her knees, theirs, for a stray pair. Robin wailed, "Tissue!" and Kate provided her with one.

Colin himself wore gloves—thick wool ones, with leather at the palms.

"We forgot their gloves," Kate said. "We're terrible parents."

His face moved with all he wanted to say—his protest at the inclusive pronoun, the shared condemnation.

"Terrible." Kate rubbed both of Robin's hands between hers.

"*I* didn't forget their gloves."

"Well, somebody did."

"Yeah." He laughed over his coffee cup. His face appeared both menacing and vulnerable, his rough cheeks red with chill. "You did."

"We're both responsible."

"Not me. You know why? Because I wasn't aware I was supposed to remember the gloves. I didn't get that memo."

"I didn't either," she said. "Get the memo. That's my point."

"What is?"

"We'll be outdoors; it's thirty degrees; they need gloves, right? So you just as easily as I could have thought, Yes, let me get the gloves; the girls will need gloves. *You* could have sent out the memo, or better yet, just done it on your own. Why do I have to delegate?"

"But you were getting them ready."

"But only because you weren't. Yes, I was getting them ready. And myself ready. And them ready again, after they took their coats and shoes off while I was putting mine on. All I'm saying is, is it impossible for you to do one small thing, the gloves?"

"But you didn't ask me to get the gloves," he said. "You didn't tell me you were counting on me to get the gloves."

She sighed extravagantly.

"This was your idea," he said.

"If I'd asked you," she said, "you'd think I was controlling."

"No, I wouldn't."

"You would. You would. I don't want to have to manage everything; I didn't remember about the gloves either. Gloves were not even on my radar at that moment when I could have asked you to get the gloves."

"Gloves weren't on *my* radar either."

"You remembered *your* gloves."

Everyone looked at his hands. The gray wool and leather gloves hugged them warmly. She waited for him to offer the girls his gloves. But he frowned and sipped his cider. The other family looked over at them and gathered more closely together. The wagon appeared over a small rise in the land, bearing pumpkins and their abductors.

"This whole day was your idea," he said.

"Okay, okay," she said softly. "Never mind. I should have remembered the gloves."

"Here." Colin removed his gloves. He pulled one onto both of Robin's hands and did the same with Lila.

The wagon settled at the makeshift stop, three haystacks tied with twine. The horses stamped and shook their heads. The driver grinned from his perch—felt-hatted, gap-toothed.

"All aboard!" he shouted.

They climbed up, Colin lifting Robin. They seated themselves on two long wooden planks, one on each side. The girls' faces and hands tensed in the wind. Kate leaned over and kissed Robin's cold little cheek. She felt the usual urge to bite into it—so winsome, delightful, and luscious it was.

The wagon bucked forward and bumped over the landscape that in spite of its fall harvest seemed depleted and torn. Trees hung to the edges of the fields, dark against the dull sky. Cornstalks rose fiercely from the uneven ground. Rocks kicked and clattered at the wagon's wheels. The motion threw

Kate and Lila, beside her, up, and gravity let them down, so that they jolted again and again off the wooden bench, their slender legs and tailbones punished. "Ouch," Lila cried, "ouch, ouch!" But she laughed anyway, her straight thin hair still upwardly waving as her behind hit the bench, hanging on with both gloved hands. Across from them, Colin and Robin defied the motion—he so solid and large in his maleness, Robin in his lap.

The happy-family husband requested in polite tones that the driver slow down. The driver did, grudgingly.

They passed a corn maze—at the entrance to indicate it as such, a decomposing wooden sign.

"Look!" Lila cried. Robin looked. "Corn maze!" Lila had begun reading last year but Kate still found herself stunned by the fact of it—when she shouted out, "Stop!" or "No Parking!" or sat silently over a book. "We want to go to the corn maze." Lila looked from one parent to the other. She functioned this way periodically, as a spokesperson for both girls. "We want to go. Can we? Can we go?"

Robin said, "Remember when we went on another time? On another day? On Saturday?"

"That was a hay maze," Colin said. He kissed her hair. Robin sucked on her doughnut. She sang a song she'd learned in preschool—"I looked out my window and what did I find, pumpkins a-growin' on my pumpkin vine, pumpkins, pumpkins are growing . . ." The happy-family mother smiled at Colin.

"We want to go. Please. Please can we go, Mommy, please can we go?"

"Not right this minute, baby girl. Maybe on the way back."

"You promise."

"Okay. Definitely we'll go on the way back." As always, they asked Mommy, not Daddy. He was not called upon to make the decisions, decisions that might inconvenience or incriminate him, might later be used against him, as proof of his poor judgment.

The wagon turned a corner. They bumped over a rut. Kate bit her lip and tasted blood. The ethanol odor of corn rose about them, sharp and dry. The stalks bristled.

She seized Lila and hugged her. "Ow," Lila said.

They parked at the foot of the field. The wagon wedged its wheels into the shallow rocky earth. The passengers climbed down off the back. Robin jumped from the third step. She held up her doughnut. She had mangled it and licked off the sugar. She pushed it into Kate's hand. "Don't want this," Robin said.

"Look," Kate said. She dug a shallow hole with her booted toe and dropped the doughnut in. She covered the pastry up, sweeping the dirt back over it with the side of her foot, Robin assisting.

"What are you doing?" Lila inserted herself between them.

"Planting a doughnut tree," Kate said. She poured her remaining coffee over the dirt patch. "There. It'll grow."

They were directed by the toothless driver to a cluster of small wheelbarrows. Colin took one and forged ahead to the field, which lay up a brief incline against the trees and the sky. Kate and the girls followed and then they were in it. Pumpkins burst from twisting green vines. Straw, tamped down by traffic, coated the ground between rows. Roots as gnarly as an old man's knuckles pushed themselves from the earth. The sun, setting garishly in the opaque sky, blacked out fellow pickers and pumpkin seekers so that the trudging human figures and their loaded carts resembled a children's shadow play.

Robin skipped ahead, flying spritelike and immune over the knotted turgid roots, singing her preschool song, improvising—"I looked out my window and what did I see, doughnuts a-growin' on my doughnut tree . . ."

"Oh, that's clever, Robin." Kate stepped around a root. Lila, beside her, compromised by old ballet slippers from the dress-up drawer, tripped on the same root, but Kate caught her and guided her on. Colin, both manservant and ultimate authority, trudged ahead, stooping over the wheelbarrow.

Again they divided—Kate and Lila, Colin and Robin. "This one is cute," Lila said. "It's just a baby. May I pick it?"

It hurt Kate to see Lila smiling over a baby, even just a squash baby. Even now, with this day—her creation—and her investment in it she was setting her daughter up for fundamental disenchantments.

"You can pick it," Kate said.

Lila twisted the diminutive pumpkin off its vine. She trudged ahead and deposited the pumpkin in the cart. Returning, she said, "Mommy?" She went quickly to Kate's side and took her hand. "I want to tell you a secret."

"A secret? Sure, baby girl. What is it?"

"Well." She leaned closer to her mother, bumping her as they walked. "Sometimes at school? The boys bother us."

"Bother you how?"

"They push us. They push all the girls. On the playground. They throw dirt at us. And also they talk about killing us. They go like this." She stopped, turned, and demonstrated, drawing an index finger across her throat.

"Have you told Maggie? Did you tell her what you just told me?"

"I told her but they weren't doing it then. She said she has to see it."

"Oh, she does, does she."

"She says we're supposed to work it out ourselves."

"Goddamn it," Kate said softly. Lila looked up, startled but gratified.

"Mommy?" She stopped walking and Kate did too. "When they do that"—again she drew her finger across her throat— "it makes me feel like I want to do it too. But I don't like how that feels. I don't really want to do it but I feel like I want to."

"Which boys? Ethan? Jeremy?"

"Ethan and Lionel and Max and Jeremy."

Kate bit her lip. She envisioned taking the offenders out behind the playground and crushing them, kicking their six-year-old behinds—horrible, horrible children!

"Don't tell Daddy," Lila said. She kicked at a root.

"Daddy will want to know."

"Also they called Addie a fat butt."

"Little monsters."

Again, Lila looked up, impressed. Then she stopped over a squash that was black and dented in spots, as if it had gotten into a fight. She put her arms around it and pulled at it.

"Let me help." Kate pulled with her. Together, they twisted the squash from its vine. "Next time one of those boys pushes you," Kate said, "you push him back."

She picked the pumpkin up in both her arms and carried it to the wheelbarrow.

"It's getting late," Colin said. "We should think about going."

"I want the corn maze!" Robin ran to Lila for support. Kate looked at Colin.

"I promised them the maze," she said.

"We need to get all the way home, guys. We got a late start, remember?"

"Maze! Maze!"

They clamored for it. Colin stepped behind the wheelbarrow, knocked back by their desire and its strenuous expression.

"I'll take them," Kate said.

"I can pay for these, load the car, I guess. Okay. Don't take forever, though."

They walked back toward the barn, Lila kicking at the beaten trodden path, Robin riding in the barrow amid the pumpkins. At the corn maze they parted.

"I'll be in the car," Colin said.

There seemed to be, even in all that tall obliterating corn, nowhere to hide from him, or he from her. She watched him tread off with the barrow, in his brown coat, his hands red around the handles. He had remembered his gloves but left his head bare—and his upper scalp practically hairless—how cold that must be. She adjusted her own dark pony. He'd been balding, of course, back in the days of Stamford, the train, the East Village, the crowded bars, the waitresses with their pencil topknots, even the night of the clogged sink. Still, Kate felt implicated—what had she done, done to him, to cause this blight! She had terrorized him, stripped him of his natural protection against the elements—sun, cold, wind. She wanted to chase him down, cover his poor bare head with a hat or with her own thick locks.

But how obstinate he was! How inflexible! His balding head loomed, symbolic of his stubbornness.

Lila pulled at her sleeve. "Come on."

They stepped in and stood, breathing in the sharp tickling smell. From outside, the maze had seemed compact, a contained and navigable unit. But inside, everything vanished but the most proximate activities: the crackling and settling of straw, the cry of a crow, the activity of insects.

"There's nobody else here," Robin observed.

Lila pointed deeper into the maze. "Maybe they're in there."

Robin bolted and ran through an opening in the corn—a sort of trapdoor through the wall to the adjacent section—and disappeared. Kate grabbed Lila's arm and set after her. Through the corn she caught a flash of red—Robin's coat. She rounded a corner and caught her younger daughter about the shoulders. "Don't do that again."

Lila giggled.

Above, the channel of gray sky darkened. "Just a little while in here, guys. Like Daddy said." The girls ran ahead, lightly, over the snapping straw. Kate ran also, reached after their flying hair. "Guys! I said no!" The clouds moved above, poured, like smoke from a burning building. The girls veered off in opposite directions. "Freeze! Stay together, guys!" She retrieved them. "Hold hands. Everyone hold hands, okay?"

They held hands then, twisting sideways like a paper-doll chain, the sort a child would make for a Christmas tree. They turned and turned again. Tough bowed leaves hooked on Kate's hair and pulled at it. "We should go back now, guys," she said. She didn't know how to get back but she didn't say so.

"But we have to get to the end," Lila said.

"Where's the end?"

"We have to find it."

Kate looked up. A crow flew along the sky tunnel and vanished.

"I can spell 'scarecrow,' " Lila said.

"Oh, yeah?"

"S-c-a-r-e-c-r-o-w!"

"Oh! Yes, good, Lila."

Kate had left her purse in the car. Her purse had her phone in it and her phone had the time. Anxiety surged in her, as in dreams where she could not get ready, someone waiting downstairs as clothing and jewelry slipped from her hands; as in days when errands stretched out and she searched, trapped in Target or Stop & Shop—late for everything, missing everything.

Had it been five minutes? Ten? Fifteen? The dense stalks repeated themselves. She started forward again, pulling the girls along now, hurrying.

"Are we lost, Mommy?"

Kate tripped over a root. She fell to the rough ground on her hands and knees. "Damn thing. Goddamn it."

"Are you okay, Mommy?"

"Can we get out?"

"Are we lost, Mommy? Are we lost?"

The girls towered over her, anxiously looking down.

Kate pulled herself up. Her palms stung. Her knees burned through her jeans. She shouted, "Hello! Hello! Help!"

"Call Daddy. On your phone."

"Lila, you're so clever. But I left it in my purse. Which I left in the car."

"Oh, Mommy!"

Robin turned and walked ahead, suddenly, on sturdy corduroy-clad legs.

"Follow her," Lila said. She hauled at Kate's arm.

They followed. The wicked stalks persisted. The maze whipped around and around again.

But—abruptly—light and land showed ahead. Robin tumbled toward the exit, compact with purpose. They broke out into dusk.

"Robin!" Kate scooped her up.

"Robin saved us!" Lila cried.

They ran, holding hands, down the rutted path toward the barn, past cornfields, past the geese and the ducks, past the pigs in their pen, past the bonfire, to the car where Colin waited, arms crossed. He saw them and got into the driver's seat without saying hello. He started the engine. Kate buckled seat belts.

"Thanks for making it quick," he said.

"We were lost," she said. She did up her own belt.

"We got lost!" Robin shouted. "Lost in the corn maze!"

"You did, did you."

He seemed unimpressed at the prospect of nearly having lost them.

"We got lost, lost, stuck!" Robin banged the back of his seat.

Lila banged Kate's seat. "And Robin led us out! She led us out of the maze!"

"An hour," he said to Kate. "You were gone an hour."

"Robin is magic," Lila said.

"Your daughter is trying to tell you something," Kate said.

"You said you'd hurry."

She looked out the window. Tears rose in her throat. She swallowed them back. "When you ignore the girls, when they're talking to you? It makes me feel . . ." She searched her vocabulary, could not find a fitting word. "Like shit."

He pressed his lips together.

She put her head to the chilly window. The other family, the happy family, piled into their Suburban, laughing, hay caught in the older girl's long hair. Colin pulled onto the road. The radio played "Positively 4th Street." Kate turned, sensing activity, and looked back. The girls were dancing in their seats, shaking their still-oversize heads to the beat.

"Okay, tell me, Lila," Colin said. "Tell me what happened."

19

THE CARVED PUMPKINS ROTTED on the porch. The favorite candy was consumed and the rest of it grew stale in the orange plastic totes. Kate, thinking of Brooke and Trey, collected sexual positions from the Internet. She and Colin sprawled on the parental bed examining their options:

The Panini Press
The Hit and Run
The Nice to Meet You
The All I Want for Christmas
The Sharper Image
The Shotgun Wedding
The Up and Adam
The Air on a G String
The Ass Menagerie

They tried a couple, both of which seemed to thrill Colin but only amused Kate.

Miles's name appeared in the *New York Times* in connection with the mayor. Kate fell down the basement stairs carrying a basket of dirty laundry. Colin came home and found her on the sofa with an ice pack and a scotch, sprawled out, watching *Dragon Tales* with the girls.

"You okay? What happened?"

She told him. "I hurt my hip. And my ankle. And my arm. And my elbow. But yes, I'm okay."

"Christ. I'm sorry."

"It's hard to see coming down those basement stairs with the laundry, that's all."

"Doesn't Beatrice do the laundry?"

"Portia? No, she doesn't. Only some of it. You know that."

"Well, have her do all of it."

"Oh, God, Colin. We've had this conversation a hundred times."

"Shush!" Robin hissed.

"Robin. Not okay." Colin held up his index finger. "I'll get them to bed," he told Kate.

He ushered the girls upstairs. Kate changed the channel. The phone rang. She reached for the handheld, askew on the coffee table. Her mother. Upstairs, Colin shouted, "Teeth!"

"Katie, I wonder how you'd feel if I went to Amelia's parents' this Thanksgiving instead of Judith's," Edie said.

Amelia was Miles's current girlfriend. Judith was Colin's mother.

"They invited me, and he seems to like her so, and I'm just thinking it would be nice for me to get to know the family a bit."

"That's fine, Mom. Not a problem."

"May I visit with the kids anyway? Take them for the night, maybe?"

"You want to? Take them?"

"You and Colin could have some time alone. . . ."

"We might kill each other."

"What?"

"No, never mind, nothing. Yes. The girls would love that. Friday?"

She hung up. Colin returned from bedtime and collapsed ponderously next to her on the couch.

"I'm taking the girls to my mom's Friday," she told him. "And she won't be at Thanksgiving because she's going to Amelia's parents'. So you should go out with the guys or something. Friday. Do you want to tell your mom or should I?"

"The guys, huh? You don't want to do date night? A little angel hair?"

"Ha, ha. Well. I don't know; I might spend the night up there too."

The words surprised her as she said them. She'd had no coherent thought to this effect. But as she spoke she knew she wanted to be away. From the house, from the mess, from Colin, just away.

On Thursday night she e-mailed Jack Auerbach.

Probably busy at such late notice, but . . .

He wrote back right away. No, he wasn't busy. Seven o'clock, the Q Club?

Friday morning she packed a small bag for the girls and a smaller one for herself. She laid out clothes. A corduroy skirt, a camisole, a half-sleeve sweater, the boots. Lace underwear and a push-up bra.

Doing so, she realized that she wanted to sleep with him. With Jack.

She understood that if she got the chance, she would. There it was, the knowledge, right in front of her like a dish she hadn't ordered.

Well, what was she to do? She could send it back or she could dig in.

She wanted to screw him. Of course she did. Why else would she bother with any of this, with the e-mail and the trip and the bra?

She paid the bills. She unloaded the dishwasher. She sent Colin an e-mail. She showered and picked the girls up at school, one, then another. She passed them their snack, graham crackers and string cheese. Then she got on 95 and headed north to New Haven.

"Wait till you see the house," Edie said at the door.

Kate and the girls followed her down the front hallway. Since their last visit, the living room had become a playroom. Sprightly children's literature filled the bookshelf. Beanbags abounded, toys, puzzles, and games neatly stacked. The girls ran joyfully in, responding to the cheery appeal of organization, brightness, and neatness, everything as it should be.

"It looks really nice in here, Mom," Kate said.

"I think it came out well too. It's not like I have company, so . . ."

"They love it." The girls frolicked amid the toys and books and games. Even the disorder the kids immediately created didn't get to Kate like it did at home. It seemed nothing to fret about, like someone else's baby crying or someone else's children fighting, just natural, a normal expression of normal needs.

Kate hurled herself into a cushy chair. Her mother got down on the floor and helped Lila and Robin put together a puzzle.

"I bet that puzzle actually still has all its pieces," Kate said. "How did you keep everything so neat when we were kids? You worked full-time. I don't get it. How did you do all the little things?"

"You didn't have as many toys, for one. And I think there was less then, in a lot of ways. Now you know so much and you're expected to address it all. But. Yes, there were still plenty of little things. Why?" Her mother looked up hopefully. "Are you thinking about going back to work?"

"I've thought about it."

"I'm sure the development office would take you back."

"Whatever."

The girls abruptly abandoned the puzzle and ran screaming upstairs to Kate's old bedroom.

"I might spend the night," Kate told her mother.

"You and Colin aren't . . . ?"

"What?"

"Don't have plans?"

"He's out with the guys. I'm going for a drink with Pam," she said.

Pam Pellegrino, a friend from Whitney Hall, lived in Hamden now with her husband and kids. Kate hadn't talked to her in a year.

Then her mother was staring at her, at her right arm. "Oh, Katie, what happened?"

"What?" Kate looked where her mother was looking. "Oh, that."

"Are you and Colin fighting?"

"Are you serious? I fell down the stairs, Mom!"

SHE PARKED in the Broadway lot. She applied lipstick as she walked from her car—she checked her compact, still walking.

"Going to meet someone, are ya?" the attendant said.

She laughed a little. "Yes!"

Well—she was!

She felt like running toward the Q Club, away from her cluttered, littered car. She anticipated the diffuse lighting, the taciturn waiters, the dish of olives and bread sticks and celery. In college, from time to time, she'd dined there with her father. She would drive her mother's car to meet him, just like this, maybe even leave the parking lot with a similar high, that of an impending encounter with an exciting person.

She hung up her coat and located Jack near the front. He stood up as she slid into the wooden booth.

"It's all the same!" she said. The sameness thrilled her: the gilt mirrors, the sconces and depictions of ducks at the back of each booth, and the middle table where her father had flipped bread from the end of his fork, where material surfaces had interrupted a possible orbit.

Jack motioned for the waiter, then looked at Kate carefully, registering all the little things about her: the way her necklace fell into her shirt, the way her hair hung about her shoulders, her collarbone, the old burn in the hollow of her throat where a match tip had flown off and struck her as she lit the grill.

"What happened there?" He tapped the base of his throat.

She explained. He raised his eyebrows in dismay. A shame, his look said—she was beautiful there!

Jack had his drink already, a scotch. Kate ordered a martini. The olives and celery and bread sticks appeared.

She took in the gap between Jack's two front teeth, the appealing irregularity of the whole set. A buzzing rose within her, a low pleasant hum—akin to that of a vibrator or a cell phone—that temporarily hid her intentions from herself. It was a familiar sound, one she registered but, by dint of its nature, could not identify. It obscured her immediate plans and actual inclinations as well as the giant fact of Colin. It hung about the table, altering the atmosphere. The buzzing interfered with the voice of the waiter, from whom Kate ordered a Caesar salad and salmon, smiling at him through the sound. The drink came, the food. They discussed Kate's father: his brilliance, his eccentricities, his abrupt passing, the project he'd been working on at the time of his death.

"I imagine he wasn't the easiest person to live with," Jack said.

"No. My poor mother."

"He talked about you a lot."

"Well. That's usually the way."

"So what the hell have you been up to?"

"Let's see. Kids. Other stuff. Kids."

"You were at Yale for a while, am I right?"

"Yes. At the development office. Now I volunteer at a shelter. I teach a class on sticking to a budget."

Another round of drinks arrived. She didn't remember more being ordered, but she moved happily into her second martini.

"You were saying." He leaned back. She felt him spread his legs under the table.

She shook her head. "So your ex-wife—was it amicable, or whatever?"

"Relatively speaking. She got an offer from Harvard. She wanted kids. I didn't. And so on. We were only together four years."

"Four years is sort of perfect. I feel like marriage should be renewable, like a driver's license or something, or a political office. Electoral terms of marriage."

She ate an olive out of her martini, registering, unrepentantly, that she'd just given away crucial information.

"You know, actually, in some primitive societies they would do just that. Mate for four years, procreate; then when the child was close to four years old—old enough to need only one caregiver—they'd move on and mate with somebody else."

"Well, then I am long overdue." She laughed dismissively.

"How old is your youngest?"

"Robin? She's four." The theme felt suddenly embarrassing. She ate another olive.

"Your kids, what are they like? Do they get along?"

"They fight, but Lila, the older one, is a dream. Robin's usually the instigator. The four-year-old. She's a menace."

"So Lila takes after you. Right? I remember you being sort of a dream child."

"Maybe for five minutes."

"Your dad thought so."

"Oh, I'm not so sure he always thought so."

"No?"

"I don't mean to talk trash about Robin. It's appropriate, of course, for your kids to defy you; you want them to learn to question authority, but also it doesn't seem right for them to run the show—sometimes you wish they'd just fall in line. You know? It's like that after-all-I've-done-for-you feeling."

"You think you'll go back to the development office at some point?"

"Oh, I just had this exact conversation with my mom."

"Sorry."

"No, no! It's fine. Let's see. The job itself, I could take it or leave it. The benefits are great, but so are Colin's. Maybe I'll work in finance again. I don't know; I guess I feel like I still haven't figured out exactly what it is I like to do." She took a roll from the breadbasket and picked at it. "Anyway, how about you; do you have some sort of research project going?"

She saw him glance at her neckline. "Well, right now we're using microwave radiation to determine the conductivity of single-electron transistors."

"Hmm. Interesting." She finished dismantling the roll. She procured another one and looked at it. "Do you remember having dinner here? With my parents? There was some Yale party. You were with a girl."

"Lindsey."

"Is that who you married?"

"God, no."

"My father was flipping the bread from the end of his fork. Shooting it at the other tables."

"Like this?" Jack took the roll from her hand and put it on the end of his fork and hit the tines. The roll soared out of the booth and into the adjacent one.

"Oh, my God." She twisted around and got on her knees and looked over. The dining room had emptied except for two male professor types sharing a slice of pie. "No. More like this." She flipped a second roll. He flipped a third one. A busboy removed plates and the breadbasket. The waiter brought the check. Jack signed it.

"Thank you," Kate said. "Right. That whole men's-club thing."

"They take women now, you know."

"Oh, thank God. Been losing sleep over that."

He reached across the table and took her hand. "This is nice, huh?"

They kissed in the parking lot, beside her car. He slid his arms under her jacket and held her waist. She felt as though she'd swallowed a string and he was pulling it out of her, a string that had made its way down her throat and through her abdomen and female internal organs and down her vaginal canal, and he was winding it around his wrists; the pressure between her legs intensified, as if yards and yards of magical thickening string moved in and through her.

"I'm a little drunk, I think," she said eventually.

"Want me to drive?"

He took her keys and drove her to his apartment. He lived, it turned out, in an industrial part of town on the wrong side of the highway and the park. His building had clearly at one point housed some sort of factory. They took the freight elevator up to his floor. She removed her coat and stood shivering in his living room while he adjusted the thermostat. Then she let him pick her up and carry her to his bedroom. At the gallery and at the Q Club he'd seemed skinny, his shoulders narrow under the flannel shirt, but his arms surprised her—they were very strong. His bed was covered in a military manner by a blue batik print. No headboard, no decorative pillows. There was something embarrassing about the bed's plainness—in that it, this lack of adornment, clearly announced the bed's functions—something delightful too.

"Hold on," she said.

From the bathroom, she called her mother and left a message saying she had decided to spend the night at home.

She returned to the bedroom, where Jack was waiting

with his beautiful arms crossed behind his neck. She stood at the end of the bed and removed her shirt. Then she lost her nerve and crawled toward him on the bed. Cold air came in around the tall ramshackle windows and brushed her skin. Across the way, a light went off and then on again. The radiator clanked. Jack had put music on, something soft and countryish.

Underneath him, under the covers, she put her arms around his neck. She laughed.

"What?" He looked around.

"*This* is something I like to do."

SHE COVERED HER FACE with her hands. She bit her arm. At one point she became dizzy and gasped on her hands and knees.

"You okay?" he asked.

"I might pass out."

She didn't.

He slapped her on the ass. He flipped her back over. "Scoot down," he said. "Like that. Good girl." He stood up at the edge of the bed and held on to her hips. She hooked her legs over his shoulders.

"You're so *pretty*," he said. "I love it."

SHE BORROWED HIS TOOTHBRUSH and an undershirt to sleep in. She burrowed into his armpit.

"How old are you, anyway?" she asked.

"Forty-eight. Old. Old man."

While she slept, love, or its alias, infatuation, took her over.

It sprang from his pungent armpit, or maybe his toes, and engaged her completely. It colonized her body and brain and turned the vague notion of him into a fully developed ideology. She woke up elated and agitated, as if she knew him and loved him already, as if he'd simply been hidden from her all these years.

20

As SHE DROVE to her mother's the next morning, then home after picking up the kids, her elation persisted.

Was that all it took? Was that all she'd wanted?

She went to get waxed at her usual place, where Olga waited critically for her at the desk.

"Hello, honey. Eyebrow?"

"No, bikini." She followed Olga to the back room. She lay quietly with her eyes closed as the older woman ripped her inner thighs apart.

"You are happy today. I never see you like this."

"Yes. I am happy."

Outside, a young girl's voice sounded. "I will leave you here just a minute, honey." Olga flicked the lights out as she left the room with a physicianlike rustle. Kate lay quietly in the dark. Her crotch itched and burned. "Hello, honey," Olga said outside.

"Oh, hi!" the girl said. "Hi!"

"What, no kiss today?" To the manicurist, Katya: "I am spoilt."

The girl laughed. "I saw your son the other day," she said. "I didn't know he was your son. But I've seen him before . . . at the Playwright. I was talking about this place in some context, I don't know what, I have no idea. But someone said, 'Oh, do you know that there's a guy who comes here whose mother works there. Curly.' And I was like, 'Oh, I know about Curly!' "

Voices rose—Katya's and one or two others. "Curly? Why Curly?"

Olga said, "Not his hair. Some—he doesn't tell me. Some secret thing."

"Because his hair is straight!"

"Yes, straight."

"So straight!"

"I don't know," Olga said—proud, bemused. "At camp, when we leave, like a celebrity. Pulling out, everybody, 'Goodbye Curly! Curly!' "

A small silence accumulated around the mystery of Curly. Then Olga went to call him.

The girl and Katya discussed polish colors. Kate heard Olga's voice at the back. "Honey? A girl here . . . ?" She called over her shoulder. "He says hello!" She hung up and returned to the group. "The Three Stooges. Moe and Curly and—"

"Larry."

"Yes, Larry."

Olga returned to Kate and her smarting crotch. "Turn over. Knees. Show me the money." She slapped on wax and ripped. "Your husband will think you are very sexy."

"Oh, yes," Kate said. "My husband."

Olga nudged Kate's hip and Kate lay on her back again. Olga examined her handiwork. She applied baby powder and cooling lotion. "I tell you, if I had choice between evening with a nice gentleman and a good book, I know what I would choose. Every time. Every time."

"Really? The book? Really?"

"Every"—she patted Kate on the thigh and gestured for her to sit up—"time."

"Because that is *so* not what I would pick."

"You would pick your husband. Good."

"No—I meant, if I were single."

"Well, you are young. Still pretty young. You get to be my age, all that just—" She snapped her fingers in the air.

"What, men, you mean?" Kate retrieved her purse and coat.

"Well, yes." Olga gathered up the paper cover, stuck here and there with wax and hair. "Men, and sex." She shrugged, raised her eyebrows. "You wake up one day and it's gone. Those feelings."

"Really?"

"Then, you know, you get back to you. Is different. Not bad."

"No." Kate stood in the doorway. She wriggled her hips against the itch in her bikini area. "No. That doesn't sound bad at all."

21

KATE CHECKED at regular intervals all weekend for an e-mail. On Sunday one materialized. Joy leaped in her like the dancing peppercorns of West Twelfth Street. On Tuesday, after dropping the girls at school, Kate sneaked off to New Haven. Jack buzzed her in and Kate wandered about the drafty apartment, fingering artifacts and piles of academic writings. Then they sat together on his weathered corduroy couch, Kate cross-legged and nervously mauling a recent issue of *Applied Physics.*

"Maybe Lila will follow in my dad's footsteps," she said. "She loves science. I mean, at least the kindergarten translation."

"I thought she wanted to be a ballerina."

"Oh, yes. Okay. Ballerina first, physicist later."

"What does your husband do again?"

"Finance. Money management. Private equity."

"Right, of course."

She looked at their hands together and admired the sight, then pulled hers away and twisted them in her lap and looked down. "We still do it, you know," she said. "Every now and then. No, but seriously. Every week. Ten days."

"You trying to make me jealous?" Jack grabbed her chin

and kissed her. He tossed the back pillows one by one off the couch. Clothing followed. Change fell from his pockets. He pulled her knees apart and examined her.

"Okay, Doctor." She shifted and tensed her thighs. She tried to align them.

"No, don't do that."

"My kids wreaked some havoc down there."

"No."

"Yes, yes, they did. I used to be . . ."

"No way." His tongue explored Olga's impeccable work. "You're so soft."

She clenched one arm over her face and grabbed the couch with the other. Then: "Get something." She reached into his pants with both hands and gripped him. "I'm ovulating."

"You are?" He caught her under her arms and picked her up. She wrapped her legs around his waist. "Beautiful."

"Get it."

He brought her into the bedroom. "I love carrying you around." Holding her, he rummaged in a bureau drawer. He put the thing on. He pushed himself up inside of her. She tightened her hold around his neck. He got them onto the bed and spread her legs and pushed her knees up to her chest. "I could fuck you like this all day."

"No false modesty, please."

"None."

"You are good at that."

"What, false modesty?"

"No. The other thing."

"I mean it. I could do this all day and all night."

She hooked a leg over his shoulder.

"You are exceptionally flexible, you know that?"

Lila, her ballerina, pirouetted through her mind. Then Robin. Colin clomped by alongside. All aroused fondness but annoyance as well. She didn't want them, at least not at the moment. She just wanted Jack. She'd rather lie around an old canning factory on a weekday afternoon engaging in baby-making activities with a near stranger than spend time with her actual babies, their actual father.

HE TAUGHT MONDAYS, Wednesdays, and Fridays. On Tuesday and Thursday mornings she drove up to New Haven and Jack's apartment in Erector Square (aptly named, she could not help but think). Thanksgiving passed—Colin's picturesque Darien childhood home, the insufferable Moira and the blue-eyed Liam now a real grown-up kid, the Cornish game hens. The following Tuesday Kate waved good-bye to Colin and the girls, swept dishes into the sink, dressed herself in what she hoped was a fetching getup, and tore out of the driveway.

"So that night at the club," she said. She curled up next to Jack under the covers and draped her arm across his chest. "My father told the waiter I flipped the bread, to tease me, remember? And it really bothered me even though I pretended it didn't. And maybe you could tell, because you said something about my arm, or my aim, and you shot a roll into my father's wine."

"You were what, thirteen, fourteen?"

"More like nine. Ten. Early developer." She put a finger in his mouth and ran it over his front teeth. "You never had braces, did you?"

"Braces. My father drove a taxi. My mother cleaned houses."

Everything, everything about him was exciting and endearing.

He examined her hip, where one bruise bloomed blue and red and another wilted into brown. "You sure you're not anemic?"

"I was tested." She poked at her bruises. "I don't even know how they happen. I don't even know they're there till I see them."

"No?"

"Nope."

"If I didn't know better I'd say you were a battered wife."

"Well, I'm not."

"You sure?"

"Trust me. He did throw pasta over my head. About a month ago? Angel hair."

"This story I need to hear."

"We went out to dinner. I ordered angel-hair pasta and I had a lot left over so we had it wrapped. We got into a fight on the way home. Then we parked in the driveway and we kept fighting and he grabbed the container from the backseat and dumped it over my head. Or kind of *at* my head, rather, through the window."

"I knew that guy was a jackass."

"I was being awful too."

"I went to this strip club once, in Chinatown. Years ago. Sort of an alternative-style strip club, if you know what I mean. And in this one act, the woman picked up linguine from a pot and kind of dropped it on herself. Through the whole number she kept picking up handfuls and smearing them on her stomach and her shoulders and her breasts. Weird but hot. And then once in a while she'd throw a handful at the audience."

"What was an upstanding citizen like you doing in a place like that?"

"You'd be surprised."

"Don't tell me my father—"

"No, no, at least, not that I know of. No. It was a long time ago. I went with this woman. We were young, well, youngish."

"Lindsey?"

"No, not her. No, the woman was my girlfriend before my ex-wife; she taught feminist theory at Barnard."

"Anyway," Kate said, moving on from the exes, toward whom she felt a brief but intense spasm of sexual jealousy, "when we're not getting on each other's nerves, Colin and I, we actually have a pretty good family dynamic."

"But . . . surely the girls can pick up on the tension."

"A little, yes, of course. But mainly, I don't think they care that much. I think they just like having us together, and they could care less if we get along when we're on our own."

"It's the atomic hypothesis," he said. "Things attract when they're a small distance apart. And when they're crowded into each other, they repel."

"Things, by that do you mean people?"

"Right. Things, people, animals. All living things are made up of atoms. All behavior can be explained accordingly."

"Accordingly . . ."

"According to atomic laws."

"Oh, Professor Auerbach, I see! So the atoms attract and repel just like we sorry married people do."

"And the rest of us. Very good, dear girl."

SARAH GARDNER BORDEN

254

"And so?"

"Well, are you happy?"

"Happiness is a dog—"

"I know. Sunning itself on a rock. Coleridge."

"So, who cares?"

"That's bullshit. I mean, do you like your life or not?"

"I *should* like it."

"Who says?"

"Well, I'm fortunate in all the crucial ways. All my basic levels of need are covered. That isn't true for the women I work with, trust me."

He stared at her and ran a finger across her belly.

"What?"

"I'm thinking about linguine sliding over this gorgeous white skin of yours."

What she loved about him, of course, was his appreciation of her—of her body, specifically. He served, gallantly, as an audience of one for a show about to close. She rolled on top of him and kissed his neck. He endured, uncomplainingly, while she gave him a hickey.

"I love that you let me do that!" She admired her work. "Colin never lets me do that. Not anymore. Not ever, actually. He's all like, 'Oh, oh, someone will see!' I wouldn't put it anywhere obvious. He could hide it under his shirt. See, you can hide yours."

"The kids wouldn't believe it was possible anyway."

He pushed her hair from her neck, his face clouded by amorous intent. "Oh, no," she said. "You can't. He'll see it."

"You could hide it under your shirt."

"Ha!" She rolled over. The head of the bed met the brick of the wall. She lay on her stomach, chin in hands. The brick, coated with some sort of protective glaze, sparkled as with bits of mica. In between, the mortar rose roughly. "Anyway," she said, "it was angel hair."

"But my girl in Chinatown, it must have been linguine, or at least spaghetti. Whatever it was, slippery. Angel hair tends to clump, no?"

"It does. Yes. It did."

From his bedside table she picked up *The Elegant Universe,* which she'd been using as a coaster. "Oh, this is so beyond me," she said, looking through it.

"No, it's not. If you get math you can get this."

"Right."

"You could if you wanted."

"In my next life."

"What do you do with your ladies? Meaning, what are some of your strategies; how do you construct the lesson?"

"Well, I have them do worksheets. Math problems. Basic addition, subtraction, multiplication, division, percentages, fractions and decimals. Et cetera. Then we get into the whole vocabulary of money and finance. I have them match words and make sentences. Some people do fine with the math but then get intimidated by the vocab. I have them keep a mock checkbook and record mock transactions. They get the practice checkbook and a calculator and a pen and paper. Oh, my God, the things they spend their imaginary money on. Six hundred dollars for hair straightening. Fifteen hundred a year on soda, fifteen hundred on cigarettes. I mean, not that I should talk. It's just basic stuff, two lists, one for deposits, one for withdrawals. They balance it every class; I want them to get in the habit of balancing it on a weekly basis. We also do this exercise with a scale; we use weights for the different amounts of money and one side is what they put in and one side is what they take out."

"What's the goal? Are they going to go on to banking jobs?"

"Maybe as tellers."

"Right."

"No. The goal is just to get them organized, help them remain solvent. That's it. That's a lot."

"That is. Your dad would be proud."

"Please."

ON THURSDAY she straddled him. She shed her sweater and T-shirt and bra. She unzipped him and got his pants down and slid off the couch and to her knees.

He grabbed her hair. "Oh, God, you're good at that."

He pulled at her hair and twisted it into a knot. Music played in the apartment below—something classical and celebratory and reflective, almost mystical, a work she knew but couldn't identify. Jack pulled her up onto his lap. "Come here for a sec." He kissed her and ran his hands over her shoulders. "Do you like that? Do you like doing that?"

"What?"

"Giving head."

"Well, not for just anybody."

"Oh. Ha. That's good." He grabbed her face and made her look at him. "You want to keep going?"

"Yes."

"I'm going to come if you keep doing that."

"I want you to. In my mouth."

22

THE SECOND WEDNESDAY in December snow appeared, and by early Thursday morning it had covered all available outdoor surfaces. The strange cold light woke Kate at six, pushing in through the too-thin drapes. She looked at Colin's sleeping profile and turned away. She could see out the window from her side of the bed. A car rolled methodically down the loaded street, wavering a little. She closed her eyes and put her face back into the pillow.

"Fuck," she whispered.

The phone sang from the carved antique bedside table, a hand-me-down from Kate's mother.

Snow day.

Kate banged her head into the pillow twice, then answered.

"What," Colin said, waking.

"School. Fucking snow day."

"Oh. Sorry." He sat up.

"No big deal." But it was a big deal. Inside of her, the Valeries bridled with frustrated longing. They strapped on their boots and began to kick things apart.

"What will you do?"

"Errands, I guess."

The girls ran in, chattering over the snow. "I'll take 'em," Colin said. "Go back to sleep."

She tried. When she couldn't she turned on her side and watched the neighbor, Ian Hesselgrove, trot with his mutt down the street. He appeared in one window, then the other. The Hesselgroves were a calm friendly couple in their fifties who always seemed to have enough time, always outside, gardening or shoveling or raking or striking up conversations. Their two boys were in their twenties and attended graduate school in Boston. Once when Lila was a baby Kate had lost control of the stroller and Mrs. Hesselgrove—Elaine—had helped chase it down the driveway.

Kate got up and tied on her robe and went downstairs for coffee. The clean dishwasher stood open, a bowl and mug removed. She retrieved a mug for herself and poured herself coffee and burrowed into the family room couch with her laptop and the girls, who were watching *Clifford's Puppy Days,* a spinoff that since John Ritter's death had replaced the original show. She sent Jack an e-mail. She watched *Clifford.* Then, "This is the perfect moment for your project, Lila," she said.

Yesterday Lila had come home from school with an assignment. With an "adult's help" she must conduct a small science experiment and record the results. She'd been given a list of ideas:

> Push an egg into a bottle without touching it
> Get a liquid to float
> Make fizzy lemon soda
> Clean a penny
> Water balloon toss
> Make an electromagnet

The ideas came with directions and illustrations, which Kate scanned and evaluated. "Let's do the last one," she said. "Let's make a magnet." This suggestion seemed the least messy.

"I want to push an egg into a bottle!" Lila cried.

"Oh, okay, okay. You can watch more TV, Rob, if you want," she said. *Super Why!* commenced. Robin nodded and wiggled more deeply into the couch, captivated. Lila followed Kate into the kitchen. The egg-in-a-bottle directions called for a widemouthed bottle, one peeled hard-boiled egg, matches, and a one-inch-by-one-inch piece of paper. "Eggs. Are there eggs?" She got up and opened the fridge. Yes, there were eggs. She put water on to boil and the egg in it. She added a few extra for the kids' lunches. She procured matches and an old milk bottle and she cut paper into a one-inch square. The water boiled; the eggs hardened. Kate scooped them out and ran them under cold water.

"Now," Kate said. "Let's see."

She read through the instructions again. She read the explanation of the concept behind the experiment. "This is all about high pressure versus low pressure," she said. "Air flows from high pressure to low. So in order to get into the bottle, the outer air is going to push into the bottle and push the egg in with it. So . . . with the matches, you see, we're going to lower the air pressure inside the bottle."

Lila nodded, biting her thumbnail.

"Do you want to peel the egg?"

Lila seized an egg and began to pick away at the shell.

"Okay, great." While Lila peeled the egg in tiny little increments, Kate unloaded the dishwasher and loaded it again.

"Done," Lila said.

Bits of shell lay scattered about the counter. Kate put the egg at the mouth of the bottle to check the fit.

"It should fit if you push," she said to Lila, "but not too easily. It should slide in but only with a nudge." She gave Lila the slippery egg to hold while she dropped three lit matches and the paper into the bottle. "Now, carefully, put the egg back on top!"

Lila did so. She put the egg at the mouth and snatched her hand away. The matches went out. The egg slid into the bottle.

"Cool! So cool!" Lila beat her hands on the counter.

"That is cool." Smoke drifted from the bottle. "Now write down what you saw, okay?"

Lila got her notebook from her backpack and sat at the counter and meticulously formed letters, breathing through her nose, her tongue protruding from between her teeth.

"You're reminding me of Daddy," Kate said, watching her.

Lila looked up and smiled.

KATE SHOVELED OFF THE CAR and got the girls into their seats and drove to Stop & Shop. A pickup truck passed with a wreath on its bumper. On the radio, Jon Bon Jovi sang "Please Come Home for Christmas." Wire reindeer and sleighs posed on the rooftops of small clapboard houses. Kate thought about Jack. She felt that if she didn't see him soon, she would collapse or die, or at least evaporate into sheer agitation. Her desire for him, for him in particular, calmed and organized and illuminated everything else. Her feelings for Colin, way back when, had done the same but had also involved specific ideas. Jack she wanted not toward any abstract end but an immediate physiological one.

The girls bickered in the backseat.

"Stop it, please!" Kate cried. "Stop fighting, you two."

"But she—"

"She—"

"Just leave each other alone. Find something else to do."

"There's nothing to do back here!" Lila wailed.

"Look out the window. Listen to the music."

"But Robin's poking me. . . ."

"Robin, *stop it.*" With one hand, Kate rummaged in her purse. She found a wrapped tampon and held it back over her shoulder. "Here." Robin seized the offering and began, passionately, to play with it.

"*I* want a tampon!" Lila cried.

Unwrapping sounds commenced. "Oh, be careful what you wish for," Kate said.

"What are we going to do after the store?"

"I don't know, Lila."

"I hate errands!"

"Me too."

"Can we go sledding when we get home?"

"Maybe."

"Please! Please!"

"If I'm not too tired."

She did feel too tired, as it turned out, after navigating the Stop & Shop with the two little girls and getting them home and out of the car along with bags and bags of groceries, out of the back and up the steps. But she pulled the snow gear out of the closet anyway, did up the girls' boots and her own. She dragged plastic sleds out from behind the lawn mower and headed, the girls shuffling behind, to the nearest hill.

Lila sledded alone and Kate rode the larger sled with

Robin. Neighborhood kids, some from Wintergreen, almost
obliterated by their coats and accessories, coasted alongside.
After an hour or so, Kate begged out. The girls went down
alone. Lila struggled up with her sled. Robin cried at the bottom of the hill.

"What happened?" Kate asked Lila, as her elder daughter
approached.

"She's tired. She says she can't walk up the hill."

Kate shuffled and slid down to Robin. "I'll carry you," she
said. "But this is the only time. If you want to go down on the
sled you have to walk back up." She lifted Robin to her hip,
grabbed the sled with her other hand. She climbed the hill,
breathing hard.

She let Robin ride the sled home, while she, Kate, pulled it.
Lila walked behind pulling her own sled. Robin's sled featured
an interfering steering contraption, which Robin tested as
they struggled across the street.

"Eyes on the road, Rob," Kate said. "Look where you want
to go. If you look at the scenery you're going to end up in the
scenery."

Lila asked, "Will you pull me on my sled too, please?"

"Oh, baby girl, I can't do that. Thanks for saying 'please,'
though."

"I'm tired too!"

"I know. I know you are. We'll be home soon."

Robin gave up the rudder and snatched a large stick from
the sidewalk and dug it into the snow, the effect of which was
to drag the sled sideways, severely compromising its trajectory.

"Don't do that, Rob," Kate said.

Robin kept doing that.

"Robin, I'm losing my patience!"

She kept doing it.

"I'm going to yell!"

"You're already yelling," Lila said.

"Take that stick out of the snow and don't put it back, or I'm going to take that stick from you and throw it away." Robin removed the stick from the snow and held it close to her body. "And it's probably dangerous for you to be holding a stick at all, while you're riding the sled . . . it could poke you in the eye or something, *Robin*!" The sled swerved again as Robin jammed the stick back into the snow. Kate ripped the stick from her daughter's hands and flung it away. Robin rolled off the sled into the snow, got up, and started walking after it.

"Robin, stay on the sled, please!"

Robin's snow pants rustled together as she walked. Her little body pitched comically from side to side.

"Or stay out and walk, whatever you want. But we are going home now, *right now*!"

She ran after Robin and picked her up. She carried Robin toward the sled. She retrieved the sled string and tried to carry Robin with one arm, but Robin slipped down. Kate caught her by the neck. Robin coughed and screamed.

"Mommy, choking me!"

"Okay, okay." She dropped the sled and held Robin with both arms. "Lila, would you pull that sled for me too, please?"

"I can't pull both."

"Just try, okay? For me? Please?"

Lila picked up the second string. She walked ahead, the sleds bumping together. "I can't. I can't." She began to cry.

"Oh, Robin, shape up!" Kate said. Holding her, she swatted the girl on her behind through the snow pants.

Robin leaned into her and bit surprisingly hard through the shoulder of Kate's down coat.

"Okay, *that's it.*" Kate dropped Robin into the snow by the impromptu tamped-down path. "I'm leaving you here. I really am."

Lila sobbed. "Don't leave her here, Mommy, don't."

Robin began to wail and kick her legs. Kate ran back to her and pulled her up by the collar of her coat. Robin resisted. Kate said, "If you don't . . . if you don't—"

She seized Robin's upper arm and shook her.

"Robin, I am going to spank you till you can't sit *down!*"

Robin stuck out her tongue.

Kate grabbed Robin's chin and squeezed. She raised her right hand.

Lila screamed.

Kate brought the hand down slowly. Her arm buzzed with irrepressible energy. She took the skin of Robin's cold pink cheek between two fingers and twisted. Robin's mouth turned down. Her lower lip protruded. A mighty wail surged from her diaphragm.

A car pulled over beside them and the driver's-side window opened. Elaine Hesselgrove looked out. "Everything all right?"

Kate let go of her child. Sanity and alarm disposed instantly of rage.

"Yes, we're okay."

Elaine scrutinized them, smiling a squinty smile, her glasses flashing in the sun. A quarter-size red spot blazed on Robin's left cheek.

"We're just coming back from the park." Kate indicated the sleds.

"Need a ride?"

"Oh, please. Bless you."

They got into the car. Kate helped Robin with the door and did up her seat belt. Robin stared—suddenly, eerily calm—at the back of Elaine's head.

"I should have driven. I thought it would be fun to walk," Kate said.

"Of course!"

Lila was crying, pressing at her eyes with the clumsy water-proof gloves.

"Are you all right, honey?" Elaine asked.

Lila nodded.

"It was at first," Kate said. "Then, not so fun."

"Mommy, there're no car seats in here," Lila said. She licked snot from her upper lip.

"I know, Lila; it's okay; it's just a few blocks," Kate said. She checked Lila's seat belt. "Thank you, thank you," she said to Elaine, climbing into the front. "Thank you."

"It's my pleasure."

"We might not have made it."

"I remember what it's like."

"Do you?"

"Like a boat full of holes."

"Yup. Just like that."

"It gets easier."

"Hope so." Kate glanced at Robin, sturdy and stoic in the backseat. The red patch, smoldering.

"WHAT'S THIS about car seats?" Colin asked.

"Car seats? What about car seats?"

"They said that you drove without car seats."

"Oh," she said. "Oh, no. Elaine Hesselgrove did."

Kate folded laundry at the kitchen table. Colin leaned against the dishwasher, eating chips.

What else would they tell, had they told him?

"And how . . . did she get ahold of our kids?"

"We were stuck. On our way back from the park. We were having a hard time. You know how Robin gets. And she drove by and offered a ride and we took it, and you know what, it was only a couple of blocks."

"And Robin's face?"

Mere hours later, the red had morphed into a light bruise.

"The sled turned over. And she bumped her face."

"Ouch."

Lila called out from bed.

"I got it." Colin tossed aside the chips.

"Thanks. I'm really tired from the day," Kate said. "I'm going to wrap up down here, then lie down for a bit."

"I recorded *ER*."

"I'm not really in the mood."

She made lunches. She put an extra cookie in Robin's Hello Kitty insulated pack. She finished folding the laundry. She poured herself a glass of red wine from a bottle she'd opened at the beginning of the week. The wine tasted dusty and sharp but instigated its usual calming effect. She hung up the snowsuits and lined up the boots, as if disposing of evidence.

But the outburst had overwhelmed her as powerfully as lust. Resistance had seemed unavailable, somehow wrong: a contorted and artificial effort, a stifling of essential energies. The discomfort of rage too much to stand.

But Robin's bruise—also wrong.

She chose school outfits from the clean laundry and laid them out. She could tend to Robin's clothes and give her an extra cookie but she couldn't bear to look at her, or even Lila, tonight.

What kind of a mess was she making here?

She folded over Colin's chips and put them away.

She went upstairs with her wine. She got onto the bed and took out her laptop. No return e-mail from Jack. She paid bills. From Colin's study, *Grand Theft Auto*. She put the laptop aside and got up and stood at his door.

"Hey," she said.

He glanced around. "Oh. Hey."

"How was work?"

"Work? Fine." Eyes on the game. Tongue between teeth. "How was the snow day?"

"It started out well. We did Lila's egg experiment. Then I fucked it up."

"You did? How?"

"Just, I don't know, with my impatience."

"Impatiens. Aren't they a little out of season?"

"Oh. Ha, ha, very funny."

He offered a smile via the screen.

She loitered in the doorway. "I really lost my temper with Robin."

"Yeah? You mean like the toothbrush?"

"Sort of like that."

She waited to see if he'd make the connection: the bruise, the temper.

"She's tough," he said.

"Sometimes I feel just like my father."

Here's how she would put it:

A rough patch.

Their marriage. Midlife, et cetera.

My adolescence. His little girl, you know. The boy next door.

Et cetera, et cetera.

So. Then. We went through this stage. Just a transitional phase. And he bullied me a bit. I'd call it that. Maybe not everyone would call it that, but I'd call it that.

"Your father?" Colin frowned into the screen. His head moved as he worked the control. "Why not your mother?"

SHE WOKE A LITTLE before five. The digital clock glowed in the dark, still frigid room. A snowplow chugged down the street. Kate sat up. No Robin beside her, no Lila either. Just Colin, snorting and turning over. His eyelids twitched. His leg jerked, as if he were in a dream of falling.

Kate got up out of bed and went downstairs. She made a cup of instant coffee. She leaned against the counter, drinking it black. The outfits lay by the door. The lunches waited in the fridge. School would resume this morning; in an hour or two the girls would wake up, call for her, want breakfast. Kate would scramble eggs and allow television or not. She would talk the girls into clothes and clean teeth. Lila would don her ballet skirt. Colin would unload one bowl from the dishwasher and pour Wheaties and finish them and leave the bowl in the sink. He would pull on his big coat and help the girls into their little ones and hustle them out the door.

Kate swallowed the remaining bitter coffee and put the cup in the sink. Back upstairs, in the master bedroom closet, she took down her overnight bag and packed underwear, socks, skin care, toothbrush and paste, several changes of clothes, her diaphragm. She sat beside Colin on the bed and tapped his shoulder.

"Hey. Hey."

"What?" He batted at the air.

"My mother's sick. Just the flu, I think. I'm going to go take care of her for a couple of days, okay?"

Kate had once known her mother to be sick. Colin never had. This would work in Kate's favor.

"Yeah. Of course."

"Can you manage? I'll call Portia?"

"I'll call her."

"Her number's on the fridge."

She stopped at an Exxon station, then got onto the highway. Light showed in the sky. Already, trucks populated I-95. She took the Blatchley Avenue exit and parked alongside Erector Square. She called Jack from the car. He buzzed her in, and when the freight elevator opened he was standing in his doorway in boxer shorts and a Yale Athletics shirt.

"Is this okay?" She dropped her bag and put her arms around him and her head into his chest. "I really need a break from my family."

"It's great. Not that you're having domestic trouble. But that you're here."

He guided her inside. She followed him to the kitchen.

"I just made coffee; you want some?"

"I'm good."

"Fight with the husband?" He poured himself coffee and drank some. Energized, he ran his hands up and down her waist.

"Worse. Robin. I—" Shame stopped her up. "I'll tell you later."

He left for class. She cautiously unpacked. She straightened up the kitchen and fanned Jack's *National Geographics* across the coffee table. At ten the radiators shut down. She crawled into Jack's disheveled bed and slept for an hour. At noon he called to check on her. Colin beeped in and she hung up with Jack.

"I couldn't get Portia," he said.

"Okay. I'll try. She doesn't know your cell. Sometimes she won't pick up if she doesn't know who it is."

Portia answered Kate's call and Kate arranged for her to pick the girls up after school. She drove to the Italian market—a new, competing one that had opened six blocks south, where she would be less likely to run into her mother, or Ella Anderson, for that matter. She purchased lamb chops, salad, bread, and two flushed pears.

"I made dinner," she told Jack. "Is that weird?"

He opened a bottle of wine and poured two glasses. "Not weird at all. It's cozy, actually. But you don't have to do all this. Sexual favors are enough."

"Yes, well." She sat at the table. "Now that I've made it I'm not hungry anymore. That always happens."

"No kidding. Look at you."

"I almost hit Robin," she said. "I totally lost it. I grabbed her face. I bruised her face."

She put her head down on the table. She heard him get up and come around to her side. He sat down next to her and rubbed her back.

"Kids," he said.

"She's a great kid. They both are. I'm a horrible parent."

"I'm no authority but I really doubt that."

"It's true. I should be arrested."

He refilled her wine. He brushed her hair from her neck. "Stay for as long as you want."

"You're sure? It's really okay?"

"Hey. I could use the company."

SHE CALLED COLIN the next day to report on her mother. She talked to the girls and said good night. Robin, inscrutably affectionate, made kissing noises into the phone. Then Kate and Jack went out to eat at Thomas Quinn's. They walked the five longish blocks and got a table in the back.

"So what was your secret, anyway?" Kate asked. She sipped at her Guinness and looked at Jack from under her eyelashes.

"My secret."

"From the gallery?"

"Oh. That secret."

"Yes, that one."

"Don't know if I should tell you."

"Of course you should."

"It's bad."

"Worse than the one about the dog?"

"Worse than that."

"Tell me."

"Well, okay. Take a swig of that beer, though. Brace yourself."

She took a swig. "Okay. Ready."

"Jail."

She gawked. *"Jail?"*

"Yup."

"*You?* Did *time?*"

"It was stupid. I was in college. I had a motorcycle and I was doing wheelies on the street outside of my house. We'd been drinking, and, well, I was over the limit. So. Yes."

"How *long* did you spend in *jail*?"

"About two months."

"Jesus. What was it like, for God's sake?"

"Not fun, but not so terrible either. It wasn't, you know, high-security prison or anything like that."

"That's . . . I mean, sort of funny."

"In a way. Yeah. Well, no. But what was funny was, when I was in there, I got this nickname: the Professor."

"The Professor? But you *are* a professor!"

"I wasn't then."

"Okay, well, that is funny. How . . . did it come about?"

"The other guys, they thought it was hilarious that here was this Cornell guy stuck in there with them. You know. Most of them were not college graduates, or even dropouts."

"What were they? I mean, what were they like, what did they do for work, what did they do to get in there?"

"Some blue-collar guys . . . some a little rougher than that. White guys, black guys. Some drug dealers, some DUIs like me."

"Didn't you share your oh-so-lowly origins with your jail-bird friends? Wouldn't they have liked you better?"

"They liked me fine. Let's see, what else. Manslaughter—you know, bar fights, gang wars. Robberies. Plenty of them were in there for beating their wives or girlfriends. Lots of them in for that. Probably the majority."

"Charming."

"They weren't terrible guys, though; they weren't terrible people. They just ... you know ..."

"Just what?"

"They work construction or whatever; they're garbage collectors or janitors or security guards or factory workers. They work shitty jobs, shitty hours. They come home, they want sympathy and a little TLC after the long shitty day; they want to eat dinner and drink something and get laid, and then they get home and the kids are screaming and the wife or girlfriend is on the phone or on the rag or on their case, or maybe even on the couch with another guy. So they lose it a little bit. They lose their tempers, one thing leads to another, and so it goes."

"Oh, I see. And the wives, the girlfriends, they don't work shitty jobs? Shitty hours?"

"I'm sure they do. Anyway," he went on, "the gist of it is, because I was a college kid, the guys called me the Professor. 'Hey, Professor' this, 'Hey, Professor' that. A couple of months after I got out I went to the grocery store with my roommate. And we were waiting to pay for our stuff, and the guy bagging the groceries—I looked at him and he looked at me, and neither of us could place each other—and then this big grin sprang out over his face and he yelled, 'Hey, Professor!' So everyone called me the Professor after that. Everyone at school."

She stared at him and bit her lip.

He reached under the table and squeezed her thigh. "Not funny?"

"No, sure. Funny. Yes."

.   .   .

BY MONDAY, Colin seemed, if not irritated, at least on the verge, at least perplexed. "Your mom, is she . . . can she . . . are you—"

"Portia made cake. I'm saving you a piece," Lila said.

And Robin said, "I miss you, I'm so lonely without you."

Kate said to Jack, "How long can my mom have the flu?"

"You might just tell him you needed a break."

"And then—no, then he'd just be mad at me. So mad." She hurled herself into the corduroy couch and put her face in a corduroy pillow.

"And?"

"And, I don't know. He wouldn't understand."

"You sure?"

"I feel like she's never going to feel safe with me again. And I wouldn't blame her."

He sat on the edge of the couch.

"I have to go home soon. Or not. They're all probably better off without me. Seriously."

She visualized shacking up with Jack, clearing out drawers and hanging dresses in his closet, doing ordinary couplelike things with him: movies, flea markets, cooking, socializing. Going back to work at Yale. Running into Ella Anderson at the Italian market. Seeing the girls on the weekends. Observing their growth spurts, their missing teeth, the way Portia did their hair. Then that would be it, the end of whatever romance she wanted from this version of motherhood. She would proofread essays when they applied to college. She would attend parents' weekends. She would do their taxes when they moved to big cities and acquired real lives; she would visit and take them out to dinner; she would call to check in while Lila wrote for the mayor and Robin slept around.

"You're being way too hard on yourself."

"Oh, how strange. I dreamed last night that the girls' pediatrician said that exact thing to me. Or to Colin, rather, about me. Dr. Epstein. He said to Colin, 'Don't be so hard on your wife.' And as he said it he was taking foot-long hot dogs out of a pack and sort of picking them up and stroking them and dusting them off. 'Don't be so hard on your wife.' " Kate laughed.

"You're asking for it." He put his hands on the seat of her black Lycra-blend pants.

"I know; I know I am."

THEY ORDERED PIZZA. She folded her slice in half and walked around, eating it, examining his very few family photographs. "Look at this." She wiped her hands on her pants and pulled a photograph in a plastic frame from behind a pile of books. "The great Professor Allison himself. Wow," she said. "Look how young you are."

He came up behind her. "My graduation. My parents showed up but left right after. They were freaked out by it all. Your dad took me out to dinner with his colleagues. It was incredibly sweet of him."

"To the club?"

"Chart House."

"Oh, I love that big fireplace."

"I ordered lobster because I'd never had it before. But then I had no clue how to go about eating it. Cracking the shells and all and which parts were good. I started with the body and in on the mushy gray stuff. I got a couple of funny looks. Then your dad set me straight."

"Awww."

"Yeah, well, he was like that. He thought, felt that education, all kinds, is meant to be shared, you know? Not reserved for an elite few."

THE FOLLOWING NIGHT, Robin screamed into the phone, "Mommy, Mommy!"

"Robin, I love you, baby girl; it's okay!"

"I want to see you, I want to see you!"

Colin got on. Robin shrieked and gagged in the background. "She's sick over missing you. Throwing up. Let's meet halfway tomorrow. For dinner or something. Then at least she'll see you."

"She's so attached to you," Jack said.

"How can she, how can she miss me? I mean, I know how, but when I hurt her like that."

"I'm sure she knows you didn't mean it."

"Oh, but I did mean it. That's the thing. I keep wondering how I could have avoided getting so mad and I just can't think of anything. Nothing."

"Valium? A lobotomy?"

"I've never come that close before. I just, you know, just—" She thumped her fist into her palm.

"What? Just what?"

23

KATE AND RUDY SNEAK PAST Topher's room and down the stairs. Kate waves good night to Ella and Max, who are watching *Letterman* on the giant television. Rudy opens the side door and touches Kate's waist under her jacket. "Talk to you later, okay?"

"Okay." She runs from the Andersons' door to her own.

Her father is waiting up in the kitchen, his papers spread out on the table. Again, he's sorry, feels sorry for her, she can see—back and forth he goes, between anger and pity, like a man who forgets the same essential item over and over, leaving it in the front hallway at home so that he must return again and again.

"You get your homework done?"

"Yes."

"Did you have fun?"

"Yes. Yes, yes."

And now she feels sorry; she feels pity. As if she's duped him somehow, cheated, made him a cuckold. How rudely she drags him from his elevated place, from his investigation of the atomic bomb! Her lips sting. Her throat burns. Her mouth tastes of sour milk and lemons and salt. She must reek of it, of her escapade, her successful experiment. She's got hickeys on her neck for all she knows, hair in her teeth, jism in her hair.

He looks at her hopefully over his papers. She hurries to her room.

RUDY DOESN'T TELL EVERYBODY what he and Kate did over the flash cards, but he does tell Topher, who in his rage (at Kate, all at Kate, not his beloved brother) tells everybody. At school, the boys make crude noises and move their thumbs in their cheeks. They write her number on their bathroom walls. She and Rudy bump into each other in the hallway between fourth period and lunch.

"I'm sorry. I didn't . . ."

She spits in his face.

Bystanders cheer. He wipes the saliva from his cheek with the back of his hand.

The older girls giggle, encountering her in the hall, the bathroom, the cafeteria. Someone plants a kosher dill in her locker. Someone sneaks a Popsicle onto her lunch tray.

All this is humiliating but bearable. What's not bearable is that the story gets back to her parents. Someone has written a note in class, discussing the episode, and a teacher has found it. Kate is called out of Latin and into the principal's office. In front of Kate, the principal calls Kate's mother at work and conducts a damning conversation. After school, Kate stays for as long as she can with her friends. Kate and her friends walk downtown to the Educated Burgher and sit around in the beat-up booths, eating French fries and toast. "You're going to get it!" her friends shriek. Her father, with his gun and his treatment of the gnomes, is considered sinister and exacting. "It was nice knowing you!" At dinnertime they walk her to her door and hug her good-bye.

On Mondays, Wednesdays, and Thursdays, Kate's family eats together at the table in the dining room. Most other nights Kate's mother serves Kate and Miles an early dinner and eats hers standing up at the counter and their father eats in his study. Tonight, a Thursday, Miles has decided that he will do the cooking and that he will make pot roast. He stands before the stove and stirs his concoction: tepid water, a bouillon cube struggling to dissolve, a hunk of carrot, a sliced potato. Beside him their mother heats up another pot roast, the one that will actually be served. Kate offers to set the table. She brings out the hand-me-down china, the set her mother allows in the dishwasher. At her parents' places she sets wineglasses. She folds cloth napkins and lays out forks and knives. Kate's father comes home and, ignoring her, heads straight for his study. Naturally, Kate's mother has contacted him at his office. Kate goes to her room. She does her algebra. She finishes it and begins tomorrow's assignment. She solves equations. She finds the distance between two points. She finds the x-intercept. She finds the slope of a line from point A to point B. She calculates the equation of a line passing through C and D. Next door Topher will be working on the same problems. He will be recording the progress of the balloon and banana. Ella Anderson will be smashing garlic and setting the table; Max Anderson will be watching the game. At some point Rudy will be getting *it* from his parents as well, though not as badly as she's going to get *it*—maybe Mr. Anderson will even pull him aside and slap him on the back, praise his sexual prowess. Mrs. Anderson will be horrified, but mildly, reparably! They will all move on without too much grief or trouble. The episode will be written off as vulgar but admissible—not ruinous, not the end of anything.

She lies on her bed. She scribbles and calculates. The bed is a four-poster that once belonged to her grandmother. It's big for a little person and so high she used to need a step stool to climb in. Her efforts, her experiments, are natural for her too, she thinks—even the bed, with its expansiveness, is asking to be filled; it wants two people, not just one. The sheets are soft and decorated with pale pink and green garlands. The wallpaper, which clashes somewhat with the sheets, is a pattern of vines and water lilies. Here and there a frog or a fish peeks through.

Here she stays. Hungry, but willing to be so. Maybe her parents will forget about her and she will be permitted to spend the evening alone with her algebra, the algebra that has nothing to do with anything—with Rudy or Topher or the kosher dill or the Popsicle or her mother's dismay or her father's scary silence.

But no. Her mother calls her down for dinner.

"A talk, young lady." This she promised as Kate walked in the door. When will it happen? Not at dinner—not with Miles there. Kate is suddenly, weepingly grateful for him. Though she, all of them, must sit, eat, and endure.

She washes her hands and idles downstairs, holding on to the banister. She rubs her bare feet against the Oriental runner, tacked at the risers. Along the wall, along the stairs, are framed photos of her parents' respective families. Her mother's from Philadelphia: her mother and grandmother pose in coming-out gowns, their chins tilted upward. Her father's from Galveston: his great-grandmother with her hair done up, her waist cinched painfully. His sloe-eyed elder sister who died at twenty in a car crash. His father, a midlevel employee at one of the big oil companies, who carried on the family tradition of corporal punishment with his sons, taking them out to the shed when they misbehaved and taking to them with his belt.

The Allisons' dining room is attached to the kitchen and across the hall from the living room. A crystal chandelier hangs, somewhat oppressively, over the table. A carpet of Persian needlepoint covers the wood floor. White Roman blinds hang in the bay windows. At the center window stands a table with a lamp on it. Kate sees that lit lamp from the street, walking through rain or cold or snow or dark down Livingston, hauling her backpack. She equates this light with her mother's mute, passive, constant kindness. She resents it but moves persistently toward it.

Kate has dressed herself in stretch pants and a giant, floppy sweatshirt, as if for protection, engulfment, as if the clothing might absorb her somehow.

Her father emerges from his study as she cracks open a 7UP.

Another mistake. He hates that she enjoys such junk, hates that Edie allows it. He sits, eyeing Kate the way he might a cockroach in the kitchen sink.

Edie puts the pot roast, fetching in an Emile Henry tureen, on the table. Kate helps her carry in buttered noodles, salad, rolls. She sits, arranges the cloth napkin on her lap. She has poured her 7UP into a glass with ice, so as not to offend her father further.

Kate's mother distributes the food. There is the clinking of forks on china. Her parents begin one of their conversations.

"Nero says the furnace will have to be replaced."

"Not this year."

"No, but next year, probably."

"Who says? Nero?"

"They tested for carbon monoxide."

"And?"

"Yes."

"How high?"

"Well, I don't recall exact percentages."

"Approximately."

"Not so high they had to shut it down."

"What's carbon monoxide?" Miles asks.

"Carbon monoxide," Kate's father says, "happens when carbon bonds to oxygen. An atom of carbon and an atom of oxygen make a carbon monoxide molecule. Too many of these molecules in the air can kill you. They bond with the hemoglobin in your blood and stop your blood from absorbing oxygen and you suffocate in your sleep." He returns his attention to his wife. "They're just trying to make a buck."

"Well, I don't know. How am I supposed to know? I call them for that reason, because I don't know."

"At the very least they're exaggerating."

"I looked at the meter."

"Probably fixed."

Kate makes an effort with her pot roast. She eats a chunk of carrot, one of potato. Another white like a carrot but sweeter. She separates the meat into strings. She shifts to the buttered noodles.

"This is delicious, Miles," Kate's mother says.

There are the awkward sounds of chewing, saliva, swallowing. They remind Kate of Rudy. "Yeah, Miles, it's good." She kicks her brother's foot under the table harder than she means to.

"Hey!" Miles says.

"What is it?" Edie asks.

"Kate kicked me."

Dennis pauses in his chewing. Puts down his utensils. Stands up from his seat. "Now you're asking for it," he says.

He walks around to her side of the table. He takes Kate by the elbow.

"It didn't hurt," Miles says.

Kate looks up at her father. What are his intentions?

He pulls her out of her chair. She is aware of her mother and Miles and of their attention on her, but she's suddenly been separated from them, whisked into a parallel universe— her father and she both have. Like two people in love, they are elevated; ordinary things are ecstatically skewed. The gold rim of the china shimmers; the red roses jump from the Persian needlepoint. He guides her roughly through the swinging door. In the kitchen it's warmer by several degrees. Magnets hold school schedules and Miles's artwork to the humming refrigerator; tacks pin a calendar, vacation days shaded in gray, to the wall. The cherry cabinets have been softened by use. Some of their porcelain knobs are missing. Open shelving holds dishes and cereal. Dough for bread rises in the yellow ceramic bowl. The countertops, bright blue-and-green tile, speak of the Mediterranean. A wooden spice rack displays nutmeg, ginger, curry powder, rosemary. The air smells of meat, of caramelized onions, of cooked red wine and vegetables that thrive underground.

"I know about you."

He faces her. She breaks away from him and backs off.

"What about me?"

"You and that kid from next door."

"Topher."

"No. The other one." He steps forward. "Robby?"

The swinging door settles in their wake.

"Rufus?" He steps closer. He cracks his knuckles.

". . . five minutes," Kate's mother says, to Miles.

His hands thump down on her shoulders.

"Rudy. His name is Rudy."

He pushes her against the warm stove.

"Rudy," he says. *"Rudy."* And all of his darkest notions about her are coalescing in the specter of Rudy. "I know all about it."

"About . . . what?"

What *does* he know, exactly? She won't give away more than she needs to; he won't dupe her into that!

"About you. And that kid."

"Rudy!"

"Rudy. Jesus H. Christ."

Vigorously, he clears his sinuses and throat. He reclaims his hold on her shoulders.

"Is that what you want? To run around town sucking cock?"

He knows, then—he knows everything.

She's going to get what's coming to her now; nothing to be done. She's going to get *it*.

She could slouch to the floor. She could cry and beg. Then—then he might stalk away in disgust. But something is rallying inside her. The Valeries are shouting for a fight.

"I'm very disappointed, Kate. Disappointed and puzzled." He releases her. Steps back. As if to surrender her, ruefully, to a career of conundrums and cocksucking. "I thought you were better than this."

Outside, snow crunches under the feet of Matilda Hellerman, walking the everlasting family dog. The furnace cycles off. The stove ticks. Kate shrugs. The gesture directed, partially, toward herself—is it? *Is* this what she wants? To run around town, etc.? Maybe . . . possibly . . . she's not sure either way, not one bit.

"Well," she says. "Guess you were wrong."

His hand flies out. He strikes one ear, then the other.

She falls against the stove. The thuggish force immediately inspires mortifying tears, but the contact also abruptly energizes her, sends invigorating messages from her skin to her brain—her ears are ringing, actually ringing, as if in misplaced celebration.

"You'd better tell that Rudy to steer clear," Dennis says. "Of both of us."

"He didn't make me do anything."

"That so?"

"I decided on my own."

"Did you!"

"What we did was . . . my choice."

"Well, congratulations. What a liberated girl you are."

"Well, I . . ."

"Your choice!"

"I . . ."

"Thousands of dollars on a private school education and what does she choose to investigate? The law of exponents? No! Not that."

"I *had* my homework done."

"The quadratic formula? The War of 1812?"

"I—"

"Nope, while the other little girls are analyzing Hamlet's fatal flaw, my daughter, Kate Leigh Allison, is sucking cock."

"Please stop saying that."

Veins jump out at his temples. He grabs her upper arm and

hauls her toward the opposite counter and shoves her face down into the ceramic bowl. The dough is cool and sticky and smells of caraway. She twists this way and that, rooting around for air. She delivers a kick to her father's shin with her bare foot. He releases her, a certain brief respect established by this aggression on her part. She rights herself. He takes one step backward, now looking quizzical and disgusted, as if she has plunged into the bowl of her own accord.

"Well, maybe . . ." She brushes dough from her forehead. "Maybe if you weren't such a total ass—"

"Christ! The mouth on you!"

He whacks her across the face with the back of his hand. She stumbles sideways. He smacks her again. With his right hand, alternating between the back and then the palm, again and again and again. Across the kitchen, on the open shelf of breakfast cereals neatly aligned, the Rice Krispies box in its bright blue and the three elves in their happy little hats jump in and out of sight. His hand flies in front of them, the blue box and the elves; the cereal veers from right to left. Sweat accumulates at his temples. She throws her arms over her head. She slumps and ducks and cringes. His hands pummel her arms and elbows. She drops to the floor and huddles abjectly there. He kicks her in the side.

Then the blitz ceases abruptly. He backs off, removing himself from the vicinity of her. His temper recedes like the noise of a passing truck. Footsteps and a squeak of hinges proclaim his departure.

And now she submits utterly to tears, finding herself in pain without even her persecutor as witness. She sobs. She runs up to her room. Later, her mother pokes her head in. "I hate you," Kate announces, apathetically, and her mother goes away.

Kate gets up and goes into the bathroom and looks in the mirror. Her face is red and scuffed but otherwise intact. The algebra, interrupted by the family dinner, no longer interests her. She drops it unfinished into her book bag. She lies on her bed. Eventually she realizes what to do. She calls her best friend, who calls another friend, who calls another friend, who calls Topher, who tells Rudy. At nine-thirty or so, Rudy calls her in a tender rage.

"I'll come over and . . . !

"I'll . . . !

"I'll . . . !"

24

NEVER WOULD HAVE GUESSED IT," Jack said. He lay next to Kate in bed with his arms crossed behind his neck. The digital clock read midnight. She'd spent the last hour telling Jack everything, the whole story: the driving lesson, the slap, the flash cards. The principal's office, the pot roast, the following struggle. And the sporadic but riveting recurrences.

"The weird thing was," she said, "that in a way, it was fun."

"I don't buy that for a minute," Jack said.

"All the time it wouldn't be, no way, like what I see at work. When it's real. But . . . in a way it wasn't; it wasn't all the time; it was just like, your kid acts out, you get mad."

"Maybe it seems that way to you now."

"It was like—Colin and I used to go to the movies every Friday night? We'd see all these totally violent ridiculous action flicks. And most of them were bad, but fun to watch. My father and me, it was kind of like that. Look, it's only relatively recently that corporal punishment hasn't been the norm."

"Is that your secret?"

"It's not a secret. It just isn't something I talk about at drop-off and pickup."

"You must talk about it with your husband."

She shrugged.

"You're kidding me."

She shook her head.

"He doesn't know?"

"It just never came up. It just hasn't. The other night, the Robin night, I thought about getting into it. But I don't know; then it just felt weird, after all this time. And I wondered if I told him, maybe he'd just think I was making excuses. Maybe I am." She put her head on Jack's chest and ran her fingers over his abdomen. "What's this?"

"What?"

"This scar. Knife fight? From your days in prison?"

"Oh, that. Hernia."

"I hate for you to think badly of him," she said.

HOURS LATER she poured herself a cup of Jack's frighteningly hot percolator coffee. "Thank you," she told him.

"What, the coffee? You're so welcome."

"No. I'm going to go. I'm going to go home now. And I guess just see what happens."

She took 95, relatively quiet this early in the morning. Another Springsteen song played, one of his early ones, about the boardwalk and amusement parks and freaky sideshows, before he started writing about cars and dreams. Last summer, the circus had come to town. Kate had watched the girl on the trapeze, watched and watched. The girl's body tensed as she grabbed the swing, her muscles readying under leotard and tights. Robin pulled at Kate's elbow. "Mommy, Mommy." A pink cloud of cotton candy had toppled into her lap. Kate shushed her and shoved the sticky stuff back down on the stick, like a hat. She watched the girl, anxious and excited, with a sensation that was somewhere between wanting to be her and wanting to fuck her. This was the problem. She wanted to fall and catch herself by her knees, to be skilled, and to express her freedom exquisitely—she wanted to be the one admired and overpowered, but she wanted to hurt the girl and hold her down too—she wanted to be a man and screw her, dominate her; she wanted that supremacy and that messy release.

She pulled into her driveway ten minutes before eight. Lila and Robin had yet to leave for school. Kate called the respective classrooms, spoke with the respective teachers. "Movie!" Lila cried, and, "Popcorn!" Robin hollered. They drove to the video store and rented a movie and watched it. They made popcorn. They made ornament strings with the leftover. They made more hard-boiled eggs and pushed them magically into the milk bottle. They made a giant mess that Kate found herself able to live with for an entire week.

KATE RETURNED to the Rose Center and assisted in the holiday decoration. Colored lights went up in the windows, an artificial tree in the common room. Pregnant Brittany gave birth to a baby girl. She returned to the shelter from the hospital and triumphantly displayed the infant, whom she'd named Latrina.

"*Latrina?*" Kate said to Ruby. They were filing case reports in the unventilated office, which gave off the same radiator and foot smell as the budgeting classroom.

"I think she made it up."

"I figured. But does she not know the word 'latrine'?"

"I don't think so."

"Does she not realize she's basically named her baby 'toilet'?"

"Don't say anything. She's very proud."

"Oh, jeez."

Ruby put her finger to her lips.

"Okay, then. Latrina it is."

Kate baked cupcakes for the holiday party and had Lila and Robin decorate them with silver sprinkles. She packed them into the Tupperware container and brought them to the party. She sat on the couch and drank a ginger ale and played with Latrina. She laid the baby on her knees and clapped the tiny feet together.

Brittany had found a job with a cleaning agency and a basement apartment for herself and the baby. She planned to leave the shelter in six weeks. Eva, on the other hand, had decided to return to Nikolai and the Bridgeport apartment they had shared.

"Why?" Kate whispered to Ruby.

"Food, rent, health insurance . . ." Ruby ticked off on her fingers.

"I'm not criticizing. But if Brittany can do it . . ."

"Frankly, I think she's jealous of that girl."

On her way out, Kate ran into Eva smoking a cigarette. Eva held the pack out to Kate and tilted her head.

"You sure? I know they're expensive these days."

"Of course. Of course." Eva leaned forward and lit Kate's Marlboro with her own.

Kate inhaled and threw her head back and blew out smoke with her lower lip.

"Oh, God, that's good."

They smoked and leaned against the building.

"So pretty, the stars," Eva said.

"Very pretty."

"You know I am leaving?"

"Ruby told me."

"You don't like it."

"No," Kate said. "I don't like it."

"He wants wife. If I stay away he will marry her, the girl. Russian men, they like to be married."

"Hmm. Yes. I bet."

"I am happy. He is my family. Family should be together. Father, mother, child." Eva conducted with her Marlboro: a brief aria of a happy family.

"You won't always want him," Kate said.

"I want him," Eva said.

"But in a couple of years you won't."

"I will want him always, always, to the end."

"Well," Kate said. "Then the end might be right around the corner."

She threw the Marlboro to the ground and stepped on it and walked away and got into her car.

25

SHE SHOWERED and exfoliated and applied lotion and dried her hair. She dressed and smeared on scented lip gloss and drove to Jack's apartment. He opened the door and she dropped her purse and car key and kissed his face and his neck and pushed him over to the couch.

"So," she said after a bit. "Anyway. What do you do for the holiday?"

"Well, I used to go to my parents'. Then my ex's parents'. But, death, divorce. So, not much of anything."

"Oh, that's sad!"

"Don't worry about it. Hanukkah is kind of a minor holiday anyhow." He ran his hands up and down her back. "And you? Tree, presents, the whole thing?"

"Yes. Then we all go to my mother-in-law's. Yuck. She makes Cornish game hens. So we each have our own individual hen and no one shares. For Thanksgiving too. She thinks it's festive but it's not; it's like the sorriest thing ever."

"Hang on." He retrieved his pants and went into the bedroom and returned with a manila folder. "Look what I found."

He held it out to her and she took it and opened it. Together, they looked at what appeared to be lecture notes.

The familiar handwriting sprang out over the yellow paper.

"These are my father's," she said. She groped around for her T-shirt and underwear and slid back into them.

"They're yours if you want 'em."

"Don't you?"

"Not particularly."

"Oh, cheer up. Look. That stuff that happened, it doesn't have anything to do with, you know, his mind. That was just how he was with me and then just a small part of how he was with me. And again, also, it was what he was used to. The way he grew up."

"Seems worse with a girl."

She smoothed out the paper. "Notes on the Feynman diagram."

"If you don't want them, someone will."

"No. I want them. Thank you." She slipped them back into the folder. "I remember him being really into Feynman."

"It kind of goes with the territory."

"Yes. I know that, at least. But he wrote that piece on the whole atom-bomb incident."

"The incident? The Manhattan Project. World War Two, Pearl Harbor, Hiroshima?"

"Yes, yes. Don't tease. He was writing about how Feynman didn't know what they were making, or rather, what they were making it for."

"No, he knew. Did you read the piece? That wasn't your dad's angle."

"But I thought he was shocked. Feynman. When they dropped the bomb."

"No, no."

"But—"

Jack got up and took a book from his shelf and opened it.

He searched for a page. "In this letter to his mother? After the experiment, the testing? He wrote, 'Everything was perfect but the aim. Next time it'll be headed for Japan.' "

Rudy, on the money after all!

Jack said, "You know, initially he thought of it, the building of the bomb, as a defensive act, as defense against the Germans. He knew the information was out there; he knew that his team could do it, and that if they could, so could the Germans. It was World War Two, he was Jewish, for what that's worth."

"But then . . ."

"The Germans pulled out of the war. But by then, as he claimed, at least, he'd forgotten why exactly he'd decided to take the project on in the first place. And by then they—the team at Los Alamos—were so caught up in it. They'd put all this time and work into it and . . . just, in a fundamental way, wanted it to succeed. Wanted to finish the job."

"The job."

"Morally, yes . . . questionable. But the whole endeavor became less and less about the reasons behind it and more and more about the thing itself, until that was the only thing. Turning matter into energy."

"Thank you, Professor."

"You're so welcome, dear girl." Jack returned the book to the shelf and himself to the couch.

"All this time, I've been . . ." She shook her head. "Misinformed." She traced the shape of his ear with her fingers. "Well. Anyway. Tell me a story. Something about when you were a kid."

"Let's see." He lay back on the couch and put his feet in her lap. "I had this friend, Rick Roberson. His dad was just . . . completely bonkers. Once he took us somewhere, maybe to

the zoo or to an amusement park, Riverside or something . . .
I'm not sure. Somewhere far enough so we had to take the
highway. He'd packed a lunch, and at some point, a ways into
the drive, he pulled onto the shoulder of the highway and we
all got out and had a picnic."

"That's dangerous!"

"I'd say so."

"So. The rest of the break? What's on the agenda? Besides
this or that landmark research project?"

"Well. Hopefully, hanging out with you. Then I wrap
things up here. Then, Sydney."

"Australia?"

"Yep. Sabbatical."

She flinched and stared at him. "What?"

"I mentioned it when you were here, didn't I?"

"You didn't."

"Swear I told you."

"Absentminded professor." She looked down at his feet and
put a hand on his toes.

"I'm renting this place to a guy from the University of Sydney. I'm renting his place and he's renting my place."

"Just like that movie with Cameron Diaz and Kate
Winslet."

"Exactly like that."

She pushed off of him and got up. She found the rest of her
clothes. She located the manila folder and slipped it into her
purse.

"Don't go yet."

"If you really wanted to you could change things around.
Right? I don't mean to put too fine a point on it. But you
could, right?"

"You're married," he said. "It's not like . . ."

"For me it is," she said. She pretended to look through her purse for the car key, which lay in plain sight, glinting up from between two floorboards.

"Come back here for a minute. Come on. Let's hear a story about you."

"You've heard them all."

"Stay anyhow."

"I'm going to go home and read my book."

"What are you reading?"

"Just this book."

"Called?"

"I don't know. Anniversary something, or something anniversary. I found it in my mom's bookshelf. Someone must have given it to her, because it's not the kind of book she'd buy for herself."

"What's it about?"

"A guy and a girl. Young, married. They break up. They get back together."

"That sounds very dull."

"The best books usually sound that way."

"If I were going to write a book," he said, "a real book, not an academic book, I would write about—okay, how's this—"

"Bye. Happy Hanukkah. And New Year and all that." She picked up her purse and pulled her coat on.

"Faculty girl grows up, falls in love, gets married, moves to the suburbs, has a couple of kids. . . ."

"Well, that does sound dull."

"Or this. Woman with abusive father—"

"Let's write a story about you."

"Already plenty of stories about me. The Professor, for one.

Then the Jack stories. 'Jack and the Beanstalk,' 'Jack and Jill,' 'The House That Jack Built' . . ."

"Honestly, 'abusive' is a word you shouldn't abuse."

"Volatile father, jackass husband, gets married, has kids. Meets brilliant older man. Experiences sexual renaissance. Then, let's see . . ."

"That story—I would guess that story does not end happily."

"No?"

"Those kinds of stories never do."

ALL AROUND HER, objects (recently purchased magazines, certain articles of clothing and jewelry) began to take on the sheen of heartache—and not just new things, but old things too, as if her whole life had become associated with him. She'd been all right without him (*had* she?) mere weeks ago, but now desolation met her at every juncture of her day. Shopping for groceries, driving to the Rose Center, she thought about Jack's shaggy armpits, his scarred abdomen, his pale, ropy arms. How flat everything else seemed.

She finished her charmingly optimistic novel. She read through her father's notes on the Feynman diagram, as if they might make some kind of sense. They didn't.

Tidying up, organizing the puzzles and games and Wood-kins and Webkinz and dolls, Kate recalled the napkin-clad Bar-bie from the gallery, the celluloid gang bang, the copulating couple. Jack had likely known what he'd wanted from her even then. He'd wanted it and gone after it and gotten it and moved past it and left her there in the middle of it, still want-ing it and unable to proceed without him. The attraction and attachment were specific to him, accidental as he was, as she knew he was—still, the attachment persisted in her body. It seemed as though they, Jack and she, had been involved in two separate, parallel experiments: his linear and goal-oriented, hers circuitous and obscure. His completed, his energies released and deposited in her; hers still in its early stages, now interrupted. The sweetly libidinous urges expanded painfully within her, finding no way out and, at any rate, nowhere to go. It was a sudden stifling of her biological inclinations, like something lying down and dying inside of her.

She read her father's notes again and this time she understood. Something, if not the notes themselves. That sexuality and autonomy—hers, at least—were at cross-purposes, the former constantly distracting from the latter. That her father had simply wanted her to identify wholly with something reliably abstract.

26

K ATE AND RUDY GO STEADY for the next three years, through her junior year at Whitney Hall and the year he takes off before college. But Kate is no longer fawned over at dinner and Ella Anderson greets her coolly from her stance at the kitchen island. In Rudy's room and in the backseat of his car Kate develops certain techniques—she learns to twist as if she's opening the jar, and to wrap her hands around his shaft and link her fingers together. She learns to make a ring with her thumb and index finger at the base. They borrow a cucumber from the Anderson family refrigerator; when finished with it they return it to the crisper and Ella slices it up for the salad. They rent a porn movie from the sleazy video store where no one they know ever goes. Rudy is reluctant to give his phone number, but the clerk insists: "In case there's an emergency, like the video is seven days late or something."

Kate's effect on Rudy, what she produces with her mouth and tongue and hands, is divinely gratifying to her, exhilarating and nifty in the manner of a science project—eggs frying on pavement, soap in the microwave, the illuminating power of crossed wires. Swearing and sighing from him, shouts of joy from the Valeries. And sex, once they get to that, is another delightfully reactive pastime. She feels about Rudy the way she does about a certain yellow cake sold at the Main Street bookstore café: yellow cake with chocolate frosting. The cake is dense and porous and textured and damp. Not terribly sweet, though the chocolate frosting is very sweet. A slab of frosting dissolves between two layers, leaking into the spongy pores so that the top of the bottom layer and the bottom of the top become saturated. It is necessary to cut the cake with the side of her fork and then look at it before eating it, necessary to observe the textured insides with the chocolate smear. She has eaten the cake for breakfast, for lunch, for a snack, for dinner. She feels the same hunger for Rudy. He is satisfying and pleasing in every way. He is satisfying yet never satisfying enough. Having had a little she wants more of the same. And the cake is volatile and meaningful as well, deliciously fraught. Possibly it resembles a cake baked for some childhood birthday. Possibly Rudy resembles her father, somehow, or her mother, or a character in a book, or a line from a song. She doesn't know. But in his arms she feels the pleasure of a dream—blurred but particular, opaque but revealing, a pleasure that has nothing to do with Rudy but is, at that moment, impossible without him.

Usually Kate returns at midnight from the Andersons' to find the first floor shut down, the refrigerator humming in the dark, her parents' bedroom door closed. But sometimes her father is up and about, listening for her. And then sometimes he stops her as she fetches her glass of water from the kitchen. Though he knows, he'll ask where she's been. He'll ask after Rudy, after the others. He'll point out the time or Kate's chafed jaw or her general disarray. The kitchen is their place, as if compromised now, as with some outbreak of the skin, susceptible to a certain altered chemistry.

Or the struggle might erupt after dinner, or on a Saturday between soccer and sundown: something Kate could avoid if she wanted to, really wanted to, but she doesn't. She defies him; she challenges him; she makes a face; she shrugs or swears. She has a hunch that what he's doing is changing her, inventing her, and that his slaps and pushes (never exorbitant, generating only a discreet bruise or two, an upset stomach) will make her into something valuable and durable and refined.

Shortly after her sixteenth birthday, she and Rudy pack an Indian blanket and a joint and a six-pack and venture out to the park. They lie on the blanket and pass the joint back and forth and look up at the stars.

Rudy says, "I saw on the Learning Channel the other day that in a billion years there won't even be any human beings left."

He is living at home during his year off and working construction in a volunteer capacity on a housing project for the city. He has become political and civic-minded. This stance has given him a certain confidence, has counterbalanced his academic struggles. He unwinds at night with a joint or two and has consequently lost some of his exuberance in bed.

"Oh, don't talk about that," Kate says.

"Why not?"

"It's sad."

"There's evidence that we're bad for the planet."

"I don't care."

"You should."

"We like it here. Maybe the Learning Channel is wrong."

"Everything changes eventually. It's evolution."

"Huh."

"Let's make out and then get you home."

He puts out the joint. Under cover of a second blanket, he goes down on her, then pushes into her. Somewhere nearby, years ago, Nelson Young raped the Hellerman girl. Kate closes her eyes. She imagines herself as Matilda, Rudy as Nelson. It's exciting, but it wouldn't be, she decides, if it were really happening. Kate and Rudy gather up their things and he walks her to her house and her front door. In the window of her father's study, the light is on.

"I'll go in with you," Rudy says.

"No, don't."

"I should."

"No. He's working." She can still feel Rudy inside of her; her vaginal canal buzzes with that particular sensation. Tears fill her nose. "It's fine. I don't want to argue about it."

Inside, she makes a racket—locking up, dropping her key in the china bowl, rummaging around the kitchen, procuring Oreos from the highest cabinet shelf. She stands and eats the cookies at the counter, taking them apart and licking the vanilla cream off the chocolate wafer. She leans her elbows on the counter and listens for her father. The typewriter clacks and Edith Piaf sings incomprehensibly of love as he labors, forges his ideas, excavating precious metals from his brilliant, cavernous mind. Eventually the study door opens and closes and his feet sound in the hallway and he enters the kitchen through the swinging door.

He looks at the Oreos, then at her body. She's gained some weight since Rudy became a pothead. He comes right up next to her to the sink for a glass of water. She hoists herself up onto the counter and sits there next to the open pack of Oreos. He sips the water and pauses. He leans toward her. He sniffs.

"You've been smoking something," he says.

She breaks an Oreo apart and looks at the two halves.

"Have you been smoking pot?"

"What do *you* think?"

She nibbles around the circumference of one Oreo half, the one with the vanilla cream stuck to it. She slouches on the counter. She waits to be pushed or pulled off.

"Are you all right?"

She shrugs and slouches. Her nose fills again.

He puts his hand to her cheek. And then he does lift her off the counter, but instead of shaking or smacking her he hugs her. This is terrible, embarrassing, almost as uncomfortable as the other business. She can smell his armpits and the onions he ate for dinner. Feebly, she hugs him back.

"Kate," he whispers. "I'm sorry."

Lying in bed the next morning, registering the smell of coffee from downstairs and the birdsong from the copper beech, she understands what's happened—she's sixteen and to continue with their ritual would give it a character he doesn't mean for it to have, would make it definitively brutal, and shameful. A certain distance, a certain respect must assert itself. She's not a child. She has sex and her boyfriend is going to college. She can and will take her driver's test, get her license, drink a glass of wine in a restaurant. Her father can no longer assume such a casual, such a familiar relationship with her body. His parental right—to punish, to handle—must be withdrawn.

They adopt a disinterested, intellectual, almost philosophical stance toward each other, that of colleagues who have collaborated intensely on a groundbreaking project. They discuss books at dinner, books neither Miles nor Edie has read. They discuss physical equations. When she passes her driver's test, he claps her on the back and gives her car privileges. He calls her from his office and asks for a ride. Kate loses the extra pounds. She breaks it off with Rudy. Like a soldier home from war, she spends her free time in unsatisfying ways, at a loss—in front of the television or in the kitchen, opening the fridge and closing it again. She hangs out in Eastwood Park at night on the weekends with her friends and they hurl discarded beer bottles at a decaying brick wall. Her father carries on with the graduate student and demands a divorce—he claims he's in love, as if it's not enough to jilt Kate's mother; he must humiliate her too. He moves out and rents an apartment on the second floor of a three-family house. There's something undignified about this but at least he's given up the once-lavender-now-red house on Livingston Street without a struggle—as he should, as he should. Kate leaves for college. She doesn't write or call. She majors in economics. She rides on the back of her boyfriend's motorcycle. The Valeries recline, inactive, at the edge of a lake. They lie on warm rocks and snuggle into sleeping bags. They read books or bite their toenails or braid one another's hair or skip stones or masturbate. Kate spends her vacations at her mother's house. She runs into Topher, also home on vacation, into Mr. and Mrs. Anderson. Nick is a lawyer, she hears, and married; Sebastian is in med school in Chicago; Rudy is majoring in environmental studies. Kate's father takes the journals from the attic and the gun from over the fireplace. Gnomes crop up in new abundance, audaciously, impishly, and pause on the slate path, the porch steps, their small white-bearded heads raised. The Hellerman girl is close to thirty. "She'll pull through it," people said, years ago, when it happened, but she never did. Kate spots her sometimes still at the market, her hair cropped short, filling her basket with sweets, dragging her feet and singing—an anecdote now, a heavy, burdensome creature with varicose veins and graying teeth and furrows across her sorry thumb-sucking face.

27

ATE AND COLIN took the girls shopping for a Christmas tree at the Bishop's farm sale. They climbed into the car around noon, the girls' hands protected this time by thick gloves—Kate had laid out all the parts and details of their dress the previous night, had searched the laundry for matching gloves and socks. They lunched in the beat-up grill room of a country restaurant where the waitress gave the girls crayons and paper. At the farm, the evergreens leaned together in splendid rows, sacrificially bound. The girls ran off immediately into them. "Stay where I can see you!" Kate cried.

Colin rubbed her shoulder and smiled at her. "I have a good feeling about this Christmas," he said.

"You do?"

"Yup." Surprisingly, he pulled her to him and wrapped his arms around her. She endured. "Maybe we should have it at our place."

"Your mom would never be okay with that. Or Moira."

"Well . . . I could put it out there."

"I'm sure your mom and sister have everything totally set already. I mean, but maybe. Sure, you could ask." She stepped back and called, "Lila! Robin!" Two raucous voices responded. "They're getting so big," she said.

He pulled her close to him again. He said, "Maybe we should have another baby."

The Valeries stirred and snickered.

Shush, she wanted to tell them. Sympathy and nostalgia coiled within her. She recalled Jack's beautiful arms. She put her forehead against Colin's chest. She didn't think she could bear to look at him. "What's all this about?"

"I think I'm going to land that account."

How could he still want her after all these years, all the bitterness? But clearly he did. He was kissing her face, kissing her like he fancied more. She put up with it but how icky it felt, akin to kissing Miles. On the train, he had hugged her and kneaded her shoulders—he could not help but touch her, and she had leaned into him, both of them stirred below their work clothes and fatigue. She had thought this perpetual wanting each other would last them the rest of their lives—years, at least. It was a trick that nature played, wanting them to couple. It was given and quickly taken away. Now all the innocent and arbitrary particulars she'd loved about him seemed like bait in a trap.

He went for her mouth and she withstood the urge to clench her lips closed. She allowed the tip of her tongue. But after a minute or so she turned her head.

She said, "We can barely handle the kids we already have."

He released her and stepped back. "You're right."

"Robin!" she called. "Lila!"

"Over there."

They chose a tree and purchased it. Colin strapped the tree to the top of the car and at home he unloaded it and carried it through the hall into the living room while Kate carried in everything else, all the frustrating odds and ends of the excursion. The girls reacquainted themselves with their things—the Woodkins, the puzzles, the Ariel head, the Play-Doh—not playing exactly but touching and examining and moving from one place to another. While Colin clamped the trunk upright Kate swept away the trail of needles.

"I'm hungry," Lila said, looking up.

"Family dinner," Colin said.

Kate knelt and brushed the needles into the dustpan. Was he mocking her?

"On the other hand," he said, "there's tomorrow."

"School night."

He shook his head at her pessimism.

"I'll order pizza," she said.

She called Gennaro's for two take-out pies. Then Colin (the man, the bringer of provisions) went out for them. Kate hosed down the girls and washed their hair. She put on the radio and hung a star in the front window—a white paper star with triangular cutouts and an electric bulb suspended inside. She switched it on. She went out front for a minute to admire it. How enchanting it looked.

She poured herself a glass of Chianti and went out into the living room, where the girls played, building something out of pillows and the more portable furniture. Lila looked up. "Will you make cinnamon rolls for tomorrow, Mommy?"

"Sure, baby girl. Why not."

She mixed the ingredients into a silky dough and set it on the counter to rise. Colin returned with the pizza and slid it onto the sideboard. Kate covered the dining room table with a cloth and lowered the lights. She set the table with the blue-and-yellow ceramic plates and cloth napkins. Colin watched disapprovingly (retreating from his earlier tenderness and subsequent rejection into censure), as if she were hurling the plates to the floor rather than lining them up in neat pairs across from one another. Standing, he took a piece of pizza from the box and began to eat it. She took the boxed pizzas off the sideboard—away from him—and took them into the kitchen and stuck them in the oven in their cardboard and set the temperature to two hundred.

"Will you round up the girls?" she asked him.

She made a salad. She set one box of pizza on the table. Her family joined her and took their places. She took her place too. Robin touched her arm. "Soft Mommy," she said.

"Did anyone dream last night?" Kate asked. "What did you guys dream? Do you remember?"

Robin said, "I dreamed there was a . . . I had a dream about . . . a dangerous dungeon. When a person walked by, it grabbed their legs." She demonstrated, clutching at the air.

"Sounds scary." Kate picked up her pizza. "You're brave, Robin, to get through the night in your bed. Good job."

She looked at Colin. *See?* her look said. *It'll all work out. She'll stop when she's ready.*

"Let's see if you can do it again, Robin," Colin said. He folded his pizza and tore it with his teeth.

"I don't want to tell you my dream," Lila said.

"Was it a bad dream, Lila? Tell me, baby girl. Tell us."

"Only if you promise not to tell . . ." She thought. "My class."

"We won't tell your class."

"My dream was, there was a desert. Three men pretending to be nice but they weren't. They cut me up into little pieces."

"Jesus," Colin said.

"It's too scary for my class. Don't tell them. Don't."

Kate had dreamed a dream she'd had before. In the dream she'd somehow forgotten all about Colin, lost track of him entirely. She waited alone while other people coupled off. Then she saw Colin, or remembered him. Sometimes when this happened they were on the train. Then excitement would spread through her like a colored tablet dissolving in the bath. And she would feel elated, relieved. Now her life could begin: T-shirts in the microwave and pumpkin-picking expeditions and Halloween costumes and school mornings. And a house lit up in the snow and a star in the window.

"What did you dream?" she asked Colin.

"I have no idea."

He poured more wine into his glass. She would have liked him to pour more into hers, but he didn't. She would have liked for him to ask her what she'd dreamed, but he didn't. She reached for the Chianti bottle and poured for herself. Though she'd lost her appetite to fatigue and no longer wanted the pizza, or the salad, or anything but the wine, she picked up her slice and took a bite.

"Something about buying a tree with two little girls?" Colin said.

"That was real, Daddy, that was real!" Lila shrieked, kicking her feet under the table. Robin laughed, her sweet rare belly laugh.

Lila tapped out a song on the table with her spoon. "Guess what song this is," she said.

Kate guessed. " 'Wheels on the Bus'?"

"No!"

" 'Clementine'?"

"Tell us."

" 'This Land Is Your Land.' "

Robin banged one out too. Under her breath she hummed "Wheels on the Bus." "Guess," she said.

"That's not fair," Lila said. "You were singing, Robin. You were singing."

"Lila," Kate said. "Come on."

Lila's pizza languished on her plate. Colin reached over and took the cheese from the top and crammed it into his mouth. Lila, turning her eyes back to her plate in time to witness the theft, began to cry.

"Oh, Colin," Kate said.

"What?" He swallowed, a frog with a fly. "There's plenty more pizza."

"I want that piece." Lila wept.

"I'm sorry, sweetie. I didn't realize." He looked at Kate. "I thought she was done. It was just sitting there."

"But, Colin, you don't just take from her plate."

"We're a family. That's what families do. Families share."

Insufferable prick, she thought. Out loud she said, "By that you mean you take what you want when you feel like it. Even if it's not yours. Even if you did nothing to get it."

"I paid for this pizza and I picked it up."

"She's a person. She's a kid but she's a person too. Have some respect."

He slammed his fist onto the table. The plates jumped. "I know she's a person, for Christ's sake!"

"Oh, damn you."

"Nice. Nice thing to say in front of your kids."

Kate put her elbows on the table and her head in her hands. She pressed her fingers, smelling of tomato and garlic, into her face. She looked down between her spread fingers at the pizza on her plate. It seemed very far away: To eat another bite would be impossible.

Robin next to her and Lila across from her vibrated with worry.

"Sorry," Kate said. "I'm sorry. Let's regroup, okay?"

She took her hands from her face and looked up. Colin reached for a fourth slice of pizza. He folded it and began to eat it fast and furiously, the way he ate when angry.

"Don't shovel your food," she said. She couldn't help it.

He banged the cardboard box closed and shoved his chair away from the table and stood up, shaking his head, still holding the folded pizza. He tramped into the kitchen.

The girls looked at her.

"You guys are the best," she said. "Sorry. Mommy had a fit. Daddy had a fit. Don't worry. Don't worry." She got up and kissed their delicious full cheeks—Robin and Lila and Lila and Robin and Robin and Lila, one cheek then the other, again and again, until they covered their heads and complained.

Colin appeared in the doorway and suggested bedtime.

"Yes," Kate said. "Thank you and please."

She swept the crumbs off the tablecloth and shook the cloth out the back door. Beneath the cold and snow and the Hesselgroves' dwindling fire she detected the scent of cannabis. The grad school sons, home for the break.

She piled the dinner plates by the sink, still crowded with cereal bowls from the morning and a pan from Thursday, a frying pan in which she'd cooked lamb chops. She loaded the bowls and the dinner plates into the dishwasher. Behind her, Colin broke up the pizza box for the recycling.

"I'm sorry," she said.

He didn't answer, just shoved the cardboard into the bin.

He sprayed and wiped the counters. She washed and dried the Sabatier knives, Chianti still at hand. She bent down to start the dishwasher. He poured the rest of her wine down the sink.

"I was drinking that," she said reflexively. Then, "That's okay."

Again he didn't answer, and it was then she realized he wasn't speaking to her.

"Colin?"

He raised an eyebrow. He filled a glass with water and drank it.

"Say something."

"What's there to say? Jesus, Kate. You don't want me. I don't think you love me."

"Of course I do."

"Then why don't you ever want to sleep with me?"

"Oh, that's so normal, Colin!"

"It's not normal."

"Brooke and Trey—"

"What?"

"Never mind. Never mind. But it is normal; it is. I'm tired. There's a lot going on. We've been married for years."

"Kate, I really don't think it's as normal as you seem to think it is."

"Oh, really. Well, aren't you the expert."

"I've talked to my friends," he said ominously.

"Your friends?"

"Yes. My friends."

"You talked to your friends about our sex life. Well, that's just great. No, I don't feel too humiliated."

"What, you never talk to your friends about our sex life? Or lack thereof?"

She recalled the conversation with Brooke and Mave. "No," she said.

"Even when we actually *have* sex, you don't enjoy it."

"No, I mean, yes, I enjoy it! Yes, yes!"

He headed toward her, suddenly, holding the lavender surface spray. She stepped back. He put the bottle away under the sink.

"You don't," he said. "You think I can't tell but I can."

She said, "We have sex once a week, or at least every ten days. That's not bad. We pass, okay? That's *enough*. That's *enough sex*. I looked it *up*."

"But you don't *want* to. You don't want me." He took hold of her waist. He pushed her gently against the counter.

"I *do* want you!" she cried. She shrank away from him. She covered her eyes with both hands.

She closed her eyes behind her fingers and breathed through her nose. Tomato and garlic, lemon and soap.

He released her. He backed off. She felt his hurt and his vulnerability, both her creation, the same way she'd felt Lila and Robin earlier vibrating at the table.

She dropped her hands from her face and, with some effort, looked at him.

He seemed all right—at least, she detected no signs of recent harm.

Calmly, he said, "I'm a grown man. And . . ."

"And . . . what?"

"And I need sex to be a part of my life."

Intolerable! Unspeakable!

"Maybe if you unloaded the dishwasher once in a while . . ."

"I see. So now you're *withholding* sex."

"Not feeling like getting down because I have too many other domestic chores on my list is *not* the same thing as withholding sex."

"Oh, go to hell."

"No, *you* go to hell!"

He plucked a paper towel from the roll by the sink and turned away and shook his head and his shoulders, shaking her off. He wiped down the range. Then he paused. He held his hand to the oven door.

"Colin?"

He ignored her, entirely preoccupied with the oven. He opened the door. Inside sat the second pizza in its cardboard box. He removed the box and opened it. He examined the pizza, cooked slowly over low heat to a crisp, black boils erupting at intervals. He clicked the oven off.

She watched him. Then she turned back to the sink and began to scrub the lamb chop pan—further evidence of her delinquency.

"I'm sorry," he said. "Did you want that on?"

She paused. Gunfire tore through her. She resumed scrubbing.

"Yes," she said. "I did. I do want it on." She threw the sponge into the sink and turned around. "I want to burn the whole fucking house down."

He closed the pizza box, walked toward her, and hit her backhanded across the cheek.

She stumbled against the dishwasher. She caught onto the lip of the sink and leaned over the basin. Her hair swung into the suds and the pan.

"You okay?"

In the pan, grease persisted. The water separated and reflected the tasteful recessed lighting in tacky little rainbows. She touched her cheek—still intact.

"Yeah. Okay."

"Fuck, Katie. I'm *sorry.*"

She straightened and seized the dishwashing soap and squirted it at him.

His arm went over his eyes. Then his hands to her shoulders. He pushed her. She fell against the counter, then to the floor.

Down there, the crumbs dismayed her. She must ask Portia to get under the table, the fridge, the cabinet doors. Hopeless, this struggle against crumbs, a magically proliferating trail of crumbs that led from the kitchen to the living room and up the stairs and into the girls' bedrooms and her own.

She got on her hands and knees. Her ears swarmed and the veins in her head thumped. She felt as though she might be sick. She clambered up and again hung over the sink, unsure of where else to go.

"You okay?" he asked again.

"I think I might throw up."

"Want some ginger ale? Or something?"

There was the pan, still sudsy, still soiled. She put her hands on it. She lifted it and turned to Colin, holding it high. Water ran down her arms and into her armpits.

"Don't even think about hitting me with that," he said.

She tried to hit him with it. He grabbed her wrists. The pan smacked the floor and, seemingly, some vulnerable part of Colin's foot.

"Motherfucker!"

She backed away. Pressed her spine against the granite over-
hang, held on with both hands. Outside, the compressed snow
creaked under the boots of one of the Hesselgrove sons. The
Hesselgrove dog yapped. A door slammed. "There, boy," the
son said. Marijuana again, through the ill-fitting windows,
evoking Rudy Anderson.

Kate recalled the moonlit park, Richard Feynman, Oreos.
Headless gnomes, breakfast cereal neatly aligned, mnemonics.
*How I Like a Drink, Alcoholic of Course. Richard of York Gave
Battle in Vain.* The flash cards, the principal's office. The night
of the pot roast.

The stove ticked, shutting down. The furnace kicked on
and warm air blew from a vent.

The Valeries elbowed her. *You see now,* they said. *You do, don't
you? Look. Look around.*

The girls' art, attached to the fridge with whimsical magnets, flapped and made whispering sounds.

The dishwasher thumped. Dough rose in the ceramic bowl.

Colin twisted Kate's wrists behind her back and turned on
the cold water and pushed her head into the sink.

She wasn't going to cry, not this time.

She tried to kick him between his legs.

He yanked her hair.

She screamed.

He put his hand over her mouth.

She bit his palm. Blood ran onto her tongue.

He let go of her and she flung her wet hair back and
straightened and swung at him. She used her weight. She kept
her thumb outside her fist.

He slapped her, hard, across the face.

No Rudy now, no Topher searching all through the house, no father waiting for her at home, no one searching or waiting for her at all. She lived here—if anyone cared or wanted to know she could be located right in her own kitchen, exactly where she was supposed to be.

28

*L*YING AWAKE THAT NIGHT, as Colin snored downstairs on the couch, Kate thought about fleeing to Miles in the city. She envisioned his shock and embarrassment. Or to Darcy on the West Coast. She thought about packing the car with clothes and books. Leaving a note for the girls. Buckling up for a long ride.

The mark on her cheek went from red to blue to brown. The girls inquired about it and she explained somehow, implausibly—poor little creatures who believed in fairies, in Santa Claus, who would believe that Portia was Miley Cyrus in yet another disguise, if Kate chose to con them so.

She avoided chitchat with the other mothers. She hid her bruise under winter gear. She quarantined herself. She avoided Colin and he avoided her.

She instituted a tumult of neatening. She picked up, put away, labeled. She cleaned the crud off of every plastic toy. She located every puzzle piece and recycled the puzzles she couldn't complete. As she organized she looked for a way around what had happened. She looked under sheaves of artwork and in abandoned containers of paint and in the baskets of breeding synthetic animals. But there wasn't a way around it. She kept looking until she'd uncovered everything but there wasn't.

That Thursday, the girls' respective schools broke for the holidays. Kate picked up Robin and headed to Wintergreen. A snow flurry commenced. Kate hustled Robin out of the car and into Lila's classroom, then both of them across the street to where the station wagon was double-parked, hazards flashing. The girls chattered in the back, unwrapping string cheese. Kate glanced into the rearview mirror. She recalled them on the pumpkin expedition, swaying to Bob Dylan.

She turned the car onto Linden Street. In the bright snow, the red globe of the abstract iron sculpture shone like a planet.

"We want to touch it! Stop!" the girls cried.

"Okay. Okay."

Kate pulled over. She put the hazards on. She got out of the car and directed the girls out—she picked Robin up and, holding Lila's hand, guided them across the street. She hoisted Robin up to touch the red globe. The little girl stood on Kate's shoulders and Kate held her waist. Then, with more effort, she hoisted Lila up in the same manner. She craned her neck to look at her older daughter, who patted the globe, then threw her head back and caught snowflakes on her tongue.

The girls finished their snack and fell asleep on the drive home. The snow stopped. Kate pulled into the driveway and shut off the engine. She turned around, assessed her slumbering daughters.

What are they doing? she might ask Colin.

Their heads hung heavily, Robin's to one side and Lila's to the other. Their coats, which they'd shed, as they did at the least opportunity, tangled between them on the middle seat like another passenger. Exhaustion transpired in the girls' damp, gently odorous breath.

If she woke them now, they'd object.

She considered the house. The paper star hung in the window like a bat. Behind the star soared the Christmas tree, which Colin had last night managed to string with lights. Kate and the girls had admired the spectacle, and then, forgotten, the bulbs had burned all night and all day. They shone dull and pale in the belated afternoon sun. In the girls' bathroom also a delinquent bulb anemically gleamed. It picked out a cluster of fairies and gnomes, frolicking above the tub. There Colin had sat, on the edge, and mopped Lila's creased neck.

How gallant he'd been, tending so sweetly to a little girl!

Still, Kate sat in the driveway, reluctant to wake her offspring, reluctant to exit the car and enter the house. The sun receded. The cold settled in, reached below her coat and felt her up. Shadows lengthened; the light flattened.

Two teenagers—the neighbor's son and his girlfriend—erupted from the house to the right. Both kids wore parkas zipped to their necks. His black, hers pink. He wore a black knit cap, she an exuberant high ponytail. Both wore gloves and blue jeans. He dragged a shovel after him down the steps. She was laughing—he was talking to her, amusing her. She swung her arms happily. She bent forward and hung from her waist. He leaned the shovel up against the side of the house and went up behind her and smacked her on the behind. She fell to her knees in the snow. She shrieked. Then she struggled to her feet and scooped snow into her gloved hands and shaped it. The boy watched her. She threw the snowball and it hit him in the chest. He brushed at himself. He packed his own snowball. She covered her head with her arms. He threw the snowball into her abdomen. While she was fashioning her second he lobbed another at her face. The snow stuck to her skin. She screwed up her eyes and nose and wiped off the white deposits. She looked at him from under her brows and ponytail, goading him. Her eyes were bright and excited.

They went at it, packing and hurling their ammunition at each other. His, for the most part, hit its mark. Hers, flung spastically from under the bombardment, fell apart in the air.

He lost interest. He slogged to the side of the house and retrieved the shovel and began to clear the walk. Kate heard his crisp footsteps, the activity of his jacket. The girl examined the house, then the occupied boy pitching dense shovelfuls this way and that. She watched the white mounds fly and scatter. She dropped and lay on her back. The pink parka rustled. She stirred her arms and legs, composing her shape in the faintly bluish snow. He finished the walk and they went inside together.

The temperature inside the car dropped. The blue intensified and sundown followed. Details disappeared; shapes emerged. Kate rubbed her arms. In her house, the bathroom bulb and Christmas tree lights began to radiate warmth and comfort.

Robin snored. Lila whimpered. Kate twisted the key in the ignition. Heat and music rolled through the wagon's interior. Kate turned the car around, pulled out onto the street and back toward the highway.

She got on and headed north, toward New Haven and Livingston Street.

She passed the exit to the steakhouse, the dangerous diner, the Showcase Cinemas, and the first-floor apartment where Lila had spent the first three months of her life, where Kate and Colin had merged their shabby furniture and unpacked their wedding presents, where they had ambitiously pursued a certain sweetness—more than just a taste, more than just a bite, more and more and more. Yellow cake every day, yellow cake for breakfast, lunch, and dinner, yellow cake for a snack, chasing the crumbs like ravenous, sensitive children.

She had no idea if at that point things could have gone one way or the other, or if only one way, this way, had been available. They'd lain awake in bed the night before leaving that apartment for the Fairfield house; they'd stayed up talking, holding hands, vaguely nostalgic already but energized and expectant. To recall this scene was crushingly sad. Again, Kate sensed Colin's sincerity throughout the whole endeavor. But she too had felt sincere in that moment. His sincerity had leaked into her anxious, porous self.

She passed familiar signs: Ferry Parking, P. J. Murphy Moving & Storage. Pleasant Moments Café, offering stag parties and fifty dancers weekly. She passed the industrial structures of Bridgeport, the convenience stores and Italian restaurants. Somewhere among them Eva, lighting an advent candle, fixing ornaments to her tree, rigging an angel on top.

Kate stuck to the middle lane. Homeward-bound cars boarded and exited the interstate. Heat blew gently around Kate's ankles. On the radio, a female country star sang about unrequited love. There was something direct and uncomplicated about the song, something internal but external also. It described the singer's interior life but also acknowledged a certain kind of heartache that had to do with critical attachments to other people.

Lights flashed in the opposite lane and the green-and-white highway signs glowed: 8 to Waterbury, 95 to New Haven. Billboards offered entertainment and sustenance. The interstate rose up on concrete legs and crossed the Long Island Sound, where tethered boats clustered against docks. A train passed below. Cement towers jutted to the left, oil tanks to the right, casting vast shadows over the sullied water. After Stratford, the highway narrowed. Little vinyl-clad houses cropped up on either side of the road. Holiday lights trimmed front doors and porches. American flags swayed from aluminum poles jammed into front lawns. Traffic cleared. The lanes darkened and opened up, beams hitting blacktop, the road to Livingston Street and the red house with the playroom and puzzles in boxes.

Kate checked the rearview mirror. She registered the sleeping girls and a truck on her tail. The mammoth headlights illuminated the wagon's interior. She accelerated. The truck did too. Then the lights abruptly vanished, and she felt the force of the truck passing on her left. The station wagon wavered as the air around the outsize vehicle separated and surrounded the wagon with a disruptive current. Kate contracted her hands and steered through it. Gorgeously stripped trees posed in white against the infinite sky. But Kate watched the road and the red taillights and the green shimmering signs, keeping her eyes on where she wanted to go.

ACKNOWLEDGMENTS

Many thanks to the following individuals: Libby Borden, Gavin Borden, Fred Borden, Jenni Ferrari-Adler, Jennifer Jackson, Dave Marsh, Tristine Skyler, Robin Black, Renata Rainier, and Jennifer and Christopher McFadden.

Printed in the United States
by Baker & Taylor Publisher Services